TEMPTING THE SAXON

VIRGINIE MARCONATO

OLIVER HEBER BOOKS

Cover art by Dar Albert at Wicked Smart Designs

Published by Oliver-Heber Books

0 9 8 7 6 5 4 3 2 1

"Caedmon? I can't believe it, it *is* you!"

Before Caedmon could answer or even open his mouth, Frigyth had fallen into his arms and wrapped him in a bear hug. His own arms closed around her, an automatic, natural response. At the contact of her familiar body against him, his heart gave a jolt. Had it been ten long years since they had last seen each other? Yes, it had. In other words, an eternity. Dear God, how he had missed her. He closed his eyes and did not resist the urge to place a kiss on the top of her head.

Finally, he was home.

All too soon, she broke away from the embrace and took a step back to take a better look at him. Her eyes were full of unshed tears.

"What are you doing here?"

He didn't want to answer, didn't quite know what to say to explain his presence in the Norsemen village. The truth was out of the question.

I left London because the woman I was supposed to marry made a fool out of me. And the worst of it was, I didn't care a jot, because I never loved her like I love you. I came because I should never have left and I miss you too much. I'm here to see if, against all odds, I can win you back.

"I'll tell you everything in good time," he grumbled. "For now, just let me look at you. You haven't changed a bit, Frig."

She laughed at what she took for an outrageous compliment, but that was no lie. Heaven help him, she'd even grown lovelier since he'd last seen her. Normal people, including himself, aged as years went by, but somehow she had only become more beautiful, more...radiant. That was the first word that came to his mind.

Radiant with happiness.

He dipped his head to inhale her feminine, unique smell. Freshly baked oat cake, with a hint of honey. Even that hadn't changed. How was that possible? Yes, now he was most definitely home.

A cough behind him made him stiffen. Without turning around, he knew who would be looking at them. Or should he say *glaring* at them...Sigurd, Frigyth's husband. In other words, the luckiest man in the country.

Caedmon slowly turned. As he'd thought, a tall, not best pleased Norseman was staring at him, his fingers bunched into fists.

"Coldman. Welcome back." The greeting was as warm as the man's ice blue eyes and the deliberate mispronunciation of his name didn't bode well. Ten years had not lessened the animosity he felt toward him. Well, it hadn't lessened his either, but he would not cower. Without this man, he might be happily married to Frigyth right now. It was enough to make Caedmon hate him.

"Seagull," he answered. "Delighted to see you."

The man's lips quivered, a reaction he had not anticipated. Was he amused? It would be a first.

"Oh, please," Frigyth interposed before he could be sure. "Stop it, you two! I'm not in the mood for your male posturing."

"No posturing, Birdie. We're just having a friendly chat, telling each other how nice it is to meet again after all these years."

With that, the Norseman wrapped an arm around his wife's shoulders, confident in his right to do so. It was not the possessiveness of the move that had Caedmon's guts writhe like angry eels. It was the way his and Frigyth's bodies seemed to fit together, as if they had been in that exact same position thousands of times, as if they were the two halves of a whole.

These two people belonged together, he could not doubt it anymore.

Well, what had he hoped?

That Frigyth would throw herself into his arms, say that she had spent the last ten years wishing he'd come back to her, that she had made a terrible mistake in refusing his offer of marriage and wanted to flee with him?

Yes, sadly, part of him had been hoping for exactly that, which went to show what a fool he was.

Caedmon stared at the sun peeking through the trees and sighed.

He should never have come. It was clear nothing but disillusion awaited him in this village.

CHAPTER ONE

EAST ANGLIA, SPRING 1047

"Come, Bee, your mother will be waiting for you. We're late already."

"Ah. She won't worry, she knows I'm with you."

Ingrid rewarded this sensible answer with a smile and followed her niece out of the door. Strictly speaking, Bee, whose real name was Dawn, was not related to her through blood, as she was only her brother's adoptive daughter. When Björn had married Dunne, a Saxon, five years ago, the four-year-old child had become his and they had become the best of friends. The Norseman never treated her differently than the two little boys who had been born since and he had made it so plain that he would skewer anyone who ever referred to the girl's real father that no one dared to even allude to the fact that he was not the one who had sired her.

She took the hand the little girl was holding out and made her way to the other side of the village.

As they came into view of the well, Bee spotted her parents deep in talk with her aunt Frigyth and her uncle Sigurd. She let go of her hand and ran to her brother Rorik with a shriek of joy. While the children hugged each other, Ingrid stopped in her tracks. A stranger was standing next to Björn. Intrigued, she joined the group. It was not often they had visitors in the village.

The man was a Saxon, it took her less than a heartbeat to see it. Not that it was hard. He was a couple of inches shorter than the men populating the village, he didn't wear a beard, his hair was cut shorter, and it was brown. No, not brown, she amended, which was far too plain a color to describe it. It was much more vibrant than that. She had always been secretly jealous of her sister-in-law's hair and eyes. Not for Dunne, washed out blonde and common blue. Her hair was as glossy as a horse's coat and her eyes a striking gold. That was the problem with having fair hair, blue eyes and pale skin, Ingrid thought. It was somehow flat, and lacked depth. Growing up surrounded by people who all shared the same coloring, she had never thought anything of it. But since meeting Frigyth and Dunne, she did. These Saxons really had the most interesting shades of irises. One could never predict their color, and the members of a same family could look markedly different. A few years ago she had even seen a woman in the village with eyes as dark as coal. Eowyn's gaze had been riveting.

What would the man's be like?

As if he'd heard her musings, he turned to look at Bee and Rorik, and Ingrid's jaw almost dropped. Green. And brown. And blue. And gray. And gold. All rolled into one. No, she had most definitely never seen eyes like these, never even suspected they could exist. It was like looking into the heart of a precious gem that captured the light as it moved. She could only stare, fascinated, and hope he would not take exception to it.

He did not. In fact, he had not even looked at her once. After a brief glance at the children, his gaze was now fastened on Frigyth, who was making introductions, because Merewen had just joined the group, her young daughter, Eyja, straddling her hip.

"This is Caedmon, the friend I've told you about many times."

"Of course!" Wolf's wife smiled in welcome. "I'm delighted to finally meet you. We've heard so much about you."

At that, Sigurd scowled, apparently not liking the idea of his wife talking about her old friend to the whole village. Ingrid could not help a smile. As if he had anything to fear...Theirs was one of the strongest marriages she had ever seen. Before anyone could say anything else, Wolf approached the group, his face like thunder. It was an expression he rarely sported and her heart instantly picked up speed. Since his arrival in the village some twelve years ago, the Icelander had been in charge of the safety of its inhabitants. If he appeared worried, then she should pay attention.

Merewen placed a hand over her husband's chest. "What is it?" She clearly agreed that something must have happened for him to look so grave.

"Someone stole Demon."

Everyone save the Saxon, who had no idea what had been said, since the words had been spoken in Norse, stared at him in stupefied silence. Demon was Wolf's stallion, an animal he'd had since his arrival in his new country. The two of them were inseparable and Ingrid guessed he would be devastated by the loss of him.

"Any idea who might have done such a thing?" she asked.

"No. He was not in the field yonder with the other horses, for once. After my visit into town last night, I was tired so I left him to graze outside my hut." He shook his head, visibly wishing he hadn't been so lazy.

Sigurd slapped him on the shoulder. "We'll find him, my friend, don't worry. There aren't many stallions like him around. Someone's bound to have seen him. Come, let us see if Magnus saw anything suspicious this morning. He's always first up and the forge is not far from your hut."

After a brief kiss to their respective wives, the two friends left in the direction of the smithy's workshop. Just then, two men came running toward them. With a shiver of disgust Ingrid recognized the taller of the two as Ivar. Though she usually did her best to avoid him, it was not always possible in a village so small. She forced herself to act naturally. It would not do to betray any discomfort when her brother was present. Fortunately, Björn was too occupied with his newborn son Ralph, who had started to fuss, to pay attention to her.

"Saxons!" the second man cried out. "They stole into the village last night and took the horses."

"All of them?" Ingrid gasped. Wolf had clearly thought only Demon had been stolen.

The question drew Ivar's attention to her. His gaze wandered over her the way it always did, slow and appraising. For five long years, she'd had to endure it and it was not getting any easier. Before she knew what she was doing, she shuffled closer to the man nearest to her, who happened to be the Saxon. Their arms touched briefly. He glanced at her in surprise then frowned and turned his attention back to the two men as if he'd guessed they were the reason for her unease.

Ivar had not missed her move, and a malevolent gleam appeared in his eyes. "It's him!" he said, pointing in Caedmon's direction. "The thief. I recognize him. He crept into the village while everyone was asleep."

By her side, the Saxon stiffened. He'd understood they were talking about him, even possibly realized they were accusing him of something but, as the conversation was being conducted in Norse, he had no idea what the problem was, or how to respond.

Her heart sank. This was all her fault. Ivar was accusing

him because he'd seen her huddle close to him. He just wanted the Saxon punished because he thought it would hurt her.

"Don't be ridiculous," Frigyth scoffed, reversing to her friend's language so he could follow what was being said. "Caedmon did not steal any horses. He would never do anything like that."

"Wouldn't he? He's a Saxon. How do you know he can be trusted?" Ivar spat to the ground. "You're a Saxon yourself, so of course you would take his defense! But I—"

"Careful," Björn growled, taking a step forward. Even though he was holding a babe in his arms, he looked as menacing as she had had ever seen him. "That's my sister-in-law you are talking to, so you will mind your tongue."

Ingrid knew her brother would not countenance anyone inconveniencing his wife or her sister for any reason, much less for being Saxons. Ivar blanched, but everyone knew he'd gotten off lightly. If Sigurd had been here, he would already be flat on his back. The hot-tempered Dane would not have anyone insulting his wife.

Knowing Björn would protect her if necessary, Frigyth stood her ground. "I've known him all my life. I'm telling you he didn't steal the horses. And if you saw him creep into the village, as you say, then why didn't you raise the alarm? And how did he manage to steal six horses on his own and in silence?" There was no answer. "This is all ridiculous. Caedmon is not the thief."

Although Ingrid had only just met Caedmon, instinct told her this was the truth. He looked too proud to be a thief, and too unruffled to be guilty of any wrongdoing. Besides, if he really had stolen the horses, he would not be so stupid as to come alone to the village the very next day, at the risk of being recognized.

No, he had to be innocent.

Ivar was not so easily beaten, however. "Are you saying that you can vouch for him because you know where he spent the night?" he sneered. "What do you think your husband would say if I told him you claim to know the man's whereabouts at such an incriminating time?"

Frigyth's cheeks flushed a violent red. "I don't advise you to try. He would tear you to shreds for spreading slander about me and well you know it."

Despite the spirited retort, a flash of panic had crossed Frigyth's eyes. She seemed desperate that her husband should not hear about her and the Saxon spending the night together, even if it was an outrageous lie. Ingrid could not see why she worried so. Surely Sigurd would not doubt her? The two of them were deeply in love. Trust Ivar to want to stir up trouble. He'd only accused Caedmon because he'd seen the way she'd shuffled next to him in search of protection and wanted to unsettle her.

The need to shut him up churned in her guts. When he smirked at her it boiled over. It was as if all the resentment, the hatred that had built up inside her since that dreadful night had finally decided to escape. For too long she had said nothing, for too long she had allowed him to have the upper hand.

No more.

"Enough!" she snapped, taking the Saxon by the arm. He stiffened but did not protest. "Caedmon did not steal the horses last night, as he was in bed with me. Or are you saying that a man can be in two places at once?"

Only a stunned silence answered her.

"I ASSUME you will explain to me at some point why you said what you said?"

Caedmon stared at the woman in front of him, who had claimed to a party of onlookers, amongst which was her own brother, that they were lovers when they had not exchanged so much as a single word in their lives. What had possessed her to utter such a lie? That she had meant to help him was obvious, as he was being accused of theft at the time, but surely she could have defended him without compromising herself?

She shrugged, as if she hadn't done anything noteworthy. "Ivar was accusing you of stealing the horses and refusing to believe in your innocence. I had to do something."

"No, you didn't." He crossed his arms over his chest. Even if he appreciated her impulse, it wasn't her responsibility to help him, and they both knew it. She could easily have kept silent and let others help him. "Don't get me wrong, I'm grateful for your help, but you might have spared yourself the trouble of lying. Frigyth had already taken my defense."

Yes, she had, and it had warmed him to hear her side with him so unconditionally. After all, she didn't know what he had been up to these last ten years, and he had reappeared out of the blue, just when a crime had been committed. She could have thought the coincidence a bit too convenient. But she hadn't hesitated in coming to his aid.

"Yes, she meant to help, I could see," the woman said. "But, unlike me, she lacked the means to provide you with an alibi for the night."

Yes, unfortunately she did. Oh, if only they had spent the night together!

Pushing the painful thought out of his mind, he took the opportunity to find out more about his old friend. "You mean that no one in the village would believe she spent the night anywhere else than in her husband's arms?"

The chuckle the woman gave was answer enough.

Evidently the mere idea was ridiculous. His gut tightened. As he'd thought.

"No one," she said unnecessarily. "She and Sigurd are just too happy together."

"I see. But why do *you* believe in my innocence? You have no idea who I am or where I spent the night. I could have stolen those horses, for all you know."

"Well, did you?" She crossed her arms over her chest, mimicking his pose. Was she mocking him? Perhaps. After all, she did not seem to be the shy kind.

He frowned and uncrossed his arms. This woman was unlike any he had ever met. She was also one of the loveliest. Up until today the only other Norse person he had seen up close was Sigurd and attractive was the last word he would have used to describe the tall Dane. But it seemed that blue eyes, blond hair and well-defined features, when they did not belong to a man you resented but a woman who intrigued you, could be rather...fascinating. No Saxon he had ever met had blue eyes quite that vibrant, or hair as shiny as gold. She was also blessed with a perfect figure.

Ironically, given the fact that they were posing as lovers, she was exactly the kind of woman he would have chosen for a night of passion. The fact that she resembled Frigyth in no way only added to the appeal. Without quite knowing why, he'd always refused to bed women who put him in mind of his childhood sweetheart.

"No, of course, I didn't steal the horses," he said, realizing the woman was still waiting for an answer.

"There you are then."

He shook his head. Clearly he was not going to win that argument. It seemed to him that she was not interested in the truth anyway. He had the feeling that she'd enjoyed getting one over that Ivar. The look on the man's face when she'd announced they were lovers had been one of surprise mingled with resentment. This might be less about defending him and more about jumping on the opportunity to get the better of someone she didn't like.

In any case, he didn't want to make her feel bad for it. Her motives mattered less than the result. She'd gotten him out of a potentially dangerous situation. If she'd settled a score with someone at the same time, he could not begrudge her the privilege. There was nothing wrong with killing two birds with one stone, it only showed resourcefulness.

"Your brother didn't seem best pleased," he said instead. In fact, he was certain the Norseman would have hit him for debauching his sister had he not been holding an infant in his arms at the time.

The woman made a grimace. "No. He wasn't. But what do you expect from a big brother? Björn still sees me as a baby."

Caedmon hid his smile. Now was not the time to tell her that she did look barely old enough to have lovers. "How old are you?"

Her answer surprised him. "Twenty-four."

He'd thought her younger. But then everything about her was not what it seemed at first glance. When she'd approached the group earlier he'd thought her timid and unassuming, but then she had gone and claimed in front of half the village that the two of them were lovers. She looked barely in her twenties but was actually of an age where she could have been married and have children. Her figure was not voluptuous enough to make men swoon but the way her clothes fit her showed it to advantage. Her face could have been described as plain until one looked into her eyes. There was a spark of mischief in the blue irises that kept you captive and she moved with an air of tranquil assurance, like someone happy with her life, that lent her an irresistible charm.

It was just as he had thought. She was intriguing, more and more with each passing moment.

"What's your name?"

"Ingrid."

"Were you born here?" Her accent, when she spoke his language, was flawless. He doubted she'd just arrived in his country.

"Yes."

"Do you live on your own?"

"As you can see." She looked around her and threw him a radiant, if slightly condescending, smile. "Do you have many more questions like this? Do you want to know if I like gruel perchance? I do, but I prefer sweet things. Do I have a dog? No, just chickens for my eggs. All of them red, except one gray one. She's my favorite."

"That's enough information, thank you. You don't need to detail what you like to wear when it's cold or why you prefer the gray hen." He couldn't help to smile back. Really he'd struck it lucky with Ingrid. The woman helping him could have been a stout matron or a vapid ninny. But his savior was both beautiful and engaging.

"Very well. My turn to ask questions then," she said, leaning a hip on the table next to her. "Why did you come to the village, if not to steal the horses? It is not often we see unknown Saxons here."

The smile vanished from his face. She had to bring this painful subject first, didn't she?

"I came to see an old acquaintance." Why did he hesitate in naming Frigyth? He had no idea and anyway, Ingrid might well have guessed who he meant. He imagined there weren't many Saxons living in the village. "But I won't linger. I stopped to say hello, but I was on my way to see my grandmother in town."

There was little point in staying here. He'd seen what he'd

wanted to see, or rather what he'd dreaded to see. The woman he had never stopped loving was blissfully happy with her husband and their brood of adorable children. Once, he had been the only thing keeping her sane but there was no place in her life for him anymore.

He'd been replaced.

"You stopped here, you say?" Ingrid carried on. "So you don't intend to stay?"

"In the village you mean? No. But..." But he had no idea what he wanted to do, or where he wanted to live. At an age where most people were settled, his future had never been more uncertain. "I spent the last ten years in London and last month I decided it was time to leave. I'll start by going to town, see what I can find there."

Ingrid threw a glance out the window. "Well, you can't go now, it's already late." Either she was worried about him being outside at night or...

Or she meant to make the most of the presence of a man in her hut. Was that what it was? Did she mean to make him reward her for her help? There was no denying that her outlandish claim had put an end to what had been about to become a very unpleasant scene. The people around her hadn't seemed to give much credence to Ivar's accusation but he might easily have convinced other villagers it was worth interrogating him.

Yes, Ingrid's intervention had been both timely and efficient.

Did that mean he should agree to it if she demanded to be bedded? No. She could ask, but she could do nothing to force him. If he refused, there was not much she would be able to do. Small as she was, she would never be able to subdue him. A sudden vision of himself tied up to the wall, at the mercy of her whims, caused his blood to surge with a suddenness he could not account for.

He cleared his throat, perplexed. Since when did the idea of being tied up get him aroused? Well since now, apparently.

"You don't expect me to sleep in your pallet, I hope?" he asked.

Ingrid couldn't help a smile at Caedmon's question. He'd made it sound as if sharing a bed with her would be the worst fate imaginable for a man, some sort of punishment. The impulse to tease him washed over her. Mischief was a side of her personality she rarely indulged. For some reason, people saw her as shy and sensible, and they didn't know how to react when she behaved differently, so she had stopped trying long ago. But this stranger would not know she usually didn't go around teasing people. He would have to accept whatever side of her she wanted to present. The temptation was too strong to resist.

She smiled. Here was an all too rare opportunity to do something unusual. She'd known the people in the village all her life, had the same predictable conversations with them all the time, and did the same things every day. But tonight there was a man she didn't know in her hut, and she could not let the opportunity for amusement pass. It might be months before she met another stranger.

"Oh, I expect you to do much more than *sleep* in my pallet," she cooed.

A deafening silence followed her declaration. She had rendered him speechless, Ingrid saw with some satisfaction.

"You expect me to give you pleasure in exchange for your help out there?" he said after a while, his voice little more than a croak.

Give her pleasure? Was that what his first thought was? Weren't men supposed to think of their own satisfaction first, if not exclusively, when bedding a woman? She had always thought so. The Saxon's question made her reassess her opinion. Perhaps they were not all like Ivar and his friends.

Her interest in him increased tenfold.

"Put it that way," she answered. "My sister-in-law, Dunne, is not going to be able to hold off Björn forever. At some point my brother is going to remonstrate with me for taking a lover. He is never going to believe I lied just to help a stranger. He will simply think I'm trying to spare you from his ire, and with good reason. So I'm thinking…Since I am to be condemned for the crime anyway, I may as well commit it."

The satisfaction she had been feeling at unsettling him transformed into alarm because then the look in his eyes became incendiary. He was considering agreeing to the offer, something she had not anticipated. She had imagined he would laugh it off and find her delightfully refreshing, maybe tease her back or even just simply refuse.

"I see," he said slowly. "You really want me to—"

"No! I was jesting, of course, I don't expect you to do anything! To me or…or to…"

Her throat went dry and she took a step backward. What had possessed her to say such a stupid thing? To jest about such matters with a man she didn't know, who didn't know her either and would take what she said at face value, who was alone with her in the hut? For all she knew, he had already decided to make the most of the opportunity of a night under her roof. It was as she had said. If he was going to get a beating in the morning for his supposed involvement with her, he might as well enjoy some benefit beforehand.

Ingrid could have kicked herself. *That* was why people behaved like what was expected of them. Because not doing so was not only silly but potentially dangerous.

Oh, what had she done? Should she demand he leave?

Would even agree? After all, she had been the one inviting him in her hut, and then all but dragged him to her bed.

"Are you—"

"Going to bed you? Sorry, no." He allowed his gaze to roam over her, as if trying to decide if he was making the right decision. "But I will accept your offer of a night in your hut and sleep on a fur in that corner, if I may. I swear I won't try anything. You have my word of honor, but you're welcome to place an axe next to you if you prefer."

Ingrid swallowed and realized that, although she didn't know him, she believed him. After all, if he'd wanted her that bad, he would simply have jumped at the offer and then pretended to ignore her protests. But he had looked appalled at the idea.

No, she would come to no harm with this man. Her shoulders relaxed.

Disaster had been avoided.

CHAPTER TWO

"I think I'll have a wash before I go."

After his long trip from London, Caedmon wanted to feel clean when he saw his grandmother for the first time in ten years. Not that she would care, she would be too busy showering him with questions. A thought suddenly tore through his mind. Was the old woman still alive? She could have died years ago and he would have been none the wiser. He shook his head and decided it was not worth worrying until he knew for certain.

"Can I borrow a piece of linen?" he asked, gesturing at the pile in the corner.

Ingrid nodded absent-mindedly. He frowned. Though she had assembled a veritable feast for him on the table, she had barely touched a thing. She was sitting opposite him, staring at the loaf of bread as if she had no idea what it was. The contrast between this subdued, pale woman and the brazen minx who had teased him about sharing a bed last night was striking. Caedmon felt a pang of guilt. Had he scared her by not immediately telling her he would never take advantage of her? Was she tired because she'd spent the night worrying he would break his word and pounce on her?

No. She didn't look scared, or tired, rather...He wasn't sure how to name it. What was certain was that he hoped to see some color in her cheeks when he came back from his dip in the river. He hated to see her like this.

"I won't be long."

There was no answer.

The river was just beyond the trees, he remembered from his earlier visits to the village. Setting off a run, he reached it in no time.

As he started to take his clothes off, Caedmon did his best to recapture the excitement he had felt at the prospect of coming back home. Was it the right choice? Going north had been the obvious option when he'd decided to leave London, but now he was not so sure. He'd been away for so long, and so much had happened since then, that he might feel like a stranger in town. Would he find peace in the place where he had spent his childhood? It was far from certain. His memories of the place were not exactly happy. Not only that, but Frigyth and her sisters were now gone, and apart from his grandmother, they were the only people he wanted to see.

Yes. Perhaps returning to his past was not the wisest decision he'd ever made.

Oh, well, it wouldn't be the first time he'd made a mistake, would it?

He dove into the cold water headfirst.

When he entered the hut later on, his hair still wet from his bath, he found Ingrid leaning against the table. Her face was chalky white and she was grimacing. He'd hoped to find her better, but she seemed much worse.

He rushed over to her and stopped before he could sweep her into his arms. For a moment he'd forgotten they didn't really know each other and he had no right to touch her so intimately. She must have seen the concern in his eyes because she tried to smile.

"Forgive me. I...I don't feel too well."

No. That much he had surmised. Not well at all, by all accounts. Had she eaten something that didn't agree with her? No. She had barely touched the bread this morning so that couldn't be it. Was that the problem then? That she was actually hungry? She had not eaten anything last night, either. Whatever it was, she looked about to faint.

"Come. You need to sit down."

He made to guide her to the only chair in the hut, but she shook her head. "I need to lie down."

She sounded dejected more than worried, as if she had experienced this discomfort before and was resigned to it. He looked at her more closely.

"Do you know what ails you?"

"Yes," she sighed, massaging her temple. A headache amongst other things, Caedmon concluded.

"Can I help?"

"No. It will pass. I just need to sleep. Would you please cover the window with the wooden panel before you go? The dark will help."

Go? He bristled at the mere suggestion. She could not think he was just going to go and leave her while she was half delirious with pain? But now was not the time for a confrontation. Without a word, he did as she'd asked and watched her burrow under the covers in search of oblivion. She looked so small, so fragile, in that moment that his protective instincts took over.

She had helped him yesterday. He would take care of her today.

Ingrid blinked. Outside it was dark, which meant she had slept all day. There was nothing odd in that, it was what always happened on the first day of her womanly flux. Still, it felt as if something was not normal. She searched her foggy brain, trying to understand what was bothering her.

Finally, she did.

There was a faint glow of light behind her that shouldn't be here. Her heartbeat instantly picked up. Someone had come into the hut while she slept and lit up a tallow candle. Who? Why? Slowly, so as not to betray the fact that she had woken up, she turned around. There was a man sitting on one of the stools, as she'd suspected, but instead of causing her to panic, the sight reassured her. Though his back was to her, there was no mistaking who he was. No one else in the village had hair that color.

"Caedmon?" He turned around at the mention of his name. "You're still here?" It was nighttime. He should be in town by now. Wasn't he supposed to have left this morning?

Before answering, he came to kneel next to the pallet. Even though his body was blocking almost all the light, she saw that his face was creased with concern. "Of course, I'm still here. I could not in all conscience leave while you were feeling so poorly. I had to see that you were all right, make sure you weren't on your own in case you needed help."

"I always knew it would pass," she whispered. Yes, she had, unfortunately, but, of course, *he* hadn't known that. If he'd thought her at death's door, he would have wanted to stay. She was touched by his thoughtfulness. "There's nothing to worry about."

He seemed to hesitate before answering. "Yes. I know that now. Frigyth told me what was happening to you."

"She—What?"

She bolted upright, shocked, mortified and angry all at once. He *knew?*

"It's all right. There's nothing to be embarrassed about. 'Tis only natural. But...I had no idea it could be that bad for some women. Is it always the same for you?"

He sounded so concerned, so matter-of-fact that her anger and embarrassment vanished. It was hard to get mad at someone who was so worried about her. "Yes. Every month. This one was particularly bad, though. How long have I been asleep? It looks like it is the middle of the night."

"It is, near enough. When you fell asleep, not knowing what to do, I went to see Frigyth to tell her you weren't well and ask her advice. Dunne was there with her and they told me you are plagued thus when your woman time comes. You don't remember they came to see you this afternoon?" he asked, sitting back on his haunches.

Yes, of course, she did remember the two women helping her putting the padding in place between her legs. She'd been grateful for the help but she'd not suspected they would have discussed such a personal topic with a man, and a stranger at that. What had they been thinking? But perhaps, having grown with him, the two women were used to discussing everything in his presence. He was no stranger to them.

Heat gushed between her legs when she moved, reminding her it was time to change the padding.

"Forgive me, I need to..."

Would there be no end to her humiliation? She felt herself flushing but Caedmon only nodded. "The women gave me what you needed. You'll find everything on the table. I brought in a pot of fresh water as well. Once you're comfortable you should eat something. I caught a rabbit earlier and Frigyth gave me some bread and honey."

"I..." She didn't know what to say. He'd seen to everything while she slept, oblivious to it all.

"I'll be outside. Just call me when you're ready."

He left before she could even thank him.

Dumbfounded, Ingrid went about washing herself and replaced the soiled padding with mechanical gestures. Then she took a deep swig of ale, wondering what to think of the Saxon who had taken care of her so well. It could be argued that it was his way of thanking her for what she had done the day before, but she had the impression that he would have done the same regardless, for anyone.

Eventually, she built up the courage to call him back inside.

He walked in, looking perfectly at ease, which helped her pretend nothing was amiss. Which, strictly speaking, was true, of course. As he'd said, there was nothing more natural than a woman having her monthly courses. It was just...well, she hadn't expected a man to be so comfortable with it. But, of course, if Ivar and his friends had not skewed her opinion of men so much, she might have been less surprised. She didn't imagine her brother shunned his wife during her flux for example. He probably attended to her as helpfully was Caedmon had done. As to Sigurd or Wolf, they always put their wives' pleasure and comfort before their own so they would not even blink at the notion of nature running its course.

Perhaps she should give men she didn't know the benefit of the doubt. After all, it would never have occurred to her to assume they were all selfish and crude before her parents' death and Ivar's betrayal.

She sat down opposite Caedmon. Not having eaten for a whole day, Ingrid was ravenous. She bit into the rabbit flesh and almost swooned. It was tender, roasted to perfection. The Saxon could certainly cook.

"Thank you, this is wonderful."

He nodded and gave a wistful smile. "I haven't roasted a rabbit in years, you know, never mind caught one. Not much call for it in a big town." He helped himself to more honey and Ingrid found herself fascinated by the way he licked his thumb when a drop landed on it. Something inside her quivered at the sight of his tongue lapping at the shiny drop, such an intimate thing to see. "And the food's nowhere near as tasty in London as it is here."

"Why did you leave your home and go so far?"

As much as she sometimes resented being part of such a small community where everyone knew her and nothing was new, she could not fathom going somewhere like London on her own. Even after the misadventure with Ivar she had not considered leaving, which went to show she didn't have an adventurous bone in her body.

Caedmon's face became an inscrutable mask and she knew without a doubt that he had been fleeing something, or someone, and didn't want to talk about it. She dipped her last piece of bread in honey and did not insist. Some burdens were not meant to be shared and didn't she know it.

"I'm rather tired. Do you mind if I get some sleep?" he asked, eyeing up the corner where he'd slept the night before.

"Of course not."

What else did he want her to say? Send him out into the night at that time? Offering him shelter was the least she could do after what he'd done for her.

"I'll wish you good night then."

Caedmon fell asleep with enviable ease, but having slept for most of the day, Ingrid was not tired. She spent long moments watching him. He was so...She searched long and hard for the best way to describe him, then when he turned and allowed his arm to unfurl on the floor by his side, she settled on "elegant".

Yes, that was a good word. Everything about him was lithe,

slender, graceful. She could have watched him for days and still be surprised by the way he opened his hand or tucked a lock of hair behind his ear. It was like watching leaves swirling in the breeze on a crisp autumn day when one had only ever seen them attached to trees before, familiar and yet, completely new.

Riveting.

In any case, it mattered not what he was. Elegant, thoughtful or exotic, the Saxon would be gone tomorrow, and she would never see him again.

CHAPTER THREE

In the morning, seeing that Ingrid was restored to her usual
self, Caedmon decided to leave. The sun was already at
its zenith and he wanted to reach the town before the end
of the afternoon, and give himself time to see if his grandmother
was still there, and find a place for the night if she was not.
There was no reason to linger in the village, anyway.

He'd gone to see Frigyth earlier that morning to say goodbye, and the meeting had not gone how he'd imagined—or
wanted—it to go. To his utter mortification, she had laughed and
jested about him still being here.

"You never came to the village to see *me*, did you," she'd
chided, a smile on her lips. "You came to see your sweetheart,
Ingrid! This, I didn't see coming, I will admit. How did you two
even meet?"

There was no way he could answer that question, as, of
course, he and Ingrid were not sweethearts, and they had met
the moment she had taken his arm and announced to the world
that they were lovers. He could not admit as much without
making a fool out of both of them. Fortunately, Frigyth's
youngest son, Moon, chose that moment to come crying that he

had a splinter stuck in his foot. While her attention was wholly on the little boy, Caedmon watched her, marveling at how content she appeared to be in her new life. Growing up with a drunkard father, she had always had a haunted look, which he'd hated and had done his best to wipe from her face. Often he'd succeeded.

But now, that look had completely disappeared, thanks to someone else.

"I don't know if you knew my youngest sister, Birgit, married a man from Mercia and now lives there?" she asked once Moon had stopped crying.

"No," he confirmed. He'd not seen or heard of Brigit since he'd left for London. But he already knew the third sister had come to live in the village and had married a Norseman herself, who happened to be none other than Ingrid's brother. He'd seen the two of them the day before with their three children. Dunne looked happy with her own husband, he had to admit. The haunted look had gone from her eyes too. Damn these Norsemen. How were Saxons like him supposed to compete when they strutted about with their muscles, their braided hair and their fierce demeanors?

Women seemed drawn to them like moths to a flame.

"Thank you, Mama." The little boy placed a kiss on his mother's cheek and, to Caedmon's surprise, another on her stomach, before running back outside.

"I'm expecting another child for the autumn," Frigyth explained, blushing slightly, when he arched a brow. "We told the children last night. Moon is ecstatic to have another little sister or brother."

Bile in his throat, Caedmon did what was expected of him. He offered his congratulations on the upcoming babe, and pretended to be happy for her when his chest felt hollow with despair. Why had he come back? Was he such a glutton for punishment? Right at that moment, Sigurd entered the hut and Caedmon had to watch as he kissed his wife full on the lips and placed a gentle hand over her stomach.

"You look beautiful this morning, Birdie," the blasted man said, stroking her with what Caedmon could only describe as reverence.

What made the whole thing worse was that it was obvious he was not trying to make him jealous. He simply loved his wife too much to keep his hands off her.

Yes, all in all the whole thing had been excruciating.

"I should get going," he declared, before emptying his cup of ale. He allowed the taste to linger on his tongue a moment before swallowing. Damn, Ingrid's ale was remarkably good, both light and floral.

But yes, he should go, before he went mad.

"I will accompany you," Ingrid said, standing up herself. "I will go as far as the meadow before the river. There might be some wild garlic left for tonight's broth."

She took her basket and they set off together. Above them a light breeze ruffled the trees' highest branches, the rustling sound mingling with the birds' chirping in perfect harmony. Sunlight weaved its way through the leaves, and the air was scented by nature in full bloom.

It was a perfect spring day, full of promise. So why could he not enjoy it? That was one of the reasons he had left London. After so long spent in a town, he had wanted to be surrounded by nature. And now that he was, instead of making the most of it, he was seething inside, reliving his painful encounter with Frigyth over and over again.

He turned to Ingrid and saw that she was doing what he didn't seem able to do, lifting her face to the sun, smiling at the birds in the trees. At one point she stopped to gather a bunch of cowslips. Bringing the yellow bells to her nose, she took a deep inhale. When she stood back up, her eyes were aglow with pleasure. Dear God, how had he ever thought her plain?

He rubbed the back of his head pensively. It had been years since he had found a woman beautiful, or rather, attractive. That he could see Ingrid's appeal whilst mulling over Frigyth's rejection was more than a little disconcerting.

"Are you all right?" Ingrid asked, and he realized he must be scowling.

He nodded. "Of course. But I never thanked you for your help the other day. I'm not sure the accusation of theft would have been dismissed so easily without your intervention."

The flowers bobbed their delicate heads when she waved his thanks away with a flick of her wrist. "'Tis nothing. You would have done the same for me. And you did me a great favor in turn."

"I did nothing to alleviate the pain of your suffering," he reminded her. "*That* would have been a great favor. I only made sure you had something to eat when you woke up."

She gave a small, defeated smile. "No one can do anything about the pain. But they can feed me and make me more comfortable. They can stay and look after me, make sure I'm all right, all without me having to ask for anything. I truly appreciated what you did."

"Well, I'm glad."

She glanced at the clearing to her right and then planted her amazing blue gaze into his. Like him, she seemed at loss as to what to say and reluctant to part ways.

"I'll leave you here, I think," she said eventually. "Goodbye, Caedmon. Come say hello if you ever visit the village again."

"Goodbye, Ingrid. I will."

But he already knew he would not visit again. What would be the point, other than cause him more pain and show him what he could never have? Frigyth had never wanted him as a husband, and now she didn't even need him as a friend. He had better try to build himself a new life well away from her.

He set off for town with renewed determination but as he approached the river Caedmon found that he was parched. He knelt by the water and took a long drink. It was refreshing, but not as good as Ingrid's ale. The thought made him smile.

The little Norsewoman had made a lasting impression on his mind and he already knew he would not be able to forget her, despite their short acquaintance. She had been surprisingly easy to be with, making no demands, thanking him for doing nothing more than roast a rabbit for her when she was out cold with pain. Her heartfelt gratitude, her irrepressible appetite for life and her penchant for mischief, combined with her beauty, had been an intoxicating combination.

And, of course, there had been her outrageous jest about the two of them sharing a bed. To his shock, the suggestion had stirred his interest. For a shameful, inexplicable moment, he had even considered agreeing to the suggestion.

Should he have? Perhaps. As much as she'd claimed to be jesting, there had been a glint in her eye telling him she would not have been averse to it if he'd played his cards right. And who knew, a woman like her might have put an end to the endless cycle of disappointing conquests. She was so different from the women he'd met in London that she might well have been the solution to his problem. Dunne and Frigyth had found happiness with men from the village, why could he not do the same with a Norsewoman? Perhaps, being different from the women he was used to, she would expect different things from him, see him differently?

No, he was getting ahead of himself. They'd met two days ago and, even if he found her beautiful and desirable, he was neither ready nor willing to get settled with anyone. It might be that he would never be able to do so.

He splashed some water into his face, determined to put such foolish thoughts from his mind. It was then that he heard the voices. A group of men was coming toward him. At the moment they were hidden behind the bushes and didn't seem to realize someone could hear them. But hear them he did.

"We stole their horses and that was a great satisfaction."

A chorus of agreement followed the declaration. Then there was a sinister laugh and a second man spoke.

"Yes, but having had their beasts between my legs, I now feel in the mood for a different kind of ride, if you know what I mean. So we'll steal a few of their women. There are some rather comely ones in that village, I think you'll agree. Why should the savages be the only ones to enjoy them?"

"Aye, you said it!"

From his place by the river, Caedmon froze.

The bastards who'd stolen the horses the other night now wanted to commit an ever bigger crime. They were about to raid the village and abduct as many women as they could carry. His gaze darted to the meadow in the distance. He'd left Ingrid there on her own, looking for wild garlic. She would be the first one the Saxons encountered. They would take her.

And they would rape her.

His decision was made in the blink of an eye. He would go with the men, pretend to want a Norsewoman for himself. That way he would make sure to be the one abducting Ingrid, and protect her. She would be safe with him and, as soon as they'd reached the scoundrels' lair, he would let her go, so she could go get help for the other women. From what he'd heard there were at least four Saxons behind the bushes. As much as he wanted to rip them to pieces now, before they even got to the women, on his own he could do nothing to stop them. But he could at least ensure Ingrid was not hurt and the others got help. It was not ideal, but it was the best he could have hoped for.

He stood up and walked over to the men, doing his best to appear calm when his blood was boiling with a rage such as he had rarely felt. He would have to appear like the worst kind of bastard when all his life he'd been praised for being a good man. The irony was not lost on him. Would he even be able to do it?

He could only hope so. Too much depended on him.

When he broke through the bushes, the startled men turned to him with scowls on their faces. He didn't let it worry him. *He* was not in danger of being raped. He could face them.

"Forgive me, but I was by the river having a drink and I could not help overhearing your conversation." The word made him cringe inwardly. That had been no conversation! Nevertheless, he had to hide his disgust or his plan would never work. "I was wondering if you'd let me come with you."

The four men looked at each other uncertainly. It was obvious they didn't quite know what to make of his offer. That was good. Confusion was better than anger. They were all younger than him, he noticed, something that would also play in his favor. If he could impress them, they would be less suspicious of his motives.

"Let him come. The more the better. There is always strength in number," a rather scrawny-looking individual said. Caedmon repressed a sneer. Of course, *he* would prefer to be surrounded by burly friends. On his own he would achieve nothing.

"Why would you want to come with us?" The man nearest to him, who was also the oldest, was not so easily won over.

Caedmon knew nothing would convince him more than proving he was as vile as they were so he palmed himself crudely. "Why do you think? I have a taste for blonde women with fair skin if you must know and I have been too long without."

The other three laughed and made rude gestures. One of

them, a tall, gangly youth, slapped him on the back. He'd been accepted into the group.

"Well, then, my friend, let's go."

ONE LAST BUNCH of leaves and then she would go. Pleased with the product of her gathering, Ingrid looked at her basket. It was almost full. She had more than enough wild garlic for an excellent broth.

Smiling, she took the path leading to the village and found herself wondering where Caedmon was now. Had he already reached the fork in the road, and turned right at the gnarled oak? Perhaps. With those long legs of his, he would be eating up ground. Just before she reached the edge of the forest, she encountered four of her friends, on their way to the river.

"Ingrid!" Helga, the healer's granddaughter, and named after her, greeted her. "Want to join us? We're going for a dip in the water."

"No, thank you, I was just getting back to—"

There was no warning. One moment she was talking to the women, the next a swarm of devils had descended upon them, shouting and brandishing sticks.

Mayhem broke loose in the clearing. The women screamed and started to run in all directions, the men gave chase, catching them up before they could go very far and throwing them to the ground. Horrified, Ingrid recognized one of the attackers. Caedmon. There was no mistaking him, after two days spent in his company, she knew his every feature, even if she had never seen such a frightful expression on his face before.

What was he doing here, in the middle of a group of attackers?

The shock was so intense that for a moment she couldn't

move. Taking advantage of her immobility, a scrawny man seized her by the wrist and started to draw her to him. How dare he? Shaken out of her trance, Ingrid kicked him. Her foot connected with a hard shin, the pain of the contact causing both the man and her to scream at the same time.

Then, just as she braced herself for retaliation, she heard Caedmon's snarl right in her ear.

"I'll take this one."

A moment later she found herself with her face pressed against his chest.

I'll take this one?

Had he just said that? Yes, he had, she wasn't dreaming, the men really meant to abduct her and her friends, and the Saxon who had slept under her roof, eaten her food, looked after her, really intended to rape *her*, who had come to his aid only the other day, in preference to the others. Fueled by rage and fear, she started to pummel at his chest. It didn't take her long to see she was inflicting little, if any, damage.

"Let's go, before the savages come running after us!" the man who was holding Helga cried out.

A moment later Ingrid was thrown over Caedmon's shoulder and held in place by iron arms. No matter how much she ranted or however much she tried to disentangle herself from his hold, she could not move. From her upside down position she saw that the other women were treated in exactly the same manner.

Then the men started to run. Caedmon was the last in the group and going slower than she had expected. Either he had no idea where he was going or she was heavier than he had expected and he was finding it hard to keep the pace with the others. Good, she thought savagely, wishing she weighed twenty more pounds.

Suddenly he stopped and knelt down. It took her a moment

to understand he had seen a cluster of mushrooms and was picking them.

He was mad, he had to be. Who in their right mind stopped to pick mushrooms in the middle of an abduction? The realization froze the marrow in her bones, because if he was really mad, then there was no telling what he would do to her. Oh, of course, she had already guessed he would rape her…Men did not abduct women to shower them with gifts and massage their feet. No, unfortunately, she was under no illusion as to the men's intentions. The women would be taken to a secluded, grimy place and then they would be raped, probably more than once, probably by more than one man. That was bad enough.

But if they were also mad, then they might do worse than that. They might well cut them with their knives during the assault or kill them afterward.

She tried to scream, even though all the air had been sucked out of her lungs by her position, tried to hit Caedmon, even if she could tell her blows had no effect. But she could not just give up, make him think she did not mind being treated like a victim, because she did mind.

"Let me go, you monster!"

No answer, no reaction. He didn't even slow down. Ingrid stopped struggling to focus on breathing. Her vision had blurred, and her head felt ten times lighter than usual, or heavier, she wasn't sure which. She already knew she would collapse when he finally placed her back on her feet, and be unable to fight him off.

It was her worst nightmare, come true. Again.

Tears pooled in her eyes when she imagined him pouncing on her.

No, not him!

Where was the kind man who had knelt by her pallet and told her he had prepared everything she needed last night?

She had only left him in the meadow a short while ago. There had been no sign of madness in him then, he had seemed perfectly normal. So what had happened? Ingrid had once heard Wolf talk about a man he'd met in town who was seemingly in possession of two identities. He could be perfectly amiable at the start of a conversation and then turn into a veritable fury for no reason that anyone could discern. Was Caedmon one of these men? Thoughtful guest one moment and evil rapist the next? And where had he found his friends? He'd come to the village alone, or so it had seemed. Had it all been premeditated? Had he been sent ahead to assess the lay of the land, establish the best place for them to strike?

It was better not to try and make sense of it all, and instead pay attention to where they were going. She wanted to be able to retrace her steps in the unlikely event that she managed to escape.

After what seemed like an eternity, they reached a hut in the middle of the forest.

This was it, the place where their ordeal was to take place. It took Ingrid all her determination not to faint.

CHAPTER FOUR

Huddled with the other women in a corner of the hut, Ingrid was doing her best to keep panic at bay. Night had fallen not so long ago and, as they had not been given any light, they could barely see their own hands. The darkness did not help her to stay calm. One of her friends was crying softly, not too far from her. Perhaps Helga, perhaps Frida, who was only eighteen and about to marry Magnar, with whom she'd been in love for years. The poor girl would be wondering if he would reject her after this, deeming her ruined.

If this happened, in one dreadful night the Saxons would have taken her innocence and destroyed her life.

The thought lent Ingrid some strength. She could not let it happen.

There *had* to be a way out of this nightmare, one she had not thought of yet. To her surprise, the men had not raped them straight away upon arriving in the clearing. Instead they had packed them all in a disused hut and bound their wrists and ankles tight to ensure they could not flee while they waited to be used for their pleasure. Why the delay, Ingrid had no idea. All she knew was that she could hear the men carousing outside by the fire, a terrifying sound, because the more they drank and egged each other on, the more determined they would become.

"Why do you think they have not come to us yet?" Helga asked in a whisper, huddling closer to her. Ingrid could feel her friend trembling and wished she could take her into her arms. They would both take comfort from the embrace.

"I know not."

It didn't make sense and she did expect the door to open any moment on the group of lechers, drunk on mead and lust. Would they each take the woman they had abducted, or would they share? Would they take them here, one by one, in full view of the others? Would they make them take part in the degradations? Every dreadful possibility crossed her mind. The men sounded in high spirits at the thought of what was to come. Although, now that she thought of it, the merry laughter and bawdy jokes seemed to have lessened a bit. All she could hear were strange groans and moans. What was going on outside? Had they found other women to assault? Was that why they hadn't come to them yet, because they were already too busy raping other innocents? No. She could not hear any screams or feminine protests.

Suddenly the door opened. Though it was dark in the hut, she recognized the man standing in the frame, alone. Caedmon. The other Saxons she had seen were far less imposing. His body, framed by the fire burning in the clearing, seemed huge. How had she ever thought him slender and elegant?

"You," he said, pointing in her direction. "Come here."

She glared at him, even if it was probably lost in the darkness. But did he really think she would obey without question? Well, he would have to think again. She might have no choice about what was going to happen, but she was not going to make it easy for him.

"How can I go anywhere? I'm tied up." He would know that

since he had done it himself, of course, but she could not resist pointing it out. Not that she expected him to feel remorse over it.

Without a word he approached, causing the women around her to scuttle backward in fright. Ingrid forced herself not to move. She would not give him the satisfaction of seeing that she was terrified of what was to come. Only that morning she and Caedmon had broken their fasts together, he had asked her how she was feeling. And now he had tied her up like a slave and was about to rip the clothes from her body before using it to slake his lust. How had she ever trusted him? Disillusion, fear and resentment churned in her gut and she wondered if she would not be sick. Perhaps she should, as she imagined that finding himself covered in vomit would cool any man's ardor.

Or...Should she remind him that she was bleeding? Perhaps it would disgust him?

It was doubtful. He already knew it and he had not let it stop him. He seemed determined to have her, whatever her opinion on the matter, whatever else was going on.

He knelt before her, and then retrieved a knife from his boot. Ingrid's heart almost failed her. As if things weren't bad enough, he was showing her that he was armed. If she was foolish enough to try and fight him off, she didn't stand a chance. The fight would be over in a heartbeat. She would have to submit, or die. Before panic could overwhelm her, he sliced through the rope at her ankles and helped her back up to her feet. She fully expected him to throw her over his shoulder again but he only nodded toward the door, then waited for her to move. The gesture was incongruous, almost like a polite invitation.

After you.

Deciding to spare the other women the horrid sight of their friend being violated in front of them, Ingrid walked to the door without a word of protest. Once out of the hut, she considered running away before rejecting the possibility. In the dark, with her wrists still bound, she wouldn't go far, and then he would make her pay for forcing him to break into a run when his blood was up.

Heart in her throat, she spotted the other men sprawled by the fire. Was Caedmon going to share her with them? Men found this arousing, she knew. No. Taking her by the arm, he led her to a corner of the clearing, stopping only when they were under the cover of the trees, as if to hide her from view.

Despite the direness of her situation, she couldn't help a sense of relief. At least she wouldn't have to endure more than one assault for now. Biting the inside of her mouth so hard she tasted blood, she waited for him to throw her to the ground.

But to her intense surprise, he left her standing where she was and went to lean against the nearest tree, his attitude wholly unthreatening. What was that? He was supposed to pounce on her, was he not? He'd taken her into the woods to rape her, had he not? So what was he waiting for? Or perhaps the mad trance was over and he had reverted to his normal behavior?

His first words seemed to confirm this impression. "Are you hurt?"

Ah, so somewhere in his addled mind he'd understood that she *could* have been hurt, or at least afraid. Hope surged through her, quickly followed by disgust. Him being concerned for her well-being right now didn't erase the fact that he had earlier abducted her with the intention of raping her.

"No. Not yet," she said with all the venom she could muster.

There was enough moonlight filtering through the trees for her to see him wince. He didn't seem happy to be reminded of what was in store for her. Well, neither did she, so it was hard to sympathize.

"How are the women faring?" he asked, shuffling on his feet.

"How do you think? They are scared. They are worried about their men and children, who will have noted their absence by now and be wondering where they are. They are waiting to be used for your friends' pleasure." Her throat went dry but she thought she had better keep talking. If there was any chance she could make him see that what he was doing was wrong, she had to seize it.

As she spoke, however, Ingrid realized that she was not putting herself in the same category as the other women. Why not? Wasn't she waiting to be used for a stranger's pleasure as well? Weren't her wrists still tied? Hadn't she been abducted by a man who'd told his friends she was his? Yes. But...oddly, fear had receded to the back of her mind.

"Why haven't the women been raped yet?" she asked.

Caedmon winced again. For someone waiting to commit a crime, he seemed to have a strong aversion to anything relating to it.

"I convinced the men we had better wait a moment in case we had been seen by some of the Norsemen and followed. Then the screams of the women would surely draw them to us, and cut their pleasure short. I argued that a little delay could not hurt."

"Well, you were right about that!" Ingrid spat. How could he talk about it all with such calm, expose his twisted reasoning with such composure? Couldn't he see that delaying an assault on innocent women was not something to be proud of? "It makes little difference to us to be raped tonight or in the morning!"

He did not appear at all ruffled by her outburst. He really *was* mad, she decided, that was the only explanation for his behavior. If he could not see the horror and ludicrousness of what he was saying, or worry about her fear or feel guilt over his betrayal of the woman who had helped him, then all hope was lost.

Suddenly he moved. Sleek as cat, he crossed the distance between them. His eyes were both transparent and dark in the moonlight, a combination she would have thought impossible until now. She shivered and then recoiled. Wasn't she supposed to be frightened rather than fascinated?

"Listen, we have no time to discuss this right now. You are going to go to the Norsemen village and bring back help. I cannot fight four men on my own. If I could, I would have stopped them from abducting you and the women and none of this would have happened."

Stop them?

Ingrid took in a sharp breath as understanding dawned. He had never intended to take part in the expedition. None of this was what it had seemed at first. Relief washed through her, making her weak. Her instinct had not failed her. He really was the considerate, kind man she'd met the other day.

"You...These men, then, they're not your friends?"

"Of course, those bastards are not my friends!" Caedmon spat. She didn't need to hear any more to know he was telling the truth. He had only been playing a role. "I'd never seen them before today but I overheard them discuss their intentions when they walked past me at the river. There was no time to elaborate any sound plans, I just knew I had to do something. I did what I could to incapacitate them but it will not last forever. That's why you need to go get help."

Incapacitate? What was he talking about now? "What did you do?"

"I found some death caps on the way here and put them in the ale as soon as we arrived. Fortunately the poison didn't take long to take effect. The men should be out of action for most of the night and leave the women alone. I don't think they will want to go anywhere near them while they're emptying their bowels and stomachs. This will give you time to reach the village and hopefully be back before dawn with some of your formidable friends. Then all together we can give the bastards what they deserve."

With those words, he took his knife out of his boot and cut at the ties binding her wrists. Then he rubbed at her skin gently, as if to apologize for tying her up and inflicting her pain.

Ingrid stared at him in disbelief. He had planned all this from the start. That was why he had made sure he would be the one to carry her away and stayed behind the group, why he had stopped to pick the deadly mushrooms while they ran. Yes, now everything made sense. She understood why the men's laughter had transformed into groans of pain as night had started to fall, why no one had been raped yet. Because Caedmon had been there.

He wasn't mad at all, just very clever and brave. He'd never meant to hurt her, but protect her.

"Why didn't you tell me what you intended to do earlier in the hut, in front of the other women?" They would have taken heart from the fact that help was coming.

Caedmon shook his head. "I didn't want to risk the men overhearing me, as I need to appear on their side until the Norsemen arrive. And I didn't want to raise the poor women's hopes up in case...Well, in case my plan doesn't work. But it might, if you hurry."

Yes, it might well work, if she ran. There was no choice anyway, it *had* to work. She simply could not have the rape of her friends on her conscience. Caedmon had done his part, she had to do hers.

She took his hand into hers and gave it a squeeze. "Thank you."

"Please do not thank me for not taking part in such a vile

enterprise as raping women." He stared at her, returning the squeeze. "Will you know the way back to the village?"

Though she had been carried upside down earlier, Ingrid knew those woods like the back of her hand. She was confident she would be able to retrace her steps without getting lost, even at night. The moon, bright and round tonight, was throwing its light over the land and all the clouds had vanished. It was as if nature wanted to aid her.

"Yes. I know where we are. I'll be back before dawn."

On impulse, she placed a hand over Caedmon's cheek. "Thank you, Saxon. I'll never forget what you did tonight."

For a brief moment, he leaned into the caress and she thought she saw him close his eyes. Then he let go of her fingers and took a step backward.

"Go. Make sure you bring back at least three men."

IN THE END, she brought four. Wolf, Sigurd, Björn and Magnus, the village blacksmith, who'd lent his cart for the expedition. If the expression on the men's faces was any indication, the Saxons didn't stand a chance. They would be ripped to pieces before they could say a word.

Not wanting to warn their enemies of their arrival with the noise of the horse's hooves, the company alighted from the cart some distance away from the clearing and traveled the rest of the way on foot.

Above the horizon, the sun threw its first rays. Dawn was just breaking, allowing them a good view of their target.

As soon as they reached the clearing, however, Ingrid knew something was wrong. She had dreaded being greeted by the women's screams but all she could hear were male grunts. It didn't take her long to understand that the men were fighting between themselves. And there was no prize guessing why. They had recovered from their indigestion and realized they had a traitor in their midst.

Heart in her throat, she started running, the men at her heels.

It was just as she'd feared. Caedmon was facing three of the Saxons. Two of them were restraining him by the arms, and the small, scrawny one was facing him. The fourth one was lying on the ground by the dying fire, either floored by an earlier blow from Caedmon or still prey to the mushroom poisoning. Either way, he was not a threat at the moment, which was all that mattered.

"Let that man go," Wolf ordered, his voice deathly cold.

The men all turned to face him, and that was when Ingrid saw it. The scrawny man was holding a knife and pointing it over Caedmon's heart. Everything within her dissolved. This changed everything. She could have brought twice as many Norsemen and it would still have been of no use. Armed, the Saxon had the upper hand.

"Don't come anywhere near or I'll bleed him like a pig," he warned, waving his weapon.

"No!" The word was torn from her throat. Caedmon could not die, not like this, not for helping her! She would never forgive herself.

Sigurd took a step forward, all menacing intent. He'd never been as patient as the Icelander, and she feared an outburst on his part, one that would have devastating consequences, but he stopped as soon as the man placed his blade against Caedmon's stomach.

"I said don't move or I swear all you'll get is his carcass."

Everyone froze. What could they do now? As soon as any of them made a move, Caedmon would die. No one would be able to reach the Saxon before he used his knife. His two friends were still holding Caedmon captive, so no escape was possible. There was nothing anyone could do to stop the massacre. If the man wanted to kill, he only had to extend his arm to do it. He could spill his victim's guts in a heartbeat. Ingrid stared at the scene in horror. Only a moment ago she had been so sure everything would be all right, that with five men against four they were assured victory. But now everything was turned on its head. They could have outnumbered the Saxons twenty to one, it would still have made no difference. Eventually the men would be overcome, but not before Caedmon paid the ultimate price.

"It's hopeless," she sobbed.

Björn's hands landed over her shoulders, providing the anchor she needed not to sink into despair. "Wait," he said in Norse. "You're forgetting Magnus."

She frowned. What did he mean by that? It was only then she noticed that the smithy was missing. What was up? Did they have a plan she was not aware of?

Wolf put his hands up. "All right. Just tell us what you want."

Ingrid bristled. Surely he wasn't going to agree to the bastard's terms? Who cared what they wanted? Everything within her rebelled. But when Björn's hands tightened over her shoulders in warning, she realized the Icelander was only trying to gain time, until Magnus could do whatever he had been sent to do.

But what was that? She could not understand how one man could overpower three.

"What do you think? We want a taste of your women," the vile Saxon had the gall to say. "We promise you can have them back after. But first, that man is going to pay for what he did."

It all happened in quick succession.

The man raised his hand, with the obvious intent of slashing through Caedmon's middle. He made contact. Blood spurted everywhere. Ingrid gagged and fell to her knees. Then a piece of wood appeared out of nowhere, and knocked the knife out of the man's hand. Wolf cried out, *"Nù!"* and the four Norsemen charged at the Saxons, three from her right, the smithy from the bushes to her left. She could only stare, while the clearing erupted into mayhem. After a while, she managed to get back to her feet and run to Caedmon. He was lying on his back, gasping for air, his face ghastly white.

Falling by his side, she pressed her hands on his wound. Hot, sticky liquid flooded her hands. No, by the gods, he could not die now!

"Don't move," she urged. "Don't move, don't move."

Ingrid could not say anything else, could not think, except for one thing. Had the smithy not thrown the branch to defect the blow so skilfully, Caedmon would be dead by now, his guts spilled on the forest floor.

"Oh!" she said in a sob. "Just...Please don't move."

"I won't."

Relief washed through Caedmon when silence finally filled the clearing. His plan had worked. The women were safe, the Saxons were out of action, possibly dead. Not that he'd cared if they were. They deserved everything they got.

By his side was Ingrid, pressing her hands on his stomach to try and stem the flow of blood oozing from his wound. It hurt like hell. He closed his eyes to focus on breathing. When he opened them again, an enormous man was standing over him.

"I'm Wolf." The Norseman introduced himself, as if he didn't think Caedmon would remember him. But he did. He was the one who'd had his stallion stolen the other day. "Ingrid explained to us what you did yesterday. On behalf of the men whose wives, sisters or daughters were taken, I thank you. You showed great bravery when you came to their aid."

"Please. I could not stand by when I overheard what the men had planned."

"I understand that. No man of honor could. But you were on your own, with no warning or time to elaborate a plan. Yet your courage and presence of mind allowed each and every one of the women to walk out of this nightmare unscathed."

"Yes," he rasped, "that is all I wanted."

Just then the other men joined them to announce that the Saxons were all unconscious.

"Are you sure you don't want them dead?" Björn asked, his voice little more than a snarl.

"Yes," Wolf sounded as if he was forcing himself to be reasonable. "After all, they didn't touch the women in the end, and the death of four Saxons will not be so easily explained. No one apart from us knows what they intended to do. If they were found dead, it would look like a gratuitous punitive expedition and questions might be asked."

Caedmon could only agree with the Icelander's reasoning but he could see that the other Norsemen were more than ready to risk being accused of summary justice. They did not go against Wolf's decision, however.

There was a silence. Then Sigurd asked. "How bad is the cut on your stomach?"

"I'll be fine," Caedmon answered sharply, hating to have to be in Frigyth's husband's debt. Then he turned to Wolf again. "Your horses. They're in the field by the river, just behind the hut." Last night, before the mushrooms had taken effect, the men had boasted about the theft and told him all he wanted to know. "If you use the ropes binding the women's hands, you can easily get them back."

Wolf nodded, then he and Sigurd went to join the other men who had already gone to the hut to free the women. Ingrid stayed next to him, urging him not to move.

He closed his eyes again. Yes. If fever didn't set in, he might well be fine. But it had been a close thing.

All too soon the clearing was a hive of activity. Wolf and a man whom Ingrid had told him was the village smithy had managed to retrieve all the horses. Demon the stallion seemed as excited to be reunited with the Icelander as any child would be to be returned to his father.

"Magnus will ride back with the women and the Saxon in his cart while we men bring the horses home," Wolf declared to the group assembled in front of him.

"Now, wait!" Björn snarled. "I'm not having my sister anywhere near the—"

He was not allowed to finished. "He saved the women, it's the least we can do for him. Besides, even if he weren't injured, he would pose no threat to her or anyone. Or have you not understood what he did?" There was no answer and Wolf pressed his advantage. "His wound needs stitching. Ingrid is skilled with the needle, she will see to it as soon as they arrive."

There was no contravening the big Icelander in his role as leader of the village. Björn did not protest further but he threw a lethal look in his direction, as if to warn him not to attempt anything. Caedmon would have laughed if the slightest movement had not caused his stomach to contract. A bad idea, considering the slash currently splitting it in half. Indeed, what could he do in his present state save lie in the cart and hope for the pain to dull? Nothing.

Sigurd placed a hand on Ingrid's brother's shoulder and said quietly, "You can trust the Saxon. He's a good man."

Ah, yes. A good man. As usual.

Caedmon barely repressed a sigh. But at least in this case he had done something to earn the name so he supposed he could not complain.

Without a word, Wolf helped him to his feet. Caedmon

would have liked to refuse, but the maneuver was just too painful for him to do it on his own. Besides, he didn't need to lose more blood than he already had. Supported by the Icelander, he slowly made his way to the smithy's cart. A moment later he was settled amongst the exhausted women, who showered him with thanks and blessings. He merely nodded.

"See you at the village," Wolf said, before giving Magnus the signal to depart.

CHAPTER FIVE

The journey over rough terrain was excruciating. Caedmon kept his eyes closed and his mouth shut throughout so as not to betray by a look or a groan just in how much pain he was. Ingrid held his hand the whole time and he was glad of it, as he took it to mean she had forgiven him. Seeing the fear in her eyes, hearing the panic in her voice when he'd abducted her had been a blow to the gut, almost as painful as the slash he'd just received. He'd had his reasons for acting the part of the villain, and if he had to do it all again, he would do the same, but she hadn't known it was not real. For too long, she would have been out of her mind with fear, thinking she was about to be raped, and possibly killed.

But despite all the anguish he had caused her, she had forgiven him.

After what felt like an eternity, they arrived at the village. Understandably, it was in upheaval. Everyone was waiting for news of the abducted women. As soon as they had alighted from the cart to be reunited with their frantic loved ones, Magnus deposited him outside Ingrid's hut. With his help, Caedmon limped over to the pallet, where he collapsed without ceremony.

Finally, he could rest and have his wound seen to. About time, too. He was shaking with pain. He'd never been the kind of man who got himself involved in fights and had never suffered anything like a knife cut before. At least it seemed to have stopped bleeding.

"So. Wolf thinks I need to stitch your wound," Ingrid said, looking nervous at the prospect.

"Yes. You probably do," he agreed grimly. Though Magnus' intervention had stopped the cut from being fatal, it was both too long and too deep to be left alone. "Could I have a drink first?" There was no use pretending this wouldn't be an ordeal. He had never needed as much as a single stitch in his life and he dreaded the prospect.

"Of course." She handed him a cup full of the excellent ale he'd enjoyed during his stay under her roof. Was it only yesterday morning he'd left? It seemed more like two years. "I'll get everything I need."

When she came back, she had a basin of water and a few pieces of cloth in her hands.

"I need to wash the blood off first, so I can see what I'm doing," she explained almost apologetically. "Will you be able to remove your shirt?"

The mere idea of having to sit up sent his guts into a tangle of knots. "Perhaps I could just lift it?" he said hopefully.

To his relief, she agreed. "It should be enough, as the cut is quite low on the stomach. May I?"

He nodded, only too happy to lie there and have her take charge. Kneeling by his side, she slowly lifted the shirt up, making sure the material wasn't sticking to the drying blood. No, he wasn't bleeding anymore. Still, Ingrid clicked her tongue in disapproval.

"What is it?" He frowned. Was the wound worse than he had thought?

She gestured at his chest. "Your shirt will have to be mended as well. It's cut clean through."

Well, yes, it would be. He gave a little mirthless laugh and regretted it when pain slashed through his middle. "That is the least of my problems," he croaked.

Ingrid's eyes widened. "Sorry, of course. I don't know why I said that."

"Probably because, like me, you've never been in such a situation. It's all right. I suspect I might start talking nonsense myself in a moment."

"I will have to lower the waistband of your braies," she whispered. "As I said, the wound is quite low on the abdomen."

He nodded his agreement but when he saw her with her bottom lip caught between her teeth and her hands poised above the laces fastening his braies, his whole body went taut—including the part that should have had the decency to lay dormant. Even though she was not trying to entice him in any way, the gesture was too evocative for him not to react. Only a moment ago he'd thought he was too weakened by the loss of blood and in too much pain to do anything but evidently he was wrong.

Apparently, he could still get aroused.

When Ingrid flushed a vivid crimson, he understood that she'd seen the effect her actions had on his body. Not that it was difficult, placed where she was. He was rethinking the wisdom of having her lower his braies, after all. Another inch and she would expose the tip of his manhood. Quickly he readjusted himself while she turned to dip a piece of cloth in the basin. It made little difference.

Dear lord, this was embarrassing.

"Pay it no mind," he growled when she turned to face him again. "I'm a man and you're a woman undressing me, I suppose it is inevitable this should happen."

"I suppose so," she answered, wringing the cloth—and stalling for time. Apparently she thought she had better wait until he regained some semblance of control before she did anything. He agreed. The only problem was, it would not happen while she looked at him with flushed cheeks and wide eyes.

"I expect it will go down as soon as you stick that needle in me."

"I expect it will. But I have to wash you first."

Oh, God. Washing. He'd forgotten about that. In other words, she was going to put her hands on him, rub him slowly in a place inches away from his straining member. It would be torture for them both. But it could not be helped. He would have offered to do it himself if his head didn't start spinning as soon as he tried to lift it, but he knew he would never be able to manage. Couldn't the blasted Saxon have cut his arm? Or at least his chest?

"I'll go and get everything ready while you...finish your drink," Ingrid murmured.

While you try to compose yourself, she meant.

And he tried, he really did, calling on all his powers of imagination to picture rotting carcasses writhing with worms and snails crawling all over his flesh. He even, when this didn't work, conjured up a memory of the man who'd lived next door to him in London, complete with rolls of fat, grimy hands and putrid breath. In vain. When Ingrid came back with her thread and needle, there was still a sizeable bulge at the front of his braies.

Acting as if she couldn't see it, Ingrid went about wiping the blood from his skin. It was as bad as he had feared. Because she was so gentle, he could not even use the pain she was inflicting as an ally. There wasn't any pain, just a beautiful, sweet-smelling woman on her knees by his side, with her head bent low over his crotch. Damn the Saxon to hell!

Closing his eyes made no difference whatsoever, because he could still feel and imagine. When she finally stopped, he was hard enough to hammer nails and Ingrid sounded distinctively out of breath.

He opened his eyes again and found her staring at him. His breath caught in his throat. How could anyone look so beautiful in the midst of such grim a task?

"All clean. Now for the hard part." She flushed at the words, as if realizing what she'd said, then threw the piece of cloth into the basin. "I'm sorry for the pain I will cause you. I will be as gentle as I can."

Caedmon only grunted and took one last swig of ale, readying himself for the ordeal. At least now his erection should go down. Small mercies. "And I'm sorry to have to inflict such a task on you."

A tense smile answered him. "Don't worry about me. I'd much rather be here stitching a wound than in that hut being raped. Again." She added that last word in such a low voice that he wasn't sure he'd heard her right.

Had she said: "*again*"? His heart skipped a beat. Had one of the Saxons raped her last night, before he could free her? When? How? It didn't seem possible. He'd been watching the door to the hut with an eagle eye all evening. If anyone had even tried to enter, he would have stopped them. Besides, the men had all been lying on the floor, trying to survive the mushroom poisoning.

He opened his mouth to ask what she meant but, at that precise moment she stuck the needle in for the first stitch and he gritted his teeth.

This would be hell.

Ingrid tried to keep her body relaxed to make sure her gestures were as fluid as possible but the whole thing was nerve-racking to say the least. Not that the wound was horrific, exactly. Thankfully, even if it was rather long, the cut was neat and would be easily mended. But Caedmon's golden skin, surprisingly muscular stomach and, well, distracting bulge just under her right hand, made the task all the more daunting. She would have stitched her brother or any of the villagers and thought nothing of it. This man though…This man was different. It was not just that he had saved her and the other women from a dire fate, or that he was objectively handsome. He drew her like no other, had from the start.

She would have liked to kiss his exposed stomach rather than stitch it, bring him pleasure rather than inflict pain, lick his skin rather than—

Kiss? Lick? Was she mad? She berated herself for such distracting thoughts and focused on the task at hand. Caedmon would bear that scar all his life. All his life he would be reminded that he had sacrificed himself for her. The least she could do was ensure it was not a horrid one.

This is just another shirt I'm mending, she kept repeating to herself. *Nothing more than rough wool or dyed linen I'm piercing.*

Mm, yes. This was like mending a shirt in the same way that fire was no hotter than sunlight and the ocean no bigger than a puddle. Thinking those things was no help whatsoever. Perhaps talking would help distract her.

She cleared her throat.

"When Dunne taught me how to sew all those years ago, I hated it. I never imagined I would ever become proficient at it or…" She gave a hollow laugh. "Or that I would end up stitching a wound one day. I don't mind admitting it is quite nerve-racking."

"I can well imagine," Caedmon said through clenched teeth. "I don't mind admitting that being the one stitched up is not pleasant either."

"No. Of course, not." What was she doing, complaining? He was the one suffering. "Forgive me, I'm doing my best not to be too rough."

"Oh, I have no doubt you're doing all you can to make the whole thing as bearable as possible." His voice sounded strained. "Still, I won't mind when it's over."

A moment later, it was. Ingrid's hands were trembling, and Caedmon's forehead was slick with sweat. She wiped it with her last clean piece of linen, lingering over the gesture. He'd been so brave, not uttering a single moan of protest throughout.

"Let me go see if Björn has something that could dull the pain," she said, standing up on shaky legs.

Dear Heavens, if she felt so unsteady she could not imagine how Caedmon, who'd had to endure having his skin pierced time and time again, would fare. This had been nothing short of an ordeal and she wasn't sure when she would build up the courage to pick up sewing again. It seemed to her that every time she stuck her needle into fabric she would see golden flesh and blood pearling to the surface.

"Why would you ask Björn?" Caedmon glanced toward the door as if he expected her irate brother to burst through at any moment, something she was dreading herself, she had to admit.

"He makes the ale for me," she explained, nodding toward the cup that was now empty. "He might have made a stronger batch for himself. That would come in handy right now."

"I thought you made the ale?" He sounded surprised, as well he might. Ale making was usually reserved to women.

"Björn has always had a talent for it, and he is kind enough to supply me and a few friends with his production. Sigurd and Frigyth for example." She thought she saw him scowl at that, but she must be imagining things. Or maybe he'd just felt a twinge of pain. "I won't be long."

Outside, the fresh air helped restore some of her composure.

It was really over. She was home, safe, she could relax now. All she had to do was find something to help Caedmon deal with the pain. That should be easy enough.

A moment later she was in front of Björn and Dunne's hut. Bee opened the door almost before she'd had time to knock. She must have seen her approach through the window.

"Aunt Ingrid!" The little girl didn't seem surprised to see her, which told her that her parents had not mentioned what had happened to her. Ingrid smiled, relieved. She would have hated for her niece to hear about the women's abduction. She was much too young for that.

"Hello, Bee. Is your father in?"

"Yes. Come in."

The whole family was around the table, enjoying a hearty meal. At the sight of the food, Ingrid's stomach growled, reminding her she had not eaten anything since yesterday morning.

"Forgive me for interrupting."

"It's no issue." Björn stood up. "How do you feel, sister?"

"I'm fine." She probably looked a bit pale, but she was fine.

"What can I do for you?"

While the children carried on eating, Dunne started to assemble a few items on a wooden plate. Cheese, smoked fish, bread, oat cakes, nuts. There was enough there for two people, Ingrid noticed, her and Caedmon. She shook her head ruefully. Trust her sister-in-law to think about everything.

"Do you have a cask of extra strong ale by any—"

"No, I don't do that, never would!" he snapped.

Ingrid recoiled at Björn's unexpected reaction. What had she said? It surprised her even more to see Dunne, who evidently understood the reason behind her husband's sudden outburst, place a soothing hand over his arm. She would have to ask her what that was about when they were alone. For now she had to see to Caedmon's comfort. That was why she had come.

"Very well then," she said, taking the plate Dunne was handing her with a grateful smile. "I'll go and see if Helga has a potion for the pain of Caedmon's injury." Why hadn't she thought about that first? It would be much more efficient than strong ale.

"The Saxon!" her brother spat. "Why are you worried about that man! Let him suffer, it's nothing more than he deserves after what he did."

Ingrid was incensed at the unfairness of the comment. "I won't let him suffer when I can do something to help! And I worry about him because he saved me and all the other women from a dreadful fate and he almost died because of it! He deserves everything I get him." How could her brother not see it? But she knew already the reason behind his animosity. He thought the two of them were lovers. She could have told him the truth now, but she didn't think he deserved to know, if he was going to be so pig-headed about it.

"Mm." The stubborn man crossed his arms over his chest. "If you say so."

"I do. Now let me go."

Unlike her brother, the healer was only too glad to give her what she needed. She only had words of praise for the brave Saxon who had ensured the women could be rescued in time.

"Make sure he drinks some of this now, even if he's asleep, and then the rest regularly throughout the night," she instructed Ingrid, handing her a small vial filled with a dark liquid. "It should help. Be careful though, it is quite potent, you don't want him to start having visions. Send for me if he falls prey to a fever. I fear it might happen. A wound such as the one he received can all too easily go putrid. I'll come see him tomorrow anyway. And make sure you get some sleep yourself, girl, you look about to drop dead."

"Yes." After all she had endured, she did feel half dead.

Thanking the woman she regarded almost as a mother, Ingrid made her way through the village. A moment later, she entered the hut.

Caedmon was lying still on the pallet, asleep, just as Helga had anticipated. She approached in silence and placed a hand over his forehead. It was still cool to the touch. Relief washed over her. No fever yet. With luck, now that his wound was closed, it would stay that way.

"Saxon," she called out, kneeling down by his side. "You need to drink some of this potion, for your pain."

He grunted and his right eye fluttered open. Slipping one arm around his shoulders, Ingrid brought the vial to his lips. With her help, he swallowed a few spoonfuls of the dark liquid and fell back on the furs, like a man determined to get to oblivion. Though she would have liked him to eat something, she did not try to wake him up further. Right now for him, sleep was more important than food. But she knew she would not be able to fall asleep before she'd had something to eat, so she reached out to the plate Dunne had prepared for her.

Nibbling at an oat cake, she watched as Caedmon slipped into the deep sleep Helga had promised. Then, once she was sated, she settled herself on the fur he'd used when he'd slept in her hut. After a night worrying herself sick about what the men had in store for her and then a day full of trepidation, she was exhausted. In moments, she was fast asleep.

When Ingrid next opened her eyes, it was full dark in the hut. How long had she slept? Only a ray of moonlight allowed her to see anything. On the pallet, Caedmon was still as a statue. A good sign? It was hard to tell from where she was. She crept up to him, intent on checking him for signs of fever. When she reached him she could not help a gasp. His eyes were wide open, two gleaming orbs in the moonlight. He was not asleep, as she had first thought, but staring at the ceiling, looking almost panicked. Without a word she extended her hand to his forehead.

Before she could touch him, he grabbed her wrist and drew her to him.

"It's you," he said in her ear, his voice cold as ice. "What are you doing here?"

"I-I live here," she replied stupidly. What sort of a question was this? Where else could she be?

Then she remembered what Helga had said, that he might have visions. Apparently he did. That had to be why he looked so panicked, why he was taking her for someone else, someone he hated. He had never spoken to her in that tone before, even when he had pretended to abduct her and played the role of a villain. When he winced and placed his other hand over his wound, she glanced at the bottle on the table. Should she give him more of the potion if he was in pain? He already seemed quite affected by it, and the healer had urged her to be careful. What if she had given him too much already?

"I have something that could bring you relief," she said hesitantly.

A sneer answered her. "I bet you do. You always seemed to use your wiles to ensnare me. You think I cannot see what you're up to, but I can."

Oh, dear, that wasn't good. Whoever he thought she was, this person was more akin to an enemy than anything else.

"I'm not up to anything, and it will help with the—"

"You think this is for you, don't you?" He forced the hand he was still holding to land over the bulge between his legs. Ingrid gasped. He was hard, harder than any man she had ever felt, and much larger. Seeing the bulge earlier had been impressive enough, touching it was a lot more disconcerting. It gave her the full measure of his potency. "But that doesn't mean a thing, sweetheart, other than I'm a man. Now, how do you propose to give me the relief I need this time? Will you use your hand? Your mouth?" He licked his lips in such a lewd manner that Ingrid felt a bolt of heat shoot between her legs and realized she was still holding his rigid member. "Your pretty little c—"

"That's not what I meant at all when I said I could help!" she cut in, scrambling away from him. "I meant I have a potion to make you sleep."

He gave something between a chuckle and a growl. "Sleep. I don't want to sleep. I need something quite different right now. So why don't you come ride me, make me come? That would help, for sure, and it's the only thing you're good at."

By the gods, who was this woman he was taking her for? She had never imagined Caedmon could be so crude, so scathing to anyone. And why did the idea of bringing him the relief he was after arouse her so? Perhaps she could do as he suggested, and ride him. That way they would both get what they needed. Because thanks to his lewd talk, she was slick with want. After all, if he were wholly unaware of who she was and would never remember what had happened come morning, she could—

Reality slammed back into her, making her shake her head.

Was she mad? Of course, she could not do such a thing, quell the need throbbing between her legs while he was unaware of what he was asking, and of whom! She could not use him so, when he was all but unconscious and injured!

Angry at herself for even entertaining such shameful ideas, Ingrid shot back to her feet. "I won't give you any more potion tonight," she told him sternly. "It seems to me you've had too much already."

He laughed again and palmed himself crudely. "Well, then, I will have to see to my needs myself, won't I? Care to watch?"

"You can't do that!" she cried out in panic. Not here, in front of her! If he started to stroke himself, she would stay and watch, she just knew it. She would not have the will to leave. "Please be reasonable, you'll tear the stitches if you...move," was all she could manage.

"Mm, yes. Maybe you're right." His hand fell back to the floor. "I don't think I'll have the strength to stroke hard enough anyway," he said, his words suddenly slurred. "Pity."

And just like that, he fell asleep.

Ingrid stared at the body lying on her pallet for a long moment, trying to regain some sense of composure. Her heart was drumming in her ears, louder than it had last night when she had thought he was about to attack her. Already knowing she wouldn't be able to get any more sleep tonight, she turned her attention to what was left of the food.

She had to do something, other than keep admiring Caedmon.

After a quick bite of bread and cheese, she picked up her needle out of habit before discarding it with a shudder. Would she ever be able to sew again? She didn't know. With no light, no wish to wake Caedmon for fear he started stroking himself or demand she do it for him, and nothing to do, she had little choice but to lie back down on the fur and try not to look in the direction of the man sleeping mere feet away from her, dreaming of a mysterious woman riding him.

Eventually she must have fallen asleep because she woke to a gray predawn light. Groaning, she stretched her numb body. How had Caedmon spent two nights in a row on this fur and not felt the worst for it? She felt as if someone had hit her all over with a hammer. With difficulty she stood up and helped herself to a cup of ale.

On the pallet, Caedmon was stirring as well. Determined to wait until she'd ascertained what mood he was in before she looked at him, she kept her gaze firmly on the cup in her hand. Was he hard and ready for a tumble? Had he recovered from his earlier madness? She wasn't sure she was brave enough to find out.

Just then there was a knock at the door of the hut. Ingrid opened to a smiling Helga.

"How is the patient faring this morning?" the healer asked, accepting the cup of ale Ingrid handed her.

"Quite well. He's just waking up. I was about to check him for signs of fever."

"I'll do that, girl."

Helga knelt by his side and placed a hand over his brow. Ingrid pinched her lips, imagining Caedmon drawing the old woman atop him in the way he had grabbed her last night and demanding relief.

"No fever. That's good. It means you took good care of him when you stitched him back up. The potion will have helped, no doubt." Helga sounded satisfied. "Mind you, that is a potent mixture. Did he have visions?"

"Erm…" Ingrid felt herself go red to the roots of her hair. That was the least she could say. "No. Not that I could tell, but after all, I'm not in his mind so I cannot be sure."

"Of course. But did he start to speak nonsense is what I mean?"

"No. Everything he said was perfectly clear."

Yes. His demands had been perfectly explicit, but she was not about to admit to the old woman that Caedmon had asked her if she preferred to suck him dry or ride him senseless. It was bad enough she had considered doing those things.

No one could ever know about that. She would take her secret to her tomb.

"I thank you for your care of—" Caedmon started, his words slightly slurred, just like last night before he'd fallen asleep.

"It is I who should thank you for what you did for our women, young man. My granddaughter was one of the ones who were abducted." Helga took Caedmon's hand in hers and gave a squeeze. Her voice, usually so steady, was wobbling. "I will never be able to repay you for saving her."

"Please. What else would you have me do? I could not let the men go through with their evil plans when I had the means to stop them."

"No. I suppose not. You're a good man, you know that?"

"Yes. I do know that." He sighed, as if weary beyond measure. Helga took it as her cue to leave. The Saxon needed to rest and recover.

"Very well. I'll leave you to it then. Send for me if you need anything else."

Caedmon could not remember ever feeling worse. His head was twice as heavy as normal, courtesy of the potion he'd been given, no doubt, blood was drumming in his temples and every movement, even the slightest, brought flames of pain licking through his middle. The stitches on his wound were taunting him, urging him to scratch himself. He could not, of course, at the risk of undoing all Ingrid's hard work.

"I'm afraid I will have to prevail on your hospitality for a few days more," he told her once they were alone. The mere idea of standing up and walking out of here was enough to make his stomach churn.

She didn't even blink. "I would not have it any other way. You are not leaving this hut until Helga deems you recovered enough."

That might take as much as a couple of weeks, he thought grimly, accepting the drink she was handing him. He suspected the old woman would not jeopardize her granddaughter's savior's health for the world and would want to keep him abed for as long as possible.

Ingrid saw his grimace and asked. "Do you have pressing business in town? Is that what the matter is? Should I send word to anyone?"

"No." In actual fact he had no business at all, no one was waiting for him, or cared what he did. He could stay here indefinitely, and it would make no difference. The thought was rather dispiriting.

"So you can stay for as long as you need, and see more of your friend while you're here? That's good."

See more of Frigyth...The innocent comment made Caedmon realize he had not given her any thought since he'd entered Ingrid's hut yesterday. Admittedly, he'd been either in pain, or asleep since then, but still, the fact was surprising. He was supposed to be in love and obsessed with her, was he not? Why had his first thought when he'd feared he was going to die not been for her? It felt like a betrayal, but it was a fact. When the scrawny Saxon had drawn his blade on him, all he'd been able to think of was Ingrid, of how he was glad to have done enough to spare her from the men's lust.

He could not explain why that might be, so he pushed the thoughts away from his mind. With nothing else to do other than lie down and think, he would try to make sense of it all later. For now there was something he needed to ask, something that had been niggling at him since he'd woken up.

"Ingrid."

"Yes?" She stopped in the act of cutting a loaf of bread in two. His stomach growled at the sight. Having not had anything to eat since yesterday morning, he was famished. But food could wait. This could not.

"Did I speak nonsense last night?"

She resumed the cutting of the bread. It was obvious she was only doing it so she could avoid meeting his eye. So his intuition was right. He had made a fool of himself.

"Why do you ask?" she said eventually. "You heard me tell Helga you did not."

"Yes. I also saw your cheeks go the color of a sunset as you did." He arched a brow. She was the same color now. Dear God, what had he said? "I think you weren't completely honest for fear of embarrassing me in front of her. I thank you for it, but I'd like to know. Did I make a fool of myself?"

"N-nothing happened, don't worry," she stammered.

This answer, far from reassuring him, only made him wince. That was even worse than he had feared. So he *had* propositioned her, as he'd suspected. He had a vague memory of her bent over him, of his body pulsing with need. He had most definitely wanted something to happen. The question was, had he told her as much? And in what terms? Had he frightened her with his crudeness, mere moments after her abduction? It didn't bear thinking about.

"Apologies," he mumbled. "I was out of my head with the healer's potion." That didn't excuse anything, but at least it explained it.

"Well, yes, I know. It was my fault. I think I gave you too much."

A pause. "So what did I say? Please tell me."

He had to know.

Ingrid worried her bottom lip as she wondered what to tell Caedmon. He seemed to be aware he had asked her something, so she would never get away with a lie. But she didn't have to be completely honest either, did she? Not when the truth was so embarrassing.

"It was nothing really. You wanted...to go fishing, no doubt a fancy brought on by the potion. When you insisted, I had to remind you that you might tear your stitches if you weren't careful." There. Innocuous enough, and if he happened to remember bits of their conversation he would remember them talking about tearing stitches. When lying, she knew it was better to stay as close to the truth as possible.

"Yes...I seem to remember wanting something desperately. So desperately it hurt."

"I suspect the pain was caused by your wound." *And not the pulsing in your groin.* "Your addled mind confused everything. It's only normal."

"Mm." He didn't sound convinced and no wonder. The urge to go fishing and the pain caused by an erection the size of his arm probably had nothing in common. But she could not change her explanation now. Heart beating hard, she waited. "Odd, as I've never been one for fishing. You would have thought I would yearn for something I actually enjoy doing at the best of times."

Oh, this was excruciating. "You don't enjoy fishing then?" she asked in her best innocent voice, handing him a piece of bread. Perhaps if he ate he would stop talking. It was worth a try, and he needed to eat anyway.

"Not really." He took the piece of bread. "Do you?"

"Er..."

Calm down, Ingrid, he's only asking about catching fish, not what you're thinking. He doesn't know, he cannot know what he asked you to do, or that you were tempted to agree.

"No. I cannot say I often go fishing."

He bit on the bread, chewed his mouthful with slow deliberation then said, "That's not what I asked."

His amazing eyes flashed in the morning light. Damn...*Did* he know what had happened after all? Was he only testing her? She decided to stop cowering and force him to reveal his hand.

"I can't really tell you what I think of it, that's why. I tried... fishing a long time ago and thought it quite a boring activity. Now I don't have the equipment or the skill to see whether it is as enjoyable as people say." She raised her chin. "Besides, I'm not sure I would know what to do if I actually caught a fish."

"I suppose you could..." The look he threw her dissolved what little was left of her composure and she knew for sure he remembered what had transpired between them the night before. "Eat it."

"Mm. Yes. I suppose. Of course, I would have to gut it and cut it to pieces beforehand and I might well butcher it through lack of practice."

He winced when she stole an involuntary glance at his groin. "That sounds painful."

"It would be for the poor beast. So I think it is better if I stay clear of fishing altogether. In fact, I suspect that if anyone tried to take me fishing I would end up breaking their rod to make sure they cannot bother anyone else with it again."

"Well, then, it is a good thing I will never ask you to...go fishing. I would hate to have my rod broken."

By now there wasn't a breath left in Ingrid's body. The moment had been far too intense for comfort, and Caedmon's new appearance didn't help. He hadn't shaved since he'd left her hut the other day and the stubble on his jaw was utterly compelling, a dark shadow that had nothing in common with the longer, blond beards the men from the village sported.

He looked magnificent, if a little pale.

The knock on the door came both as a relief and an unpleasant interruption. When Ingrid opened the door, her heart sank in her chest.

Her brother was the last person she wanted to see right now.

CHAPTER SIX

"So let me get this straight, Saxon."

Jaw clenched, Björn straightened to his full, impressive height. Ingrid barely stopped herself from kicking him the way she often had when they were children. What was the oaf doing? There was no need for such a show of intimidation, not when Caedmon was lying on the floor, unable to defend himself. Really, her brother could be insufferable when he wanted to be. And what did he mean by using the word "Saxon" like an insult when his own wife was a Saxon and there was no one in the world he loved more?

"You mingle with a bunch of bastards who steal horses and abduct women?"

"No." Caedmon sounded oddly calm, considering what he was being told. He'd been unruffled when Ivar had accused him of stealing the horses and that had been commendable enough but this was too much. She wished he would show Björn just how outrageous the accusation was. "I only joined them so I could help the—"

"You took my sister," Björn carried on as if Caedmon had

not spoken. "You made her fear for her life, you placed her in unspeakable danger and then you—"

"Enough, Björn!" she interrupted. "He did all that so he could save us. There was no other choice, as I explained before. He was on his own, there was nothing else he could have done. And it worked! Without him no one would have found us in time, and we would have been raped over and over again by vile men. He saved us all, he placed *himself* in danger, not me, and he almost got killed in the process. Now he needs to rest and recover from his ordeal and you need to leave."

Her brother arched a brow, no doubt surprised to hear her talk so assertively. But she was too incensed to care. Why couldn't he be grateful for what Caedmon had done? Couldn't he see she was hurt by his lack of trust?

"If you're sure you—" he started in Norse.

"I am," she snapped in the same language. "What is he going to do anyway, in the state he's in? If he attempted anything, I would only have to punch him straight on his wound and he would crumple to the floor like a sack of grain. Not that it would come to that anyway. Now, leave."

Björn threw one last menacing look at Caedmon. The meaning of that look was clear.

If you lay one finger on my sister, I'll break all the bones in your body.

Goaded beyond endurance, Ingrid ushered him through the door without ceremony. A moment later he was gone.

"Well. That told him, whatever you said."

Caedmon sounded amused but she could not share in the merriment. Really, what was her brother thinking? How could he berate someone who'd just saved five innocent women at great risk to himself? Not only that but, as far as he was concerned, she and Caedmon were lovers, which meant she had gone to him willingly in the first place. What business did he have threatening the man she had chosen for herself? What would he have said if she'd objected to his relationship with Dunne? Not that she would have, of course, the woman was perfect for him. But that was not the point. The point was she should be free to choose her own life.

Independence was her most prized possession and up until now Björn had never tried to rob her of it.

"I'm sorry about my brother. He means well, but he's very protective of me and often unreasonable." It had become worse after their parents' sudden death. Aged only nineteen, Björn had taken his role of protector and head of the family very seriously and she had been grateful, because without him she might well have collapsed under the weight of her grief. But she was now a grown woman, and he had his own family to worry over. She didn't need a watch dog. "I dread to think what he will do to the poor boys who will start sniffing around his daughter soon. They will have to prove themselves three times over before they're allowed even a moment alone with Bee."

"I should hope so. If I had a little sister, or a daughter, I wouldn't want them alone with a strange man either."

She could not help rolling her eyes at that. Really, were all men so predictable? If ever she'd needed confirmation that she didn't need one in her life, this was it. "You wouldn't trust them?"

"I wouldn't trust *him*," he growled, reminding her of Björn for a moment.

"Are you saying I shouldn't trust you?"

He made a grimace. "Oh, no. I'm no danger to anyone, much less women. We all know I'm a good man."

The bitterness with which he said the words seemed unwarranted to her. What was the problem with that? He *was* a good man, he had proved it only the other night.

"Do you want some more bread? A bit of cheese?" she

asked, turning her attention back to the table. She didn't want to discuss the relationship between men and women any longer. It could lead nowhere.

"Please." She gathered what was left of Dunne's food, but he raised a hand before she could bring it to him. "I would like to sit at the table to eat."

"You—" The look he threw her was enough to stop the protest on her lips. He didn't want to be seen as an invalid. She could understand that. Hadn't she just bemoaned the fact that she would like to be allowed to make her own decisions? Besides, he didn't look on the verge of a swoon. Perhaps it would do him no harm to sit down. "Very well."

Ingrid handed her arm out to him. It was one thing allowing him to hold on to some dignity, quite another to have him hurt himself further by trying too much too soon. He took it without a word and started the painful process of getting to his feet.

By the time he was sitting on the chair, he was pale and breathing hard.

"I will go to the vegetable patch, get some onions while you eat," she said, feeling he needed a moment alone to compose himself. He nodded curtly.

By the time she was back, Caedmon was looking more like himself again. She placed the unpeeled onions on the fire pit before covering them first with cinders then with the almost extinguished embers. In the residual, gentle heat, they would become meltingly tender and be a tasty addition to tonight's supper.

Then she turned to face Caedmon, who had finished eating. Some color had returned to his cheeks, she was pleased to see.

"Now that you're up, I'd like you to remove your shirt." The moment the words left her lips she realized how it sounded. Heat suffused her chest. Had she really told him she'd like him to remove his shirt in front of her? Yes, she had. To his credit, he did not even arch a brow. She started to explain hurriedly. "I need to wash the blood, you see."

"Of course," he said, standing up.

The moment he lifted his arm she averted her eyes. How had she not anticipated what it would do to her to see him undress? He was too attractive, and the action too evocative for her to remain unruffled.

"I think I should go ask Björn if he can lend you a shirt," she mumbled.

There was a snort from somewhere behind her. "Do you really want to draw the man's attention to the fact that I am half-naked in front of you? Didn't you say earlier that I should take care not to rip my stitches? Well, I don't fancy having them ripped for me either."

Privately, she had to acknowledge the wisdom of this observation. She had better keep Björn out of this.

"Don't worry about another shirt, I'm not cold, I can wait while mine dries. In this weather it will take no time at all. But I will be the one washing it."

"Nonsense, you will do no such thing while your stomach is bandaged and your wound so fresh!" Was he mad?

Ingrid turned around and snatched the garment from him. Which meant he now stood in front of her, just as he'd said, half-naked. And the sight was not one she'd been prepared for.

By the gods, had Helga put something in the potion to make him grow even bigger during the night? When she had met him, because he'd been standing next to three of the most strapping men in the village, she had thought him rather slender. He was anything but. The muscles on his chest were well-defined, and the skin was taut over them. The overall effect was one of grace and elegance rather than power and brute strength, and much more appealing in her opinion.

But what fascinated her were the hairs. They appeared silky

soft and were a shade darker than the hair on his head. It was a revelation. She had only ever seen men with blond or no hair on their chest before. Caedmon was different, in every way, more masculine despite the lack of bulging muscles. He could have looked menacing, he only looked protective. His pectorals were covered with dark swirls that narrowed to a V just above his navel, leaving the part she had stitched up almost bare, before flaring up again above the waistband of his hose and disappearing under the garment as if the draw the eye.

Everything within her leapt in approval—or was it arousal? Probably both.

She took a step back, fearing her body's reaction. At the moment it was urging her to go pet this man, run her hands through the fascinating hairs and possibly even test how it would feel against her mouth when she kissed him, all things she could not, and should not, want to do.

"It is so dreadful?" he asked, his voice rough.

"Dreadful?" she repeated. Of all the words she could have chosen to describe his chest, this was the last she would have picked. It was not dreadful in the least.

"My wound." He placed a hand over it to hide it from her. "You recoiled. I should have thought. I'm sorry."

"I..." What could she say? Nothing that would be wise, or acceptable. She cleared her throat. "Forgive me. I am not used to such sights." That, at least, was no lie.

The tension in his shoulders relaxed. "I see."

Yes, unfortunately, he seemed to see all too well and understood that his wound was not responsible for her unease. She tightened her fingers on the warm shirt she was holding as if it would help her appear composed.

"I will go wash it now. Then I will also need to stitch it."

Which would require him to be half-naked for even longer. Ingrid swallowed hard, but there was no other solution. There was nothing in the hut he could wear. Oh well, she would just have to make sure to keep her eyes averted until he got dressed again.

"Stitch the shirt like you stitched me, you mean?" A smile was floating on his lips.

"No. Better, because I doubt it will squirm and complain as I do it."

"Ah, Ingrid." It was the first time he had used her name and her insides gave a little flip. "I did not squirm or complain."

No, he had not. What had possessed her to say such a thing? But how was she supposed to think straight in front a half-dressed Caedmon? Some things could not be helped. She might as well try to remain calm when faced with a wild animal about to ravage her. "No, I know. I'm sorry. I don't know why I said that. It was both a lie and unkind. In truth I was most impressed by your fortitude."

"And I by your gentleness. I'm sure no one would have a done a better job. Now. Is there some of that potion left?" He grimaced. "I promise not to drink overmuch, I need just enough to take the edge off the pain."

"Of course. Take what you need."

She handed him the small vial. As he took it, their fingers touched, and it was as if thunder and lightning had struck the hut. They both stilled, eyes locked, then Ingrid cleared her throat. Her brother was the only man she had been in such close proximity to, at least while he was bare-chested and standing. But because Björn was not a man in her mind, but her brother, she had never felt self-conscious, and because he was so tall and she only reached to his neck, she always felt slightly ludicrous next to him. With Caedmon, it was the opposite. She was defi-nitely aware of every inch of his body, of every single one of his intakes of breath. And when she was facing him, she could see his jaw and his mouth. She still had to lift her head to meet his gaze, but it made all the difference. Next to him she did not feel ridiculous, but feminine.

And aroused, unsettlingly so.

"Thank you," he said, and she could have sworn his voice made her core quiver. "I promise to drink the potion wisely and not bother you with my urges to...go fishing again."

All the air left Ingrid's lungs. Was she right? *Did* he remember what he'd asked her last night? She would never dare ask the question. It was better not to know anyway, as it could only lead to all sorts of trouble. Shirt in hand, she hurried out of the hut, then rushed back in to get the soap she'd forgotten, exited it again and ran toward the river, as flustered as she'd ever been. She could have used a bucket with water from the well to wash the shirt, but the farther she went while Caedmon was in a state of undress, the better.

Kneeling in her favorite spot in the shade of a tree, she plunged the garment in the cold water and started to rub the soap over it, careful not to damage it further. It took time to wash away the dried blood, and even then she wasn't certain she had gotten rid of the last of the stains. Once she was satisfied she could not do any better, she laid the shirt on a patch of tall grass just behind her. In the sunshine, it would be dry in no time. While she waited she went to the vegetable patch to get some beans for the pot, then to the chicken coop to see if the hens had been generous. It was unlikely they would have laid more eggs since the morning but she had to at least appear as if she was not trying to avoid getting back inside the hut while Caedmon was half-naked.

Fortunately the sun and wind were on her side and the shirt was soon ready. By the time she had done all her useless jobs, it was dry enough for her to start sewing. Heart beating, she knocked on the door of the hut. No answer. With luck the potion would have sent him to sleep. Gingerly, she entered.

Caedmon was lying on the pallet, head thrown to the side, one long arm extended on the floor, the other resting lightly over his chest. It was a sight she found both arousing and moving. The veins along his exposed forearm in particular fascinated her, as did the soft dip in the inside of his elbow, the ridge of his collarbone, the strong column of his neck, the color of his nipples, the shape of his navel, the—Everything.

Everything she saw fascinated her.

As soon as she had ascertained his unconsciousness, she threw a light blanket over his all too tempting chest and started sewing the shirt.

The night before she had feared never to be able to sew again, but her fingers just took over and the familiar action helped to settle her nerves.

She was just finishing when he stirred. Ingrid was instantly on her guard. What if he'd drunk too much of the potion? Would he recognize her or take her for that woman again? What would she do if he started to make advances on her? This time if he drew her to him she would feel his naked skin under her palms. He would be warm, hard and silky soft all at once, and she would not resist stroking him.

It was better to stay where she was.

"Feeling better?" she asked, cutting her thread with great flourish. If she appeared busy, he would not guess she was trying to avoid having to look at him.

"Yes. The potion did me good. But I...I don't remember having a blanket when I fell asleep," he observed, his voice hoarse from sleep.

"You started to shiver a while ago so I threw one over you," she answered, her gaze firmly on her fingers. She didn't need to know whether he had removed the blanket or not, and if he had, she certainly didn't need to see his chest. "It's getting chilly."

"Is it?"

In truth, Ingrid had no idea. She certainly felt hot enough. "Stay where you are," she warned when he made to stand up. "Your shirt is ready. Do you need help to put it back on?"

She waited, both dreading having to help him and hoping he would ask for her assistance.

He hesitated and then said, "No. I'll be fine."

JUST BEFORE SUNSET, Frigyth came to visit. The first thing Caedmon thought when she walked into the hut was that he was glad not to be bare-chested. The oddness of the thought struck him. Shouldn't he be thinking that he was glad to see her instead? Shouldn't he find her more radiant than ever or rejoice over the fact that she was not accompanied by her husband for once? Perhaps. But all he could think was that he was glad she had not seen him half-naked. And he had no idea why. It was not as if it would be the first time, after all.

She knelt by his side. He started to say that she should not trouble herself, not in her condition, but she waved his protests away.

"I'm not exactly full term, as you can see." No. She was hardly showing yet. Still. "How do you feel?"

"I'm fine, thanks."

"I'll go get more beans for the stew," Ingrid said, taking her basket before exiting the hut. He understood she wanted to give him and his friend privacy and he was grateful for her discretion.

"You look well for a man who was almost cut in half. Ingrid is clearly taking good care of you," Frigyth observed, smiling. "I'm so happy for you. She's a good woman."

Ah, yes, a good woman for a good man, Caedmon thought wryly. It always came down to this with him.

He didn't answer. For no reason that he could understand, today he felt ill at ease in front of Frigyth. That had never happened before, and he wasn't sure what to make of it. What was certain was that he didn't like it. What was happening to him? It was as if the Saxon had changed something within him when he'd cut his body, dislodged something that had been bothering him.

Mm, perhaps he had taken too much of that potion, after all, because that was a strange thought to say the least.

"I'm so happy to have you back here. I've missed you, you know," Frigyth was still smiling but her eyes had gone misty.

"Not as much as I've missed you, Frig."

She couldn't have. Happily married to the man of her dreams, she would not have felt the same yearning for him as he had for her.

"Are you going to live here, or is it just a visit?"

"I'm never going back to London."

Caedmon was well aware he had not answered her question, had not said whether he intended to stay or not. But that was because he had no idea. He had set out with no real plan in mind, except to flee Mildred and the disaster his life had become, and to see the woman he was still pining after.

"What made you come back?"

He stared at her and had the satisfaction of seeing her blush. Ah, so she had guessed that she was part of the answer, if not the main part. Good. He didn't see why he should have to pretend she didn't mean anything to him anymore, when it was not the case.

"I had my reasons," he said eventually.

"You know," she carried on, "when you left I was certain you would be back within a few months. After a couple of years, however, I stopped hoping I would ever see you again. It seemed obvious that you had left your old life behind and had no intention of coming back. The thought even crossed my mind that you had died. After all, I wouldn't have been any the wiser if you had, for who would have told me?"

She closed her eyes, and Caedmon understood that, even if she did not return his feelings, at least she still cared about him. The thought brought warmth to his chest.

"I'm sorry to have caused you pain."

She nodded and opened her eyes again. "About a year ago I bumped into your grandmother in town. She told me she hadn't seen you in years, even if she'd gotten the occasional message from you when a peddler who'd been to London visited the town. It made me think...That you'd forgotten about me,"

He inhaled sharply. "I could never forget you, Frig. But I thought...Well, I thought *you*'d forgotten about *me*, what with your husband and growing family."

"I could never forget about you!" she protested, placing a hand over her stomach. "But you're right about the family. There is this new babe, of course, but did you know we adopted a son?"

"No." How could he have?

Frigyth smiled. "Little Elwyn, Osric the chandler's son. He lived in our road, remember?"

Osric. Yes, Caedmon remembered the man, an unsavory character. Why on earth had Frigyth adopted the boy? He waited for the explanation that was sure to come. "A few weeks after you'd left, his father died and Elwyn found himself on his own. He needed a family. We gave it to him. He's fifteen now. You wouldn't know him. He's already taller than me, though I doubt he'll ever match Sigurd's height."

There was so much pride in her eyes, so much love in her voice that Caedmon's insides twisted. He ran a hand over his face. The stubble was starting to irritate his skin. He would have to shave soon. Perhaps when Ingrid came back he would ask if she could find what he needed. He sighed and, realizing he was stalling, finally looked at Frigyth.

"You know, the day you told me you had married Sigurd, I didn't quite believe it."

Where had that admission come from? He had not meant to tell her as much, ever. But it was true all the same. When she'd told him she had married a Norseman in his absence, he'd held on to the hope that it was just a lie, that he still had a chance to woo her. But when he had seen them together, that hope had died. She and the Dane were destined to be together, any fool could have seen it.

He expected her to laugh away the comment, but her answer shocked him.

"I was not married to him at the time, that may be why."

"What do you mean?"

A pause. "I lied."

He stared at her stupidly. She'd *lied* about being married? "Why?"

Frigyth didn't meet his eye when she replied, as if embarrassed. "I always knew we would not suit as husband and wife, but you didn't seem to see that what was between us was not love, merely the deepest affection. I didn't want you to waste time pining after me. I thought that telling you I was married was the best way to make you see there was no future for us. I'm sorry, I should just have been honest, but I didn't have the courage to break your heart."

Well, her good intentions notwithstanding, she *had* broken his heart.

"But you did marry Sigurd in the end?" Surely she wasn't lying now. He'd seen them together these last few days. These two were definitely a couple. And she was carrying his child.

"Yes. I had fallen in love with him while pretending to be his wife but I didn't see how it could work between us so I left the village. Then, a few weeks after you'd gone to London, I found out I had fallen with child from the...from the attack I told you about."

She swallowed and placed a hand on her stomach as if to draw strength from it. Fury sliced through Caedmon, blurring his vision. Frigyth had been raped by a Norseman from the village ten years ago. She had told him as much, but he hadn't known she'd had to bear the bastard's child.

His chest tightened at the thought of all she'd had to endure and had he not been bed-ridden, he might well have punched something.

"I told Sigurd. That day he told me he loved me and wanted to raise the babe as his own. He asked me to marry him for real, and not once has he made me regret saying yes." Emotion caused her voice to wobble. "He was with me the night the baby was born. Eirik is his son in every way, just like Elwyn, Moon and our daughter."

Caedmon's throat tightened. "You are making it hard for me to think ill of your Norseman," he mumbled.

"Why would you want to think ill of him?"

Too many reasons, he thought wryly, none of which put him in a good light. It was best not to answer. He stared at the ceiling, trying to make sense of and absorb all he'd been told. Frigyth had never thought they could be husband and wife. She had lied to avoid having to marry him. She had adopted a child with the Dane and was happier than anyone he had ever seen. All hope of anything happening between them was well and truly dead.

"I'll leave you to rest now," she said, mistaking his sudden silence for weariness. To his surprise, she leaned in and kissed his cheek. He stilled, savoring the moment. It was not the kiss he'd dreamed of sharing with her, but it seemed all the more meaningful for it. "I'm so happy to have you back."

"Thank you. It's good to be back."

When the door closed, Caedmon had the impression his life had been changed forever. The last of his illusion had been torn from him. It was as if a veil had been removed from his eyes, allowing him to see things as they truly were.

It was disconcerting, and not really pleasant. He felt rather like a child who'd persuaded himself he lived in an enchanted forest populated by magical beings, only to find out once he'd gone back as an adult that the trees were just ordinary oaks and the creatures only the fruit of his imagination. Had his love for Frigyth been based on nothing but wrong impressions? She'd been convinced, even at the time, that they wouldn't suit, when he'd wanted to think that what they had really was love. Was she right? Had it only been affection? Suddenly he wasn't so sure.

A moment later Ingrid came back, her basket groaning under the weight of vegetables.

"I'll put these to boil," she said, reaching for her knife.

"Ingrid?"

"Yes?"

Caedmon blinked, not sure why he had called her or what he wanted to say.

He considered asking her if she knew Eirik was not Sigurd's son, but he could not be so indiscreet. She might not be aware of it and he did not want to expose Frigyth's painful, personal past.

Then he wondered if he should ask for her opinion. Did she think he and Frigyth could have worked as a couple? No, that was silly. Even supposing it wasn't an inappropriate question, how would Ingrid know? They had met mere days ago. Days that somehow seemed a lifetime.

It was then that he understood what he really wanted from her.

He wanted her to sort his life out for him, make him whole

again, repair the gap in his soul in the same way she had stitched the wound on his body.

But, of course, such a thing was impossible.

"Do you have something I could use to shave?" he asked instead.

"Of course. Let me go find what you need." She smiled faintly. "I promise I won't ask Björn."

CHAPTER SEVEN

"Now what has you looking like a beast, I wonder?"

Instead of answering, Sigurd glared at Wolf. Ingrid's mouth quivered. She knew the Dane had been nicknamed Beast as a child and hated it. Only Wolf would dare call him that when he was already riled up. The two friends were like brothers but they never missed an opportunity to rankle each other.

"I just caught Elwyn kissing a girl behind the hut," Sigurd said in a snarl. Really, for someone who hated being likened to a beast, he had quite a temper on...Not daunted in the least by her formidable husband, Frigyth placed a hand over his arm.

"And?"

"And nothing! Isn't that enough?"

The people assembled by the well looked at each other, evidently doing their best to hold on to their composure. It was obvious they had expected something of quite a different nature —and magnitude—to explain the outburst but they didn't dare admit as much out loud. Unsurprisingly, the Icelander was the first one to speak.

"Calm down, my friend. It's just a kiss. It's part of life." He shrugged. "Don't you remember your first kiss? You must have been a similar age."

Sigurd grumbled. "I can't have been that young. And, anyway, I'd like to see your face when your daughter Eyja starts seeing boys! I doubt you'll like being reminded it is only part of life then!"

All the blood seemed to drain from Wolf's face at the words. "Mm. Yes. You might have a point."

"A first kiss is always special," Merewen said with a laugh, placing a hand on her husband's arm in much the same way Frigyth had done with hers. No one quite knew how to manage those fierce men as their unassuming wives. They always seemed to be able to soothe them.

"Yes, it is special," Ingrid was surprised to hear Caedmon reply.

This morning, making the most of a sunny interval, they had decided to take a walk around the village. After days cooped up inside, he'd been about to tear his hair out in frustration. Impressed by his patience thus far, Ingrid had agreed he would benefit from a change of scenery and some fresh air.

Soon, a group had started to assemble around them, eager for news of the hero of the moment, which Ingrid had fully expected. What she had not anticipated was that the conversation would turn to kissing, or that Caedmon would take part in it so readily. But his smile was wistful at the memory of his first ever kiss. She felt a highly unwelcome pang of jealousy at sight of that smile.

"I think the first girl you kissed must have been very dear to you," she murmured. Perhaps if she acted as if she didn't mind it, it would lessen the sting.

"Who's to say it was with a woman?" Sigurd snapped.

Her eyebrows shot upward. What was he insinuating? "Are you saying he—"

"Oh, no, it was most definitely with a girl," Caedmon cut in. "A sweet, warm, delicious girl. One day we went to spend the day outside the town gates. We had a lovely time frolicking in the flower-strewn fields. By the time we got back into town, though, it was raining and we took refuge between—"

"I don't think we need to hear about that!" Sigurd, who had managed to calm down, looked on the verge of another outburst.

"No," Frigyth agreed, her cheeks going an alarming shade of red.

"I mean," the Dane grumbled. "'Frolicking in the flower-strewn fields.' What are you, to talk like that, some kind of poet?"

Everyone laughed but Ingrid found herself frowning. What was going on? Her friends seemed desperate to bring the subject to an end and Caedmon was behaving oddly, talking about his personal life with surprising eagerness in front of a crowd. Frolicking in flower-strewn fields...Indeed it was an unusually poetic way to describe what he and his first conquest had done.

"Sigurd is right," Wolf intervened. "I'm not in the mood to talk about this and I'm sure we all have better things to do."

Though it was not precisely an order, everyone started to scatter. Once they were alone, Caedmon turned to her. There was an odd expression on his face.

"I will stay here a while, take the sun, if you don't mind," he said, not quite meeting her eye.

"Of course."

It was clear he wanted to be alone. She walked back toward the hut, telling herself she didn't mind. She still had to make bread, anyway.

Caedmon sat on the nearby bench, closed his eyes and started to think.

Now that he was able to walk with relative ease, he had to leave the village, and to hell with his injury. He'd meant to stay only one night at first, and in the end had stayed for two because of Ingrid's indisposition. He hadn't minded but then when he'd finally left, he'd found himself being carried back to her hut the very same day. It was as if he could not take his distance from the Norsemen village. Or perhaps from a certain woman residing in it. Was fate trying to tell him something? Was it a sign that he could not seem to get away from Ingrid, no matter how much he tried?

But a sign of what? Surely the only woman he was interested in was Frigyth?

Yes…Although, if he were honest, something seemed to have changed within him. After their discussion the other day, his feelings for her, which he had never questioned before, seemed to have taken on a different form. He had always assumed they would end up as husband and wife because they got on so well growing up but he had never stopped to ask himself if that was really what he wanted. Same for his love. He had taken it for the real thing, but what if had been the sweet love of a boy toward his only friend, nothing more, what if it had just been the tenderness he'd felt for the sister he had never had? He'd seen Frigyth's misery and he had wanted to be there for her. It had worked, for a time. But then he had left. And now someone else was here for her.

Sigurd.

It was hard to imagine her happier with anyone, himself included, than she was with her husband. The blasted Norseman had done everything right from the start, married her, adopted her son, given her the life she deserved and the kind of love she wanted. What if Frigyth was right? What if they weren't suited to each other and had only realized it after getting married, when it was too late, and they could do nothing but resent a choice made for the wrong reasons? He'd never asked himself the uncomfortable question before but now he was.

He hesitated in answering it, however, because if he admitted to himself that he'd never really been in love with Frigyth then he'd have to accept that he'd never been in love with anyone. And it was easier to hold on to the fantasy that he could have been happy with Frigyth than to accept he'd been wrong all this time. He'd held on to what they'd once shared for nostalgia's sake, because he resented the fact that he had been left behind while she was happy, married to a man who doted on her and gave her everything she needed. She had a family, and he was alone and away from home, with no one to wait for him at night when he got home.

That was why he had agreed to get married to Mildred in the end. To finally have the life he'd wanted. But his heart had never been in that union. When her treachery had been discovered, he'd been more hurt in his pride than in his feelings.

He sighed and opened his eyes. A man was standing in front of him, intent etched on his face. Who was he? Ivar's friend from the other day, the one who'd been with him when the man had accused him of stealing the horses? Caedmon could not recall his face but he seemed to be about the right age, just over twenty. Was he about to accuse him of some other ludicrous crime?

He waited. If the man wanted to say something, he would eventually speak.

The youth cleared his throat and started. "Hello. I'm Magnar."

Caedmon just stared. Was that supposed to help him? It did not.

"Frida's betrothed."

Still nothing. He didn't know any Fridas, even if he could easily guess she was a Norsewoman from the village.

"One of the women who were abducted the other day. I wanted to thank you for what you did."

Ah. Now he understood. He was about to be called a "good man." It seemed inevitable. The youth seemed very emotional, embarrassed about it, but determined to do the right thing, whatever the cost to his dignity. It brought a lump to Caedmon's throat to be faced with such genuine gratitude.

"'Tis nothing," he said in a rumble.

"It's not and you know it. So I had to thank you." Magnar shifted on his feet and then lifted his head, as if to signify that they would not broach the topic again. It suited Caedmon fine, for he really felt as if he'd done no more than what anyone else would have done in his place. "Anyway, I came to invite you to our wedding tomorrow. We had decided to get married in the summer, but after what happened, I can't wait to make her mine. I need to feel...I know that her being married will not prevent evil men from doing what they want if they ever cross her path, but I need to feel as if I've done at least *something* to try and protect her. I need to make her feel loved, to make sure she knows I'll always be there for her, no matter what." Another pause, during which Magnar cleared his throat again. "Will you come, wish us well?"

"Oh." Caedmon had not seen this coming. "Of course. It would be my pleasure."

He was moved. It was one thing helping people because you knew it was the right thing to do, quite another to see the consequences of your actions firsthand. It felt good. Perhaps being a good man, or at least doing good deeds, wasn't a bad thing after all.

"Do you know what Frida told me when she got back to the village that morning?"

"No." Caedmon already knew he would hate it but he could not refuse to hear it.

Magnar bunched his hands into fists. "She said all she could think about while she waited for those bastards to come to get her was that if she were 'soiled' she—" From the anger in the man's voice and the way he spat out the word, Caedmon guessed that was the word Frida had used, not what he thought. "She told me that if she'd been 'soiled' that day then she would have been unworthy of me. As if I'd ever think that! As if it would make me change my mind about marrying her! As if I'd only offered to marry her because she was a virgin! As if I'd only wanted to be the first! I don't care about being the first, I only ask to be the last to take her in my arms."

The youth ran a hand over his face, looking on the verge of collapse.

"I understand," Caedmon murmured.

The day Frigyth had told him she had been raped, she'd added that she was now unsuitable to be his wife. It seemed she'd thought the same thing as Frida. But it was as Magnar said. He hadn't cared a jot about not being the one to deflower her, but the thought of what she'd had to endure at the hands of that Norseman had nearly destroyed him. How could she have thought him so shallow as to reject her over that?

Now, of course, he knew it had only been an excuse to refuse his offer of marriage. But at the time it had torn him apart to see that she thought him so unreliable as to abandon her for something that was not her fault and should only have rendered her more precious to him.

"Be easy with Frida," he told Magnar. "I know it's hard not to, but don't take her comment personally. She has reasons to doubt your reaction. Unfortunately, we both know there are too many bastards out there who would reject a woman over something like that."

He stood up and placed a hand on the youth's shoulder. He was almost old enough to be his father and in that moment he was as proud of him as if he had been. A pang of longing tore through his chest. Would he one day have his own son to give advice to? His own daughter to cherish?

The possibility had never been more remote.

"As men, we have no idea how we would react after such an ordeal. It might be that we would feel the same. But you marrying Frida without delay will show your support better than any words could. You're doing exactly the right thing, Magnar. You're a good man."

Never had he told anyone those hated words before. As they escaped his mouth, he realized that people genuinely meant them as a compliment when they said them and that there were worst things to be called than "a good man." It was a revelation.

Caedmon blinked. He seemed to have had a lot of revelations as of late, too many to deal with.

"Well, anyway." Magnar nodded. "Thank you."

"You're welcome. I'll see you both tomorrow to wish you well in your new life."

Caedmon stared at the retreating Norseman until he had disappeared into the distance and sighed. Another man marrying the woman of his dreams. Would he be the only one left behind?

Feeling a hundred years old, he made his way back to the hut. His injury, much as he would have liked to ignore it, was itching something fierce. It needed to be bathed, and more ointment applied. The bandage needed to be changed at the very least. And he needed…He needed company to distract him from his maudlin thoughts.

"Ah, Caedmon, there you are. I was waiting for you."

Ingrid was waiting for him? It was almost as if she'd heard all his doubts and questions and wanted to reassure him, make him see that he was not alone in the world. He cleared his throat, absurdly moved.

Damn, that was twice in the space of one afternoon that he'd felt close to tears. First with Magnar and now with Ingrid. What was he turning into?

"Why were you waiting for me? What did you want me to do?"

She appeared nonplussed at the question. "Nothing. And you're not to do anything while you're recovering, do you hear me?"

"What did you need me for then?" He didn't understand.

"Well, I wanted to eat with you and I was starting to get hungry if you must know."

He stared at her. She hadn't *needed* him for anything, she had simply wanted to be with him and share a meal together. It was exactly what he'd thought lacked in his life. Someone wanting to be with him for no other reason than the pleasure of his company, a sense of belonging, a home.

"I'm hungry too," he said, not quite sure what else to say.

"Then let's eat."

It was that simple. As ever with her, everything was simple, natural. Caedmon sat down and a moment later he was handed a steaming bowl of stew. A rich smell of herbs reached his nostrils. He already knew Ingrid could cook, but this smelled heavenly.

"After we've eaten, I will check your injury," she said as she sat opposite him. "I expect it's itching. If it's dry enough, we won't bandage it again. It will be more comfortable that way."

He didn't answer. He couldn't have. Suddenly there was an odd tightening in his throat that he could not account for. To distract himself, he gestured toward the basket in the middle of the table, the one she used to gather eggs every morning.

"That's excellent craftsmanship. I'm impressed. Basket weaving is one talent I've never been able to master."

She smiled. "Oh, I didn't make this! Like you, I'm not talented enough. This was a present from Sigurd."

He barely repressed a groan. Not that damned Dane again! Would the man best him at everything, do everything he could not, charm everyone he could not? "He's a talented man," he forced himself to say before talking a spoonful of stew.

And a lucky bastard.

"Yes. But you should have seen the necklace he tried to make for Frigyth last summer." Ingrid burst out laughing. It was such a happy sound, Caedmon couldn't help but smile in turn. "It was a disaster. I'm told the pendant was supposed to look like a bird but it ended up looking like a fat turnip. Oh, well. I suppose everyone has their strengths and weaknesses."

"I suppose so," he said, feeling suddenly cheered. "You know, making jewelry is what I did in London. I was a goldsmith."

Ingrid stared at him as if he'd revealed that his fingers were made of actual gold. "You're a goldsmith?"

He nodded. "I learned the trade with an old man I befriended just after my arrival. He'd lost his only son and was looking for someone to pass on his knowledge to. He insisted on showing me and it quickly became apparent that I had an aptitude for it. I can now make all the jewelry a woman could want." He paused, considering. "Perhaps I should make a necklace for Frigyth, to replace the one Sigurd tried to make. It would be easy for me to make a bird that doesn't look like a vegetable. She might like that."

"I'm sure you could, but there's no need. She said she loved the creation, and wears it often." Ingrid twisted her lips and her eyes sparkled, just as if they were made of actual sapphires, which had always been his favorite gem. "You know, I think she did not even lie."

"No," he said darkly. "I suppose she did not."

CHAPTER EIGHT

The following morning, before they went to Magnar and Frida's wedding, Ingrid declared that it was time to remove the stitches on Caedmon's injury.

"It's been more than a week and you slept without a bandage last night. It is perfectly dry. You don't want to wait any longer, or they will become embedded in the skin and hurt when I take them out."

"You?" She would offer to do that for him? Surely there was no need. Placed where it was, he could easily access the wound. "I can manage on my own."

"Please. I'm sure you can but it will be quicker and less painful if you have help. I don't mind. It will be a lot easier to remove the stitches than it was to make them."

In the end he could not resist the offer. She was right. It would be better if he lay down and relaxed while she took care of him. Eyes fastened on to her, he grabbed the back of his collar and tugged. When he freed his head from the shirt Ingrid had moved. She was by the table, looking into a small basket.

"I need my scissors." She was muttering to herself like an old woman. "Some fresh linens, the ointment..."

Caedmon arched a brow. Was she embarrassed to see him bare-chested? It would be odd if she were, considering how often she'd seen him without his shirt in the last week, but she was acting all strange all of a sudden and her cheeks had acquired a suspicious flush. A smile tugged at his lips. For some reason he found her shyness endearing.

He lay on the pallet. "I'm ready. Do your worst."

She whipped around, scowling. "I would never inflict you pain if I can help it!"

"I know," he soothed. "I don't know why I said that. It's just a phrase."

She knelt by his side and bent down to examine the stitches with featherlight touches. It was his turn to be embarrassed, because once again, the evocative position and maddening caresses were creating havoc with his senses. Just like the other day, when she had washed him, he could not help his body's natural response to the touch of a beautiful woman. Fortunately this time he'd anticipated it and he was holding his bunched up shirt over his groin like a shield. With luck Ingrid would not realize that under it all he'd gone hard as wood.

Apparently she had not. She was cutting at the stiches carefully, and appeared lost in thought.

"I'm so glad for Frida and Magnar," she said in a low voice. "That night in the hut, I...I admit I thought he might turn away from her after the assault."

"Why would he do such a thing?"

She hesitated. "Men don't seem to want women who've been—"

"Men," he cut in before she could use the word "soiled", "don't want to hear that women have been raped, because the thought is unbearable, that's not quite the same."

Frida, Frigyth, and now Ingrid...Why were they all convinced that an assault reflected badly on *them*? Why couldn't they see that a normal man would not hold something like that against her? And what did Ingrid know about being spurned after being the victim of a rape? He suddenly remembered what she'd said while she sewed his wound.

Don't worry about me. I'd much rather be here stitching a wound than in that hut being raped. Again.

All the blood froze in his veins. He'd been forced to ignore the comment at the time because she'd started to stitch him up and, to his shame, he'd forgotten about it afterward. He would not make the same mistake twice.

"Ingrid," he started slowly, "were you—"

"There. All finished."

She raised her head and gave him such a pointed, imploring look that he didn't insist. If she ever wanted to tell him why she thought men would spurn a woman who'd been the victim of a rape, she would. But he would not cause her pain by making her talk about something she clearly didn't want to discuss.

"Thank you. I didn't feel a thing."

The urge to place a hand on her cheek was too strong for him to even try to resist it. He heard her inhale when his fingers touched her skin but she didn't shy away from the caress. For a long moment they stayed like this, looking at each other.

Then he broke the spell. "Let's go and see Magnar marry his beautiful bride, shall we?"

Perhaps that would go some way into restoring her faith in men.

After putting some order to their clothes, they made their way to the center of the village, where everyone one was assembled in the spring sunshine. The atmosphere was one of pure joy. Birds were chirping away, music was playing, children were running around. Caedmon recognized Frigyth's son Moon chasing Wolf's daughter, a little blonde girl who screamed in delight when he finally caught her.

The ceremony was short and sweet, quite unlike any Caedmon had seen before, quite unlike his wedding in London would have been. He felt privileged to be able to witness such a moment. The women all wiped a tear from their cheek when Magnar lifted his new bride into his arms and kissed her soundly on the lips.

Usually one to look upon weddings with suspicion, today Ingrid was finding it hard to contain her emotion.

Without thinking, she took Caedmon's hand in hers. The gesture was intimate but he did not protest. Just when she was thinking that she ought to remove her hand, he tightened his fingers over hers and drew her even closer. In that moment they undoubtedly appeared like the lovers they were supposed to be. Fortunately, Björn was deep in discussion with his newly married friend.

"Thank you," she said, her voice taut with emotion.

It made no doubt in her mind that this wedding was happening thanks to the man next to her. Had she been raped, Frida would have considered herself soiled, unworthy of Magnar and would have fled the village, never to be seen again. She had told her as much while they traveled in the cart after their rescue. Ingrid had not known what to answer. She knew all too well the shame associated with having a man you didn't want enter your body. Besides, whatever Caedmon thought, some men didn't want women who'd been soiled, and she'd had no idea then whether Magnar was one of them or not, so she had been unable to comfort Frida. It turned out that he was as steadfast as she could have wished.

Caedmon leaned in toward her. "If you mean that without me this wedding wouldn't have taken place, then you are mistaken. Magnar told me yesterday that he would have married Frida regardless of what happened with the Saxons."

She squeezed his fingers. He'd read her mind and she was

grateful for the reassurance. "I'm proud of him. He's one of Björn's friends and I always thought him more sensible than the others. I'm glad to be proven right."

"I told you. A man worthy of the name would not think any less of a woman for being abused."

Ingrid bit her bottom lip and nodded slowly, eager to put an end to that particular discussion. She had already said too much and they were in full view of everyone, Ivar included. She could not betray herself now.

They watched as the newlyweds walked toward the hut that had been allocated to them under the cheers of the onlookers.

Ingrid felt a pang of envy. It was one thing telling herself she was happy on her own, quite another to believe it when she saw the love and joy on someone else's faces and felt the warmth of Caedmon's hand around hers.

"Come. Let's go and feast," she said, pasting a smile on her face. Today was not a day to be sad. "And then we'll dance long into the night."

Caedmon returned the smile. Only his was genuine, and made his eyes shimmer like a bright summer's day. "Dancing? Is that what you'd recommend to a man who's just had his stitches removed? May I remind you that only yesterday you forbade me to lift your basket when it was only half full with vegetables?"

She twisted her lips, feeling caught out. Of course, he couldn't dance! What had she been thinking? "Let me rephrase, Saxon. *I* will dance, and you will watch."

Something flit across his face, like a ripple over water, too elusive to catch. "Oh, I will."

"Forgive me, I can see you're busy, but I had to get away from the forge for a moment," Agnes fell on the stool with a sigh.

"Magnus is tearing his hair out and trying my temper sorely. I had to leave for fear we would come to an argument."

An argument!

Shaking her head, Ingrid poured them both a cup of ale from the cask Björn had brought only that morning. She found it hard to believe that things were as dire as her friend was making out. The blacksmith was one of the most even-tempered men she knew and Agnes had the patience of a saint. They were a perfect match in that way, so a pointless argument between them seemed unlikely. Theirs was another shining example of how successful marriages between a Saxon woman and a Norseman could be. Those were becoming quite common in the village. Would it be the same the other way around, she wondered? The thought made her flush because she knew of only one Saxon man and he was just outside, cleaning the coop. He had wanted to chop wood for the fire but she had forbidden him to go anywhere near an axe. Though he was recovering from his life-threatening wound with surprising speed, he was still on the mend.

Ingrid took a long swig of ale.

Ever since Magnar and Frida's wedding a week ago she had been feeling oddly despondent. From the age of eighteen she had known she would never live with a man. But now she was, in effect, doing just that. Even if it was no romantic arrangement, even if it was temporary and had only been brought on by necessity, the result was the same. She *was* living with Caedmon and she could not help but find it comforting to have a presence in the hut, someone to rely on and share a meal and a laugh with at night.

Someone she felt desire for...

There was no point denying it any longer. She was lusting after him. Over the last few days she had tried to convince herself that what she felt when he was near was nothing out of the ordinary but she was losing the battle, fast.

She most definitely felt desire for Caedmon, a bit more every day, and she had no idea where that would lead her.

With some effort, she brought her mind back to the present and Agnes, who was complaining about Magnus' unusual behavior.

"So tell me, what happened that made you both so out of sorts?"

"A man from town came visiting the other day. A Saxon. He had business with Wolf." Ingrid nodded, not in the least surprised. Everyone within a twenty-mile radius had had something to do with the Icelander at some point or other. This was nothing new. "While he was there, his wife felt a bit hot in the forge. She undid her cloak and somehow her brooch snapped open. It fell to the ground and Growler ran away with it. By the time Magnus had prised it from his jaw, it was quite mangled."

Ingrid could not help a laugh at the scene going through her mind. The smithy's dog Growler was still a puppy, and as excitable as they came. "Yes, I can imagine."

"Magnus was mortified and promised the poor woman he could repair it. Her husband, a prosperous land owner, was delighted and assured him he would commission work from him and mention his name to his friends if he did a satisfactory job on the brooch. This is a golden opportunity to gain some wealthy customers. But, as talented as he is, Magnus cannot get it right. He lacks the dexterity needed for delicate work." Agnes reddened. "At least, for jewelry making," she finished in a whisper.

Another bubble of laughter rose in Ingrid's throat. Apparently after five years of marriage and two children, the two of them were still as in love as ever. She had once thought that the little Saxon might marry her brother. But it had quickly become clear that Björn only had eyes for Dunne, who had since then become his wife, and that Magnus was the perfect man for Agnes. Between the two of them, it had been love at first sight.

And apparently, he was seeing to her needs quite satisfactorily.

A highly unwelcome pang of envy tore through Ingrid. Would that she too had a man seeing to her needs. A man with dextrous fingers and a fascinating body covered in dark hairs...

"He dreads admitting to the woman that her brooch is ruined," her friend carried on, oblivious to her lewd musings. "Not to mention that after his accident, we could do with the money the commissions would bring in."

Yes, that Ingrid could easily believe. Last fall Magnus had broken his arm while playing with his eldest son and had been unable to work for weeks as a result. Though the villagers had done what they could to compensate the loss of revenue by ordering twice as many nails, chains and axes than they normally would, the long inactivity would have taken its toll on the family. Becoming the supplier of a group of wealthy customers was an opportunity to be seized with both hands.

"I think I can help," Ingrid said. "Well, not me, really, but Caedmon. As luck would have it, I found out the other day that he's a goldsmith."

The revelation had struck her. A more fitting occupation for a man whose eyes sparkled like precious gems she could not imagine. It was like being told that Wolf was in fact descended from a pack of wolves or that her parents were still watching over her from where they were. It just...made sense.

"Caedmon? Your lover, you mean?" Agnes' eyes were aglow with mischief. "He's rather dashing, is he not?"

Ingrid felt herself go red to the roots of her hair. After the initial lie destined to placate Ivar, she had not told anyone, not even her closest friends, that Caedmon was not really her lover.

She had a suspicion no one would believe her if she said it now anyway. After all, she herself had announced what they supposedly were to each other in front of her own brother. Then he had rescued her from a mob of Saxons and almost gotten killed in the process, and they had been living together for over two weeks now. It certainly didn't look as if they did not care for one another.

"I'm sure he can solve Magnus' problem," she said instead of answering.

As if he'd heard her, Caedmon chose this moment to enter the hut, a stack of logs cradled in his arms. Dear, he did look rather dashing. Yes...And wasn't that the problem? If he had not, she might have been able to keep a clear head around him.

"Are you all right? Did anything happen while I was out?" he asked, stopping in his tracks. The questions made Ingrid realize that she and Agnes were staring at him as if he had grown two heads. She cleared her throat, feeling foolish.

"Yes. I mean no, nothing happened. Only...We were talking about you. Agnes and Magnus could do with your help." She stood up. "Do you think you could repair a brooch that has been chewed on by a dog?"

"Chewed by a dog...My. That would be a first." A corner of his lips curled up. "I could try. I always enjoy a challenge." He dropped the logs on the fire pit and nodded. "Does he want me to go now?"

"Please." Agnes stood up in turn, looking relieved. "Thank you, that would be most kind. He's probably—"

"Wait!" Ingrid cut in, as realization hit. "You've been cutting wood! I told you not to go anywhere near the axe!"

"Did you?" Caedmon threw her his most innocent look. "I must have missed that over the hens clucking. The gray one is incredibly noisy, isn't she?"

"You're impossible!"

"Don't worry. I promise I'll spend the rest of the day sitting down, handling nothing bigger than files and pliers. No chance of hurting myself then. Does that satisfy you?"

She had to smile. He *was* impossible, but in a good way, and she could not stay mad at him. "Yes."

Without another word, he went to retrieve his bag, which she imagined contained all the tools he needed, and left.

"Let us hope he can solve the problem," Agnes said.

Ingrid didn't answer but, she didn't doubt it for a moment.

Later that evening she and Agnes made their way to Magnus' workshop. The sun had started to disappear below the horizon and a velvety sky was slowly replacing the sheet of blue they'd had overhead all day.

As soon as they walked through the door, the smithy lifted his wife into his arms. "My angel. Thanks to you, our problems are over."

Agnes laughed. "I didn't do anything. Ingrid was the one who mentioned Caedmon could help, and he was the one who repaired the brooch."

Her husband kissed her full on the mouth. "Yes, but if you hadn't gone to see them, I would still be here, messing it up even further."

"I take it that it is now fixed?" Ingrid asked. She was glad for her friends and grateful to Caedmon for helping them.

"See for yourself."

Magnus led the two women to the table by the window. On it was a gold flower, so realistic Ingrid had the impression that it had just been picked from a shiny, enchanted bush. With its delicate petals, the flower seemed so real that she almost bent down to smell it.

"My! That is incredible," she breathed, unable to believe her eyes.

"Astounding," Agnes agreed.

As one, they turned to face Caedmon, who shrugged as if he had not just created something extraordinary. "It's easy enough to do when you know how and you have the proper tools."

No one appeared in the least convinced. With infinite care Ingrid took the brooch in her hand and was surprised to find it so sturdy when it appeared so fragile. She could not help but think that were she to take it outside, it would be blown away by the breeze in a blink.

"A dog rose," she murmured, looking at the brooch resting in her palm. The petals had just unfurled and she could see every stamen in the middle, fashioned from little dots of pure gold. It was beautiful, and unlike anything she had ever seen.

"Dog roses are my favorite flowers and relatively easy to reproduce," Caedmon explained in an apologetic tone, as if he thought she would have been more impressed by a more majestic flower. She would not. This was perfect, elevating something common into a work of art. It was as if he were the first man to see the plain flowers for the marvel they were and wanting to do them justice. "I had no idea how the brooch looked originally so I took a guess but I don't think the woman will complain. Considering how badly it was damaged, this can only be an improvement."

Magnus gave a laugh. "Yes, and not all of it was Growler's fault, unfortunately. My attempts at repairing it took their toll. But it is close enough to the original, I'd say, only better, because before it was just an indistinct flower. She will be delighted." He turned to his wife and rubbed a hand over his face. "Shall we? After the last few days spent worrying about that damn brooch, I'm exhausted. I would like to sleep a bit before I face our potential client tomorrow."

Agnes nodded. "You've earned it." She turned and faced Caedmon with a smile. "Thank you for your help. How can we repay you for what you did?"

Caedmon waved her offer away. He was glad to have helped and did not need any reward for doing something that came so easily to him, especially when Magnus had been amongst the men coming to his aid against the Saxons. How could he take money from the man he owed his life to? Had the smithy not been so skilled at throwing objects, the cut on his stomach would have been fatal. This was priceless.

"I never got the chance to thank you for what you did the other day," he'd told him once he'd finished working on the brooch. "Without you, I would be dead."

"Please. The whole thing was Wolf's idea. When he saw the man holding the blade to you he told me to go around the back before the Saxons could see me. He knows that as a child I used to practice throwing stones at birds. Don't ask me why, but I thought it a more satisfactory way to hunt. And eventually, it worked. Of course, I went to bed hungry more than once before that."

Caedmon had smiled at that. Never had a skill come in more handy.

"I don't need anything," he said, slapping the smithy on the shoulder.

He would not take anything from a man who had saved his life. If anything, *he* should be repaying Magnus for what he'd done. And then an idea popped into his head. There was something he wanted to do and the smithy was the only man who could help.

"If I may," he started, taking a pair of pliers in his hand, "I would like to use the workshop to create something while I'm here. It would stop me from going mad while I wait for the injury to heal."

He'd missed his work in the last few weeks. Creating jewelry was what he did best. More to the point, he wanted to take this opportunity to make something for Frigyth. Magnus, for all that he was no goldsmith, was well equipped. He had scraps of metal and a furnace. It was petty but Caedmon needed to make something better than Sigurd, he needed to make Frigyth see there was at least one thing he could do that the Norseman couldn't. His ego demanded it. He was not proud of it but there it was, he had to know he had somehow succeeded in giving this woman at least one thing of his.

So he would make a necklace, the best he had ever created. He would put all his disillusion, his pain, his lost hopes in it as he worked and then he would give it to her. It would be a way of freeing himself of all he had felt for her. Would it work?

It was worth a try at least.

"Of course, my friend. Use what you need," Magnus gestured to the tool bench. In that moment Caedmon had the impression that he could have asked him for anything and the man would have agreed.

"Thank you."

Ingrid lingered a moment after Magnus and Agnes had left, looking rather...The word that come to Caedmon's mind was "awed." Ever since she had seen the brooch he'd created, something had changed within her. It was as if she credited him with magical powers and wasn't sure how to behave in front of him anymore. Absurdly, it warmed something inside of him. No one had looked at him like that before, as if he were extraordinary.

"Do you need anything?" she asked. "I could bring you something to eat or—"

"No, thank you, I'm not hungry."

His fingers were itching to start on the necklace, even though he had no idea what he wanted to make yet. What kind of pendant would Frigyth like? A flower, an animal, something more abstract? Or perhaps he could do a ring, a brooch, earrings instead? No, it had to be a necklace and pendant, he decided, so she could compare it with the one Sigurd had attempted to make and see the difference.

"I'll leave you to work then," Ingrid murmured. "Good night."

"Thank you. Good night."

As soon as the door was closed, he sat down on the bench and started to think.

What now?

Not knowing what to do, he took a piece of metal and started to turn it this way and that. And just like that, his fingers took over. It was always the same. It was as if the less he thought about a project, the easier ideas came to him. His hands seemed to know what he could do better than his mind did. Today was no exception.

Fanning the fire, Caedmon smiled to himself. He already knew he was about to create one of his best pieces.

CHAPTER NINE

"So you *are* fucking the Saxon, then."

Ingrid didn't need to turn around to know who was behind her. Even if she had not recognized Ivar's voice, no one else would have talked to her so crudely. She threw a quick glance around to confirm that, though no one would be able to hear their conversation, she was in easy distance of help, if need be. Just beyond the fence, she spotted Björn, talking to Magnar and Frida.

She relaxed, knowing nothing could happen to her today.

"Yes, I am," she said with a calm she didn't feel. But she was not about to humiliate herself by admitting that Caedmon was not, in fact, sharing her bed, and never had. As far as Ivar was concerned, the two of them were lovers and that was how it would remain. Her self-esteem demanded he believe it. He'd once told her no one would want her, she needed him to think someone did. And not just anyone. An honorable, dashing man.

"My, you weren't lying when you claimed you didn't want just anyone between your legs. You really do choose your men carefully. The hero of the village, the savior of women, no less!"

She tightened her hold on the leek in her hand. Forget the

taunt about her supposed superior attitude, he made it sound as if having helped the women and saved them from rape was something shameful, or at the very least unworthy of praise. Well, she shouldn't be surprised, should she? For him, rape was a game, nothing more, certainly not something a man should feel any guilt over.

Instead of answering, she reached for another leek and pulled. He wanted to make a scene, but she was not going to indulge him. She just wanted him gone.

"A Saxon!" Ivar spat. Her lack of reaction seemed to infuriate him. While she worked hard at composure, he seemed to get himself closer and closer to an outburst. "Have you no dignity? Don't you think you should—"

"Here's what I think," she snarled, finally standing up to face him, "I think that you should stop talking and leave. Now. I have nothing to say to you."

Why was he bothering with her all of a sudden? For five years they had not exchanged a single word in private. At first she had feared he would constantly seek her out, but to her great relief, he had left her alone. And now, because he thought she had found herself a lover, he was sniffing at her door. Why?

Was he jealous?

Anger seared her veins at the notion. How dare he be jealous, or anything, where she was concerned? Her fingers tightened into fists and she considered throwing the leek at him—or shoving it up a place where one did not usually store vegetables.

"I've missed you, you know, Ingrid," he said, taking a step toward her. If he took another, he would be too close for comfort. Then she *would* use whatever weapon she had. The mere idea of him putting his hands on her was enough to make her heave.

"You've missed me?" she repeated, incredulous.

"Yes. You were my first conquest and I've never been able to forget you. I still have feelings for you, I still want you in my bed. We never had time to see where things could go between us, all because of a stupid misunderstanding."

He still wanted her in his bed? Was that what he meant by having feelings for her? And he thought that what had happened was a misunderstanding? Was that really how he remembered it? This time anger caused her vision to blur.

"Go now, or I swear you won't leave in one piece," she hissed, pointing her leek at him as she would a dagger.

Ivar bared his teeth in a grimace, but she was too incensed to be afraid. Let him try to touch her if he dared! Then he would see how much she had missed him.

"I'll leave. Enjoy your Saxon while you can, but know that I'll be waiting for when you get fed up with him. I'll give you what you need then."

She didn't respond, didn't move one inch. Finally, he left.

For a long moment Ingrid stared at the vegetable patch without seeing anything.

"Are you all right?"

Caedmon approached. From a distance he'd seen Ingrid deep in conversation with a man. He'd recognized the tall Norseman who had accused him of stealing the horses the other day. That simple fact had set him on edge. He remembered how she had seemed to want to put him in his place. These two were not the best of friends, and no good could come from the confrontation. His instincts had been confirmed a moment later. Even from where he was, it had been obvious that the conversation was tense.

Before he'd known what he was doing, he'd gone to join her. By the time he'd drawn to her side the man, Ivar, if he remembered his name correctly, had left, but Ingrid still appeared riled up. She was holding a leek as she would a weapon, the gesture betraying her thoughts more efficiently than any explanation would have. What had happened? What had the man told her?

Slowly, she looked up at him and he saw that it was going to take her some effort to shake herself off from the emotion taking hold of her. It was fury, he realized, not fear, as he had first thought. It hardly reassured him. The man had no business making her angry any more than scared.

He fought the urge to draw her into his arms. They had not seen each other since the evening before. When he had finally made it back to the hut in the middle of the night after working on the necklace, she had been asleep. And when he'd woken up this morning, she'd already left.

"Let's go back home," she said, as if speaking to herself, before dropping the leek into her basket.

Caedmon had no choice but to follow her.

That night they ate in uncomfortable silence. The tense atmosphere was a far cry from the usual easy intimacy between them and he could not rid himself of the impression that Ivar was responsible for the change.

"What did the man tell you this afternoon?" he asked as they swapped their empty bowls for pastries filled with wild fruit. The meal had been sumptuous, as usual.

Ingrid bit into her pastry before answering. "What man?"

What man?

He started at her incredulously. As if she'd forgotten the incident, or how she had wanted to bludgeon him to death with a leek. It was obvious from the icy tone that she wouldn't welcome any more questions on the topic, however, so he remained silent.

"Tomorrow I'll leave," he announced once they had finished eating.

It was more than time. His injury was healing well and, in truth, he should probably have left days ago, only he had put off the inevitable for as long as he dared. But now, seeing how much it bothered him to see Ingrid upset, he understood that he had better leave before his feelings for her developed into something even more problematic. He had a history of falling for the wrong woman and suffering as a result. He was just about thinking he might survive the loss of Frigyth, now was not the time to get himself entangled in another web of his own making.

"You're leaving already?" She lifted wide, blue eyes to him. Would he ever be able to see sapphires without being reminded of her? He doubted it.

"I've been here for more than two weeks," he reminded her. It was a lot more time than he needed to recover, and she knew it. He'd been walking about for days and even old Helga had declared herself satisfied with his recovery.

"Yes." Ingrid gathered the last of the pastry crumbs up in her bowl and stood up. "I need more thread for my sewing, so I will go with you into town to buy some if you don't mind."

He nodded, glad of the reprieve. As soon as he had announced his intention to leave, he'd realized that he wasn't quite ready to say good bye, but he could not change his mind now without appearing like a fool.

Once she'd come back from washing the bowls, Ingrid seemed restored to her usual self and started to talk. It was as if she wanted to make the most of their last night together. He welcomed it, because he wanted the exact same thing.

"How old were you when you left town?"

"Twenty-four summers."

She seemed to mull on this, as if it were of great significance. "The same age I am now."

"Yes."

He smiled. Upon first meeting her, he'd thought her young but now that he knew her better, he found it hard to believe she was ten years younger than he was. In his mind they were of an age. She was so much more mature than he'd been then, and perhaps would ever be. Living on her own didn't seem to weigh her down, like it did him. She was happy with her own company, and obviously didn't need anyone to feel complete. He envied her this confidence.

"Tell me about London," she said, settling herself more comfortably in the chair.

"Why?"

She shrugged, as if not quite sure why she wanted to hear about it. "I know everyone in the village. I was born in this house, I grew up here, I have never traveled farther than the town or the coast, I hardly ever meet new people. Next to you, who's lived in a strange city and crossed the country many times, I feel ridiculous."

"You're not ridiculous!" Caedmon protested. Such a word applied to her was what was ridiculous.

"Well, maybe not ridiculous but you know what I mean. You have no idea how wonderful it is to talk to someone who doesn't know all there is to know about me already, who asks unexpected questions, who doesn't presume he can guess what my answers would be, who doesn't mind the eccentric side of me I never allow myself to show."

He could not help another smile and found himself thinking that he had smiled more in three weeks with her than he had in three years in London. "No, I don't mind your eccentric side at all." In fact he loved it.

"With you I feel at ease, without knowing quite why. Usually I don't trust strange men. Not that I meet many, as I just told you."

At the mention of strange men, he instantly sobered. "I cannot say I blame you, considering what the Saxons did the other day."

"Yes. It's not only Saxons, though," she said under her breath.

Everything within Caedmon tightened. There it was again, the allusion to some dark event in her past. This time he would not let it pass. He was leaving tomorrow, if he didn't ask now, he would never know. It shouldn't matter, but somehow it did. He needed to know exactly what had happened to this woman he'd come to care about or it would eat up at him.

"Why are you afraid of men? Did someone hurt you?" he asked gently.

For a moment he thought she wouldn't answer, which only confirmed his suspicions. Someone had hurt her, and she was finding it hard to talk about it. Blood boiling, he waited. If she didn't want to say anymore, then there was nothing he would be able to do. He would not force a confession out of her. But just when he'd lost hope that she would ever answer, she did.

"When I was eighteen I got involved with a boy from the village. For a while, everything was good. We shared a few kisses, and it was enough for me, but then he started to want more."

"Why am I not surprised?" Caedmon growled to himself. This was all too predictable.

She misunderstood his reaction for lack of interest. "I'm sorry, this is of no interest to you. If you'd rather not—"

"No. Please carry on. I asked, so I might as well hear the rest of the story now." He had better not let her see how important her answer was to him. Far from being uninteresting, it was of utmost importance. There was a pause, too long for his liking so he asked: "Did you agree to the man's proposition?"

"Yes. It made me feel beautiful, desired, like a woman. I'd never been seen like a woman by anyone before, only a child."

Well. He was surprised by how readily she admitted to such

feelings. But he should have known. The woman was anything but predictable. Her next sentence, however, shocked him.

"We started sleeping together. Then one evening he took me to his parents' hay loft and asked if he could blindfold me. I agreed."

Holy hell.

Blood shot straight to his groin.

"What happened?" he asked, more aroused than he had been in months. And this time it was not because Ingrid was bent over him. It was because of what she was saying, because she had revealed an adventurous, wild side to her that could not fail to rouse his interest. He was not very proud of this reaction, after all, they were discussing something painful to her, but he was a man, and imagining the beautiful Norsewoman naked with her eyes veiled with a cloth was an enticing image.

"We started to..." Her voice trailed and she flushed.

"Yes. I understand. No need to be more specific," Caedmon growled. It was one thing imagining her spread eagled on a bed of hay, quite another picturing a man laboring on top of her.

"It was fine but after a while I thought something was odd. It felt different, he moved differently, *smelled* differently." She shivered, like someone remembering something unpleasant. Ice spread through his veins and the pulsing in his groin instantly stopped. What would she reveal? "And no wonder. I removed the piece of cloth covering my eyes and saw...saw that it wasn't him inside me at all, but one of his friends."

Caedmon started when a rude word escaped his lips. He very rarely swore out loud but if ever an occasion warranted it, this was it. She'd been tricked into sleeping with a stranger by none other than her lover? This had to be the single most outrageous thing he'd ever heard.

"Where was the boy while this was happening?"

Had he let his friend into the loft and abandoned her to her fate, with no guarantee of how she would be treated? No, he had done even worse, as her answer revealed.

"He was on the side, watching us, and...touching himself." A pause. "Next to him was a third man, watching and touching himself, also. For a moment, I was too stunned to react. Then I pushed the boy off me and ran to the door."

This time Caedmon was too shocked to even swear. He just stared at Ingrid, who had not looked at him once since she'd started her tale. So not only had her lover offered her to two of his friends without her agreement but he'd found the idea of her being used against her knowledge so arousing that he'd masturbated to the scene. The whole thing was sickening and he wasn't sure what to say.

Eventually he cleared his throat to ask. "Did they...did they let you leave?"

He could not be sure they had. She'd been alone and in a state of shock. If the two friends had been promised they could enjoy her favors, then they would not have been best pleased to be denied their pleasure, and what could she have done against the three of them?

"Yes. I ran, and reached the hut before they could catch me. Fortunately, as I was naked, it was nighttime and no one saw me. My brother was away at the time, he'd gone to visit his wife's sister in Mercia. I bolted my door and spent the night crying over my stupidity."

"Stupidity?" he hissed. "You don't think this was in any way your fault?"

She bit her bottom lip. "I should have—"

"You should nothing. How could you have imagined such a devious idea? The boys are all to blame for this, not you. Their youth was no excuse."

She was still staring at her hands. He waited. "The worst of it was..."

Caedmon braced himself to hear what she thought was worse than what she had just described because he sure as hell could not think of anything.

"I was raped but I didn't even know it until *after* it happened. All the while, I was being used against my will but I was not aware of it. I did not struggle, I did not protest. I even..." She closed her eyes. "I even enjoyed some of it. It's humiliating. It makes me feel like a...Do you have any idea how that makes me feel? They laughed as I ran, saying that I had not been so prudish a moment ago. And I had not!"

Oh, she was right. That made it all worse. Her body had welcomed her attacker in, her mind had not raised the alarm, her senses had been won over. As a result she was not able to rid herself of the notion that she had been complicit to the assault, even if she hadn't been. She had been tricked, not seduced. And her lover and his despicable friends had laughed at their own cleverness.

Caedmon wanted to howl.

"In the morning, I decided I would be better off on my own, that men could not be relied upon. In any case, there was no other choice, for who would want me after this?"

Not want her? Who on earth had put such ideas into her head? As if he needed to ask. The boys. As they'd laughed while she scrambled back to her feet, they would have told her she was now spoiled goods and would never find a decent man to have her. Now he knew where her ridiculous notion of women being unworthy after a rape came from. From the three bastards who had put it there.

"They said I had better keep my mouth shut about what happened because if anyone knew I'd already slept with two men and enjoyed every moment of it, they would never want to have anything to do with me." Ingrid sounded defeated, which was worse than angry. It was as if she didn't even question the truth of the statement.

"But, of course, they would tell you that!" Caedmon exploded. "Don't you see? They wanted you to keep silent to save their miserable hides! It was for their benefit, not yours. They knew that if people found out what they had done, they would have to pay for it. And they were right about that, at least. Wolf, your brother, or anyone would have taken them to task over it."

She shook her head as if she wasn't interested in establishing the truth. "It matters not, anyway. It's all in the past. But now you know why I think that men cannot be trusted. I was reminded of it only the other day with the Saxons."

"Yes." What could he say? "It is clear that some of them can't. But not everyone is like those bastards."

"I know," she sighed and finally looked at him. The pain he saw in her eyes almost floored him. "Deep down, I know it. Still, it's not worth the risk. I will never marry. Better to be on my own than to be used and disappointed, don't you think?"

Silence stretched in the hut.

How does one recover after such a confession? Caedmon had no idea.

"I don't trust women, either," he said after a while.

What had pushed him to say that he wasn't sure. But Ingrid had just confided her painful, very personal story to him, and he wanted to confide his with her, even if it was not as traumatic. He'd not told anyone about his humiliation, would most likely never tell anyone else but all of a sudden he wanted to tell Ingrid. It wasn't fair for her to be the only one feeling ill at ease because of something she'd revealed, especially when she was in no way to blame for what had happened. She'd not been stupid, contrary to what she thought, she had agreed to a little erotic game with someone she thought cared about her, and had then been taken advantage of, it was not the same at all. It was his role to make her see that she was not alone in having been made a fool.

She stared at him, as if she'd guessed all he was not saying. "Why don't you trust women? What happened to you?"

He ran a hand down the back of his head. "You wanted to know about London. Well. This is what happened in London. After years spent on my own, doing little else than honing my craft, I became betrothed to a woman called Mildred."

Why did that sound ominous, Ingrid wondered? Usually a betrothal was a good thing. So, had the woman died? Had Caedmon fled the town in grief? Was that why he had decided to go back to his hometown? She had not thought that could be the case before but, after all, why not? She looked at him more closely and decided that he seemed angry rather than heart-broken at the thought of this Mildred. In all probability, she was still alive. Besides, the death of someone dear wouldn't explain why he didn't trust women.

She waited for the rest of the explanation.

"It all happened very quickly between us. One day she came to the shop to have a ring repaired and she took a shine to me. She was beautiful, and not shy with her advances." He averted his gaze as if ashamed of his weakness. "I was only too happy to be seduced."

Ingrid's chest tightened. It was not hard to imagine that he attracted women and, as an unattached man at the height of his virility, he would have had no reason to refuse a beautiful woman coming on to him. There was no need to feel embar-rassed about it, not in front of her, who had slept with Ivar, all the while knowing she would never marry him.

"About a week after we'd met she started talking of marriage."

At that, Ingrid couldn't hide her surprise. A week was no

time at all to get to know someone, never mind agreeing to share the rest of their life with them. Why, Caedmon had been living under her roof for three weeks now, three times the length of his and Mildred's courtship, and she could not say she knew him well enough to decide whether they would suit as husband and wife.

She blinked.

Where had that thought come from? She'd just told him that she didn't trust men and never wanted to marry and she'd meant it. Now she was thinking about the best way to decide if someone was suited for marriage?

"Did you agree?" she asked more brusquely than she intended. They were talking about what had happened to him, not about her foolish ideas.

"Yes. When she came to live with me, she asked if her brother could join us. He didn't get on with their parents and she worried he would one day come to blows with his violent father, she explained, and get seriously injured, if not worse." When Caedmon met her gaze Ingrid saw that his irises, green a moment ago, had veered more toward brown, betraying an intense emotion. Disgust? Self-hatred? Shame? She couldn't tell. "I agreed, even if I wasn't thrilled by the prospect. But what could I do? She kept telling me I was her only hope. It would only be temporary, time for her bother to learn a trade to support himself. I could not see how I could refuse."

"No, of course not." No one would want to have a young man's death on their conscience.

Ingrid wasn't quite sure where this was going. She was grateful to Caedmon for trying to make her feel better by sharing his own embarrassing story but she had not yet heard anything that even started to compare with what had happened to her. So far he'd only proved that he had been hasty in his decision to marry and generous with his future wife's brother, hardly something anyone could criticize him for.

"The day before we were supposed to marry, I got home earlier than usual and found them in bed together."

A gasp escaped her lips. The tale had taken a sudden, shocking turn. "In *bed*?" Did he mean what she thought he meant...The look he threw her confirmed that the pair had not been sleeping at the time. "Brother and sister? That's monstrous!"

Caedmon let out a brittle laugh. "It turns out that they weren't brother and sister after all, but lovers. Some time before we met, Mildred had fallen with his child but her parents didn't think the man would make a good husband, and I have to agree with them. He was as lazy as anyone I'd ever met." He shrugged, as if the man's character didn't matter. "But they didn't see a problem with her getting married to me, a respectable gold-smith, a good man. I never met them and I don't think they knew she had asked for her lover to live with us. In any case, I care not. That night I left London, never to come back."

"You left them the house, the shop?" Surely not?

He shrugged again. "They're welcome to it. The poor child will need somewhere to live and without me to operate it, the shop is worth nothing anyway. I took all that was important with me, my tools, the gems and precious metal. That's why I was able to repair Magnus' brooch so easily."

"So..." Ingrid was dumbfounded—and not a little bit outraged on his behalf. "If you'd not seen them together that night, you would have found yourself married to a woman involved with someone else and already with child?"

He would have found out a few weeks after their wedding, when it was too late, the depth of her deception. It hardly bore thinking about. Now she understood Mildred's haste to get married. She'd had to bind him to her before she started to show.

Caedmon nodded. "Eventually, I would have found out she never had any brothers, and only meant to use me. The baby would have been born full term only five or six months after we'd first slept together and I would have understood her real motives for marrying me. But it would have been too late."

Ingrid felt a surge of hatred toward this Mildred, whom she imagined as a sultry seductress. The unscrupulous woman had wanted to give her lazy lover a roof and her bastard child a name, and never once had she thought to the pain she was causing Caedmon.

"Why did you agree to the match with a near stranger?"

Seeing as they were being honest with each other, she might as well ask the question burning her lips. Caedmon was no idiot. He must have sensed there was something odd in Mildred's haste to be married. A woman as deceitful as she appeared to be should have roused his suspicion. Or...Perhaps he'd been head over heels in love with her. That would explain a lot. He'd just told her she was very beautiful and very free with her favors, and didn't people say that love was blind? But Ingrid couldn't hear any pain in Caedmon's voice when he spoke about what had happened. He had not been hurt by the betrayal, only angered.

No, she decided. He had not been in love with the woman.

So why had he agreed to marry her so quickly? And why had he still been unmarried two months ago, for that matter? Women would have fallen over themselves to lure such a handsome, personable man into marriage. Had he, like her, deliberately shunned all to do with marriage and family until that moment? But if he'd held out for so long, why then had he fallen so easily for someone as unsuitable as Mildred? No one renounced years of conviction in such a short time, unless they had fallen in love.

Try as she might, she could not make sense of it.

Why had he agreed to the match?

Caedmon sighed at Ingrid's question. What could he say? He could tell her he hadn't known the extent of Mildred's treachery, and that was true, but deep down he had always felt something was off. Mildred had treated him too casually for him to believe she was in love with him, but he had not let it bother him. After all, he had not been in love with her either so it mattered little. Theirs would not have been the first union contracted for reasons other than love and he didn't think Ingrid would judge him for agreeing to such a cold arrangement.

Still he hesitated in being honest because he was ashamed of his reasoning.

Mildred had wanted to use him, but he too had meant to use her, albeit in a different way. He'd thought that as a married man, he might spend less time obsessing over a woman who'd disappeared from his life. He'd hoped that having a lusty partner in his bed at night would allow him to ease some of his frustration and he was not proud of the idea.

In the end, he decided to be honest with Ingrid, withholding only the name of the woman who had hurt him. It would not be fair to Frigyth, who was one of her friends. What did he have to lose anyway? If Ingrid thought him a fool for remaining fixated on one woman for so long, it mattered little. Tomorrow he would be gone, and they would in all probability never see each other again.

"I never felt anything for Mildred, except lust, and I never placed any real hope in a marriage with her," he said bluntly.

There.

With luck, having admitted it out loud would stop him from making the same mistake the next time a woman he barely knew asked to wed him.

As for him, he knew he would never ask anyone to marry him again. He would never be able to handle another refusal.

"Ten years ago I asked a woman to marry me. Twice. She refused me. Twice. And then she married someone else. I thought I would eventually forget her and meet someone I wanted to be with, but it never happened." Now came the embarrassing part. "And I didn't want to be the only man I knew who lived on his own. Damn it all, I'm almost five and thirty, I should have a wife, a family by now! I'm a good man, everyone keeps telling me that, and yet I'm not good enough, apparently! But why should I not be considered as a potential husband just because I am not a big, hulking Norseman?"

He was getting himself into a lather and he could tell his vehemence was surprising Ingrid, if not worrying her. But he couldn't stop now that he had started. Frigyth had felt something for him once, he was certain of it, then she had rejected him in favor of that damned Sigurd and since then, he'd not been able to attract any woman worthy of attention. All they ever wanted from him was a tumble in bed. Or, he amended in an effort at honesty, perhaps that was not quite the truth. Perhaps some of them had been willing and ready for something more meaningful, but he had been unable to see it, too obsessed by memories of his childhood sweetheart and embittered by her refusal to marry him.

In any case, the result had been the same. He'd ended up alone.

And he was thoroughly sick of it.

"You think Norsemen are the only men women want?" Ingrid sounded nonplussed. But he knew that was the case. Hadn't he seen countless proof of it?

"Saxons apparently do!" he erupted. At least Frigyth did. And he had heard women gush about the tall, strapping warriors enough times to doubt she was the only one. Why was Ingrid even surprised? Wasn't the village full of Saxon women who'd fallen under the spell of the men living here? Merewen,

Frigyth, Dunne, Agnes...Her own brother was married to one of them, surely she knew the appeal the blond giants exerted over the female population? And yet there wasn't a single Saxon man around. It seemed that even Norsewomen preferred men who towered over them with their damn beards and damn braids. "They trip over themselves to land in their arms."

There was a pause. "Some women don't think Norsemen particularly appealing, you know."

"No?" He smirked. "I'd like to meet one of these elusive women, and ask her..."

His voice trailed when he understood what Ingrid was saying. That he had already met one. Her. Hadn't she told him earlier she liked him because he was different from the people she had known all her life? In other words, Norsemen. Hadn't she just admitted to having suffered at the hands of three of the villagers? Yes. Perhaps he had met the one Norsewoman who would prefer to have any man but a blond giant in her bed.

Well, so what if he had? It could lead nowhere. He was leaving tomorrow, he was not willing or able to offer her anything while his mind was still confused, still full of Frigyth, and Ingrid had made it clear she was happy on her own.

In the circumstances, sleeping together would only be a mistake.

Yes, it would, he told himself sternly, as if to ward off temptation.

"Forgive me, I am rather tired and I would like to set off early tomorrow," he said brusquely. Too brusquely. But despite his resolve to do the right thing, he could feel his senses start a war with his reason and he could not let them win. "I'll go to bed now."

There was no answer.

CHAPTER TEN

They set off just after dawn. Walking side by side, they barely exchanged a word but every chance she got, Ingrid stole a glance in Caedmon's direction.

Why did this man call to every part of her, when she had sworn never to get herself tangled with anyone? Why did he appeal to her so? She did not understand. He was handsome, for sure, extremely so, but that could not be the only reason for her growing obsession, surely?

No, it was not the only reason, she decided. He was also amusing, patient and helpful. He saw her for who she was and didn't give her the impression he was only interested in what she had between her legs. Hadn't he refused her barely veiled invitation to sleep with her last night? Clearly, he was not like the men she despised, and all he wanted from her was company. Which was fine, as she'd kept telling herself all night, while she tossed and turned in her bed. She didn't want more than his company either. Conversation was the only thing she should and did want from him. A conversation with him was more than satisfactory anyway, as it allowed her to look him straight in the eye. She could have gazed at him for days and still discover in his irises a hue she had not seen before.

As they got nearer to town, she grew increasingly agitated.

Where had her peace of mind gone? Since Caedmon had appeared in the village she had been oddly restless. She felt like someone who'd been allowed to walk at her own pace all her life and then without warning had been bundled onto a galloping horse over which she had no mastery. She did not like the loss of control, not one little bit.

That the horse in question was a headstrong, impetuous stallion only made matters worse. She lacked the strength or the experience needed to handle such a mount and she feared a disaster.

For years, her independence had been her most cherished possession, and she had thought nothing would take precedence over her need for freedom. That was why she had tried to remain detached, though what she felt for Caedmon had been getting stronger with each passing day. But it seemed that there was something she valued more than freedom: a bond to someone worthy of her affection, someone who saw her more than a body to use for his pleasure. It wasn't demeaning or suffocating to live with someone when it made you feel special. Caedmon had looked after her of his own initiative when she'd gotten her flux, he'd taken it upon himself to save her from the men's assault without asking for anything in return, he helped around the house as if it was natural. What could have felt like high-handedness, with him, just felt...right.

The time spent with Caedmon had made her see that independence was not so desirable if it meant loneliness. After years of craving freedom she had gone to the other extreme and rejected everything and everyone that might compromise her tranquility. No more.

From now on, she would accept letting other people in.

It took her less than a heartbeat to understand that she wanted to start with the man walking next to her.

In other words, the man who was leaving her. Today she would have to say goodbye to him. Tomorrow she would wake up alone in the hut. Her revelation had come too late.

For a moment she was tempted to ask Caedmon to change his mind and walk back to the village with her, to stay a while longer. She didn't, as she was not brave enough to risk a refusal.

They walked through the gates just as the sun parted the clouds.

Caedmon had expected to feel, if not joy exactly, at least something when entering the town of his youth for the first time in ten years. But he felt nothing, save that same tightening in his chest he'd felt the other day, and last night, when he'd understood he was going to have to say goodbye to Ingrid.

It only told him he was right to leave while he could. Things were getting too personal.

They walked on past the church, then, for no reason that he could discern, she stopped next to a crumbling building.

"Is anything the matter?" he enquired, glancing around. Had he missed something? Did she think the damaged walls were about to fall on top of her?

"This is where my..." Her voice trailed. "Where my parents died."

Oh. "I'm sorry. I had no idea." Why did he have to go in through the South gate? If only he'd chosen the other one, she wouldn't have had to be reminded of her loss.

"It's not your fault. You weren't to know. But their death hit me hard. I was only seventeen and..."

Her lips started to tremble. Caedmon placed a hand over her shoulder. Could he do more? Could he draw her into his arms? He dearly wanted to, as ever. "I think it had nothing to do with your age, and more with the suddenness of it. That, and the fact that you loved them very much. If you'd been less happy with them, their loss would not have been so hard to bear."

His mother's death had certainly not devastated him and he had not been much older than seventeen himself.

She nodded as if she'd understood exactly what he'd just thought.

"How did they die?"

"In a cart accident. Here, at the corner of this road. A dog shot out of nowhere and spooked their horse, who became uncontrollable. They broke their necks when the cart overturned in a bend." She shook her head. "I was told they didn't suffer. I'm not sure it is quite the truth, but I try to believe it."

Yes. It was probably for the best. No point in thinking they had endured agony before dying of their wounds or had time to realize they were going leave their beloved children behind.

"I'm so sorry." The shock must have been awful. One moment they were a happy family, the next she was an orphan, and all for a stupid reason.

"I was too young to accept their loss as an inevitable part of life and too old not to understand exactly what it meant. I remember every moment of happiness spent together."

"At least knowing you had made the most of your time together must help, in some small way."

Ingrid nodded. "It does. Now. But at first it only made the loss more shocking." Of course. One misses more what one loves. "Did you know your parents?" she asked.

He let go of her shoulder and stared into the distance, in the direction where their house had been. Was it still standing or was it falling apart, like the house in front of them? It wouldn't surprise him if it was. It had been in a bad state ten years ago. It might well have fallen to dust since he'd left.

"I knew my mother," he said eventually.

Something about Caedmon's answer caused the hairs at the back of Ingrid's neck to stand on end. He'd known the woman, but clearly he did not have good memories of his time with her.

"And your father?" she could not help but ask.

"I might have met him, but I don't remember him." This was said with such bitterness that she knew she would not insist. This was a sensitive topic. "I only have my grandmother left. If she is still alive, of course...After all this time I cannot be sure."

"Of course." Ingrid knew about the old woman, since that was why they were here, but she'd had no idea she was his only remaining family. "No siblings?" she asked in a small voice. At least she had Björn, and now Dunne and the children. She could not imagine a childhood with no company and parents who weren't there or didn't love her.

"No. My mother miscarried a few times after she had me and I suspect the last one damaged her body. She never bore another child after that, despite having numerous lovers, each more disagreeable than the last. They made my life a misery, not that I ever told her about it. She had her own issues with them."

"Oh, Caedmon." She placed a hand on his arm. What a way to live.

"It's all right." He gave her a small, wistful smile. "It's all in the past."

Yes, it was. But that did not make it less awful.

Having said all there was to say on the subject of their childhood, they walked on. Just as they entered a narrow road leading to the wash house, a cart loaded with barrels came from the opposite end, blocking their way. Instead of retracing their steps, they took refuge in a crevice between two houses while the wide vehicle trundled past. The space was just big enough to allow them to squeeze in.

For a moment they stood face to face, so close their bodies touched and their scents mingled.

Ingrid forgot to breathe. The sun shone directly overhead, making Caedmon's eyes shine a brilliant gold. There was an odd expression on his face, like that of a man debating on his next course of action. Before she had time to wonder what that might be, he leaned in—and kissed her.

Everything within her surged. Caedmon was kissing her. It made no sense. Why was he kissing her? She had no idea. Did it matter? Probably. Did she care? Not even one little bit. Was she supposed to push him away and demand an explanation? Without a doubt. Should she just stop thinking and just enjoy it? *Yes.*

Most definitely yes.

She closed her arms around his neck and drew him closer, pressing her body against his, allowing him to explore her mouth exactly how he wanted. He did so with exquisite tenderness and consummate skill, teasing her lips with his own, coaxing them open, licking her into surrender. Everything within her was melting. Never had she been kissed like this. If he carried on, she might well allow him to take more than a kiss, here, in the little crevice that seemed created for such scandalous encounters.

After a long moment that still managed to be too short, he drew away. Ingrid stared at him, her trembling fingers at her lips.

"You kissed me."

As soon as the words were out, she kicked herself. What a ridiculous thing to say. Of course, he already knew that! "You kissed me" had to be the worst thing anyone had ever said after a kiss.

"I know. Yes. I kissed you. I'm sorry."

Uh. Ingrid stared at Caedmon in disbelief. No, *that* had to be the worst thing anyone had ever said after a kiss. He was sorry? That had to mean he had not intended to kiss her at best, that he regretted it at worst. Neither proposition was flattering.

Her heart plummeted in her chest when she realized she had hoped to hear something quite different.

Only moments ago she had been bemoaning the fact that they were to part ways before she was ready. After he'd kissed her, a part of her had jumped to the conclusion that he must feel the same and wanted to make the most of their last moments together, or even prolong them.

Evidently he did not.

"It's all right. You don't need to apologize." Not when it made her feel so wretched. "I think we should just forget it happened," she mumbled, staring at the wall, at her feet, anywhere but at him. She would have taken a step back but she could not, in the tight space.

"But I do need to apologize. I need to explain why I kissed you."

Ingrid barely repressed a groan. This was getting worse by the moment. If he needed to explain the impulse, it meant that it had been motivated by something other than the usual desire men felt for women.

"I really would prefer it if you—"

"Please."

Oh, this would be bad, she just knew it. Nevertheless, Ingrid nodded, indicating she would listen. What other choice did she have? She could not run away, give herself time to think, when she knew that if she left she would never see him again. Their parting could not be so pathetic. She waited while he seemed to build up the courage to speak.

"This is where I shared my first kiss."

Oh. She had guessed this would be bad, but it was even worse than she had anticipated. He regretted kissing her. As if that wasn't humiliating enough, he'd kissed her in the same place he'd kissed the infamous "sweet, warm, delicious girl" who made his eyes go all dreamy and his lips spout poetry when he thought about her. The girl she'd started to hate with unreasonable ferocity.

"I found myself pressed against you just now and it just—"

"Yes, I understand."

He'd only wanted to recreate a fond memory, nothing more. She bit back the impulse to cry. How had she thought it would be any different? Only last night he'd refused to bed her. Why would he want to kiss her now?

Caedmon could see from the expression on Ingrid's face that he was making a mess of his explanation but he didn't know how to justify his bewildering impulse to kiss her, when he was not quite sure why it had been so important.

Because it had felt important to do it, vital even.

The only problem was, it was making her cry. And he hated it.

"No, I don't think you understand," he murmured. "I'm not sure I do myself."

Confusedly, he'd felt as if he'd wanted to exchange one memory with another, more satisfying one. Today it was sunny and warm. The night he had kissed Frigyth it had been cold and miserable, they had both been drenched and shivering. With hindsight it appeared like an ill omen, one he should have heeded. But right now he and Ingrid were basking in sunshine and there was no discomfort, only pleasure. He'd felt her supple body against his and suddenly he'd wanted to erase the memory of a woman who didn't want him, never had.

"I felt it was time to leave behind the boy I was and the girl I obsessed about for years." Just like the evening before, he refused to name Frigyth or to admit how long the infatuation had lasted, because for the first time he saw the ludicrousness in it all. Who remained fixated for so long on someone who did not love them, who had refused their offer of marriage twice, who was married to another man and living at the other end of the country? "I want to leave my miserable past behind, be another man."

One who was not in love with a woman out of his reach. He wanted to be free of Frigyth at last. In the last few weeks he'd come to understand that they could never be together and the prospect of spending the rest of his life hankering after someone he could never have scared him witless. It had made him too miserable for too long. It was time to do something about it.

For a reason he could not fathom, he now felt strong enough, brave enough to try.

Coming back here, seeing her happy with her Norseman, pregnant with his child, raising his family, had put an end to the painful hopes he had entertained about Frigyth. The two of them were only friends, they would never be more. He should have understood it years ago. Well, at least he'd seen it now.

It was not too late. He could try and salvage what was left of him.

The only regret he had was having brought Ingrid into this mess when it was not her fight. He should never have used her thus. And yet...yet he could not regret the kiss. It had been sweet, hot, slow, deep, more satisfying than any he had ever shared with anyone. As far as experiments went, it had been a success, and it was a comfort to know that every time he thought about this place he would no longer see Frigyth, or at least, not only her.

It was clear that neither he nor Ingrid knew how to recover after the awkwardness of the moment, however. The cart had long since disappeared yet they seemed rooted to the spot in the gap between houses.

They needed time apart. It was the only thing that would help.

"You go get your thread, while I buy something for us to eat. We'll meet by the wash house when you've finished."

She fled without a word.

"I swear I'm going to swoon. Those eyes!"

"That smile!"

"That *body*!"

The three women giggled in unison then stopped when they saw Ingrid just behind them. Looking caught out, they hurried away whispering to each other like excitable children. Ingrid didn't need to hear the rest of their conversation to know they were still talking about the man who had captured their interest and describing what they would like to do to that amazing body of his. As to his identity, she didn't doubt it for a moment.

A moment later, Caedmon exited the baker's shop, confirming her suspicion. The Saxons had been struck by none other than the man who was supposed to be her lover, the man who had kissed her earlier that afternoon, who had burst into her tranquil, ordered life like a tempest When he saw her, the smile that had just been praised bloomed on his lips, making her catch her breath. The eyes that had almost made the women swoon lit up, reducing her insides to warm butter. As for the body—

"All finished?"

"Finished?" Ingrid repeated, jolted out of her contemplation. What was he talking about?

"Did you find the thread you wanted?" he asked, eyeing up the bundle in her hand. Oh, the thread, of course. She'd forgotten all about that.

"Y-yes."

"Are you all right?" The smile disappeared from Caedmon's lips as he edged closer to her.

"Yes," she repeated, this time without the stammer. Damnation, no wonder he thought there was a problem, she was acting like someone who'd been scared out of her wits—or a besotted fool. She should be used to the effect he had on her by now. But...Only moments ago he'd held her close in his arms, his tongue had stroked hers in a sensual dance, their bodies had shared their heat. She could be forgiven for being a bit overwhelmed in his presence.

"Did anything happen while you were alone?" Frowning, he glanced around in search of a potential threat. "Did anyone bother you?"

"No, but someone might well bother *you* if I leave you on your own."

It was best to joke about it, Ingrid thought, rather than allow misplaced jealousy to get the better of her. She only felt that way about the women's comments because Caedmon had kissed her moments ago, she assured herself. At any other time she would have barely registered them. Although he had told her the kiss didn't mean anything, she already knew that she would remember it all her life and mull over what might have happened for weeks. But for now it was better to follow his lead and act as if nothing unusual had happened. She was grateful to the women for providing them with a topic of conversation.

"What do you mean, someone might bother me? Who?" Caedmon asked.

"The three women in the baker's shop with you just now?" He nodded, indicating he knew who she was talking about. "They seemed highly interested in you."

That was the least she could say. However, he didn't appear pleased or even interested. He shrugged and a part of her, the part that was fighting an ill-placed jealousy, inwardly rejoiced. He didn't care a jot about those women.

"Did they? Well, don't worry. I'm sure I'll be fine, even if the three of them gang up on me."

The moment the words passed his lips Caedmon wished he'd kept his mouth shut. Ingrid had gone the color of whey and looked about to retch. What was wrong with him? Being assaulted was no laughing matter, especially for a woman who'd been set upon by men, not just once but twice.

"All three gang up on you," he thought he heard her say.

She wasn't talking about the women anymore, but about the man who had offered her to two others without her knowledge or consent. She was not worried about what could happen to him, but rather remembering what *had* happened to her with her lover's friends and then the other day in the forest with the Saxons who'd wanted to rape her.

He moved forward but stopped before he could draw her into his arms. After his tactless comment, he didn't feel he had the right to touch her. "Ingrid, I'm so sorry, please forgive me, I don't know why I said that. I should never have—"

She shook her head, interrupting the pathetic apology. "Don't worry about it. I...I think we should eat. I'm hungry."

"Of course."

If she chose to be brave and behave as if his ill-advised comment had not affected her, then he should respect her wishes and make it easier for her. It was all his fault she had been reminded of her ordeal. What had possessed him to say such a callous thing? He could only blame a temporary madness, similar to the one that had made him kiss her earlier.

They made their way toward the wash house where they found a stone bench tucked in the shade of a tall beech. There they ate the bread and pies he'd bought.

"It's not the best bread I've ever had," he observed after a while.

It was an inane comment but he wasn't sure what else to say and he couldn't bear the silence between them. Really, he had done everything wrong today. Not only had he reminded Ingrid of her terrible night with the three Norsemen, but moments before that he had kissed her out of the blue and almost made her cry. Though she had fought the tears with all her might, he had not missed the effort it had cost her. As a result, there was a new awkwardness between them. He wanted nothing more than to recapture the ease between them, so that they could part ways with no ill feelings.

Ingrid chewed on her mouthful of bread before answering. "It's not wonderful, but it's not the worst I've ever had either. And I was hungry."

He stood up as fast as if he'd been poked in the back with a spike. What the *hell* was wrong with him today? Couldn't he do anything right for her? Apparently not.

"Let me go and get you another pie." He'd not bought much in the shop, and if she was hungry, she would need more food.

"It's all right." She looked surprised by his eagerness, and no wonder. He felt rather like a puppy trying to please its master after having been caught reducing his most precious possession to shreds. But he felt guilty for making her think of the bastards who had used her and he was ready to do whatever it took to make amends, just like that guilty puppy.

"Stay where you are. I won't be long."

***

"Look at that hair."

"That skin."

"She has to be a Norsewoman."

Ingrid stiffened. The three Saxon women were back. Only this time they were talking about her and the whispered comments were not compliments.

Quite the contrary.

She did her best to appear as if she could not hear them, even if they were not making any effort to be discreet. They probably thought she couldn't understand their language and did not see the need to lower their voices. Either that or they knew only too well what they were doing and they wanted to goad her into reacting. Well, they were wasting their time. She took another bite of bread and forced herself to remain calm.

Let them play their childish game if it pleased them, she would not be a part of it.

"I wonder how anyone could find such a woman attractive," the tallest one was saying, looking as disgusted as she would in front of a disembowelled rabbit. "They look odd and they sound even worse. Their language resembles boar grunts to my ear. It's bad enough when a man speaks it, but a woman!"

"Yes. And everything about her is so pale it's almost transparent. Really, what's attractive about that? Her skin looks like watered milk. "

"No sane man would want such a cold, strange creature in their bed, that's for sure."

The comments, crass as they were, hit a nerve. Ingrid was not confident enough in her appeal to dismiss the women's opinion as simple malice. She knew she was not the most beautiful of women.

The Saxons' teasing had brought her back to some ten years ago. One of Björn's friends' sister, Gertrud, a stunning girl, had taken great delight in disparaging her appearance every time they met. That she was doing it to make herself seem even more attractive by comparison had been clear and her brother had urged her to ignore the ill-intentioned comments. She'd known it was the wisest thing to do, of course. Still, it had hurt to constantly be called "scrawny" and "plain" in front of the village boys, none of which had ever contested it.

Ingrid gritted her teeth and waited for the storm to pass. If she didn't react, eventually the women would tire of their little game and walk away. She was not a shy, gangly fourteen-year-old girl anymore, she could take it.

The scathing comments drifting to him caused Caedmon to stop in his tracks.

Cold, strange creature. Skin like watered milk. Unattractive.

It was so far removed from what he thought of Ingrid that it took him a moment to understand that was who the women were talking about. Hearing his approach, they turned and stared at him with open mouths. Understanding tore through him. They had to be the three Saxons Ingrid had warned him about, the ones who had ogled him in the baker's shop earlier, the ones who wanted to gang up on him.

Fury caused his vision to blur. They dared simper at him after having disparaged one of the most beautiful woman he knew? They dared insult the sweetest soul he'd ever met and expected him to ignore the slurs? They had just revealed how mean and spiteful they were and yet they thought he would respond to their advances?

That they didn't know he and Ingrid were acquainted was not an excuse. He had to make them understand he was not interested in them, and at the same time prove how wrong they were to suppose Ingrid could not attract anyone.

He could only think of one way.

"Ah, there you are," he said, fastening his gaze onto Ingrid. Walking past the three women as if they were transparent, he went straight to her. After placing the pies he'd bought on the bench, he swooped her into his arms. "My lovely bride, the most beautiful woman I've ever seen."

"Caedmon."

His name was said in a throaty whisper that caused every single hair on his body to stand up to attention. The moment was almost too intense for comfort. Ingrid was in his arms and looking at him with her amazing blue eyes. He could tell she was grateful for his intervention, which had shown the women in the most unequivocal manner that some men found Norse-women in general, and her in particular, desirable. He certainly did.

In that moment she *was* the most beautiful woman he had ever seen—and he dearly wanted to kiss her again. Not because he wanted to erase a memory this time, not even because he wanted to teach the Saxons a lesson but because she was Ingrid, she was in his arms, and it just felt right. Behind them, he heard the women walk away with scandalized whispers. Good riddance.

"Thank you," Ingrid murmured.

"Please. I could not let them speak about you in such a way," he said in her ear. At least he had done one thing right today, he thought with satisfaction. "Ignore them, they have no idea what they're talking about.

Silence stretched between them. Then—

"Caedmon! My boy. Finally, you're back."

The voice he had not heard for ten years, speared through him. Caedmon turned around slowly, already knowing who would be standing behind him with tears in her eyes.

But when he saw her, the old woman was not crying, contrary to what he'd imagined. She was beaming at him.

"Oh, it *is* you. And you've brought your bride for me to meet!"

CHAPTER ELEVEN

D ear Lord.

Not only was his grandmother still alive, but she was now standing in front of him, looking just like he remembered her.

"Gran." He almost dropped Ingrid in his shock. She gripped his neck more tightly and let out a little squeak of alarm. He instantly tightened his hold around her, securing her in place against his chest. "Apologies."

"You can let me go now," she whispered, sounding rather daunted at being seen in such an intimate position with him. And then he remembered what his grandmother had just said.

You've brought your bride for me to meet.

Yes, from the way he was holding Ingrid, it certainly looked like he had come back from London with a wife in tow. And if the old woman had heard him call the woman in his arms his beautiful bride, as he suspected, then there would be no convincing her it was not the case.

There was no time to think. No sooner had he released Ingrid than his grandmother threw herself into his arms. "My boy! I had not hoped to see you again before I left this life. And now not only do I see you hale and hearty, but I get to meet your lovely wife as well. I was so worried about you, on your own in a strange city. Oh, you have brought me such joy this day."

He should speak out, Caedmon knew, he should rectify the mistake, tell her Ingrid was not his wife, but just a friend. But how? His first words to his grandmother, his only living relative, in more than ten years, could not be to crush her hopes that he was happily settled when it was all she'd ever wanted to see. He stole a glance at Ingrid and saw she understood his dilemma and was letting him decide on the best way to handle the situation. He cleared his throat, unsure what to do.

Just then two men rounded the corner and the old woman beckoned them over.

"Aethelred, Baldwin, come met my grandson, Caedmon. I told you about him many times." The two men exchanged knowing looks. Apparently she had mentioned him many, *many* times. Caedmon was not surprised. "He's freshly returned from London with his wife."

This was excruciating. Soon the whole town would know he was back and married. He should have spoken immediately, because it was now too late. As much as he didn't want the two men to think he and Ingrid were husband and wife, he was loath to reveal the painful truth to his grandmother in front of witnesses when he knew she would be crushed.

He stole another glance at Ingrid, hoping she was not taking exception to the farce. It was one thing indulging an old woman and his only living relative, quite another allowing complete strangers to think her his wife. Thankfully she appeared more amused than anything else. Such misunderstandings seemed to be the way it worked between them. She had pretended they were lovers the moment they'd met, he had then faked an abduction, and they were now playing the role of husband and wife. It seemed like a natural progression. He found his lips curling of their own accord. What next? One thing was sure, there was never a dull moment when this woman was around.

"London?" one of the wizened old men said, eyeing up Ingrid suspiciously. "I would say this woman comes from much farther away, wouldn't you, Baldwin?"

His friend nodded, as if that was the wisest thing he'd heard all week. "Indeed."

All hints of amusement vanished from Caedmon's face. He bristled and took Ingrid's hand in his. "She's a Dane but she was born here, in the village just beyond the valley. Not that it matters one way or the other where she comes from."

The man raised both hands in surrender. "Of course, it doesn't, son, not when she looks so lovely. And I suppose being foreign she might know some tricks in bed Saxon women do not even—"

"She also speaks—and understands—our language," Caedmon barked, "so I would watch your mouth, if I were you, old man! I will not have anyone speak ill of her."

"Yes, what is the matter with you, Baldwin!" his grandmother chided, giving the man a swat on the arm. "No need to be rude! Now be gone with you."

The two men shuffled along, a scowl on their faces.

"I'm sorry," Ingrid murmured while Caedmon glared in their direction. "I had no wish to see you fall out with your friends."

"They are not my friends, merely neighbors, and if they are going to be so dumb then I'm sure I don't want to have anything to do with them," his grandmother assured her. "Come. You two will need a drink and I need to sit down. This heat is getting to me."

Without waiting for an answer she headed toward the northern gate and there was no other choice but to follow her back to the house he remembered. This was the only place where he had been happy growing up, cherished by a grandmother who thought the sun shone in his eyes. A wave of nostalgia hit him hard when he walked through the door and the smell of dried herbs, cheese and woodsmoke reached his nostrils. Suddenly he was a child again, no bigger than the old woman stooping over the fire.

Immune to the evocative smells, Ingrid waited in the middle of the room, unsure what to do, while his grandmother placed a few branches on the glowing embers and stirred the fire back to life. She looked rather anxious and his chest constricted. The misunderstanding had lasted long enough. Now that they were alone, he had to speak out. The more he waited, the harder this would be. He owed it to the two women to tell the truth.

"There," his grandmother said with satisfaction. "While the pottage simmers, you are going to tell me all about how the two of you met."

"Erm, Gran, actually, there's something you need to know," he started cautiously. "Ingrid and I are—"

"Do not tell me you have a babe on the way? I knew it! That's why you came back, to tell me the happy news in person. Oh, that is all I needed to hear before I went to meet my maker. Thank you, thank you."

And with those words, the old woman wrapped Ingrid in a fierce hug.

I'm so sorry, he mouthed when she threw him a glance over his grandmother's shoulder. She shook her head as if to indicate it didn't matter and even gave him a small smile that warmed his chest.

"No. No. Gran. We do not have a babe on the way," he said, laying a gentle hand over the old woman's shoulder. This misunderstanding, at least, he would nip right in the bud. "But we—"

"But we hope it might happen very soon," Ingrid cut in, smiling at his grandmother.

"Oh, I do hope so, my girl, and it will, if my grandson applies himself to the task properly."

"Erm, quite."

Caedmon stared at the two women, stunned. Well, it was too late to tell the truth now. They were in league against him.

His grandmother let go of Ingrid and took his hand in hers, squeezing it with surprising force. "I spent the last few years bemoaning the fact that with you living at the other end of the world, I would never know about any family you might have. To know I have actually been reunited with you, met the love of your life and might get to see my first great grandchild soon means everything. Your mother would have been so proud. I know she never told you she loved you, but she did, in her own way. She wanted the best for you, a family life such as she had never been able to offer you."

Caedmon's throat went so tight he thought he was going to cry. What a fool! But in that moment he felt proud to have brought the old woman some joy and comfort, even if it was all a lie. Gratitude toward Ingrid invaded him. She could have fled in protest, blurted out the truth, or even mocked the old woman for making ridiculous assumptions. Instead she had decided to indulge her.

"Shall we eat?"

It was only then that Caedmon remembered the pies he'd left on the bench under the tree. Too stunned by all that had happened, he had completely forgotten about them. "I bought food this afternoon but I'm afraid I left it by the wash house. There's little point me going to get it back. Someone will have taken it by now."

"It matters not, there's enough to eat here. My friend brought me a couple of trout this morning to go with the pottage, and I have plenty of cheese left."

Caedmon's mouth instantly started to water. "Gran makes the best cheese I've ever eaten," he told Ingrid. "You'll see."

"I don't doubt it. Grandmothers usually do, or so everyone says."

Ingrid sounded wistful. So despite her happy childhood, it seemed she hadn't known her grandparents. His heart went out to her.

"We do," his grandmother confirmed. "Now, do you mind gutting the trout, my girl?"

He stepped up, a smile blooming on his lips. "I'll do that, Gran. I'm afraid Ingrid will only butcher the poor beasts. She told me once she's not very experienced with anything relating to fish and fishing."

Seeing Ingrid blush all the way to the roots of her hair gave him such satisfaction that it was almost indecent. Deciding he had tormented her enough, he went in search of the trout and they all started to work in companiable silence.

Later, when they all sat down to a hearty meal, his grandmother asked. "I say, you have such an unusual name, Ingrid. What does it mean?"

Caedmon watched as Ingrid bit her bottom lip. She appeared reluctant to answer. He knew that Norse names could sometimes be animal names. Wolf, Bear, Eagle to name a few. That was not bad, but what if she was called something she was ashamed of? Cow? Mole? Perhaps he should make something up to spare her from embarrassment, but what could he choose? No animal seemed fitting for her.

"It means 'fair', 'beautiful', " she said eventually, keeping her eyes lowered.

"Well, look at that!" his grandmother was delighted. "No name could suit you better."

"No," he confirmed.

Indeed, no name would be better for her. Mole…Really,

what had he been thinking? Of course, the parents who had loved her would have chosen an appropriate name for her. Briefly, he wondered what the three women who'd disparaged her looks earlier would say if they knew what her name meant before pushing them out of his mind. They did not deserve another moment of his time.

Instead of commenting, Ingrid took another bite of the cheese. "Caedmon was right. This is the best cheese I've ever eaten. You'll have to tell me your secret before we leave."

He understood that she was trying to avoid having to talk about the meaning of her name and he did his best to help her along. After what she'd done for him, he owed it to her to make the stay under his grandmother's house as comfortable as possible.

"I would be surprised if you managed to extract that secret. Gran has always refused to reveal it to anyone."

"Bah! I think I can make an exception for my grandson's wife, can't you? In fact, I know I should. You're my only family and it would be a pity to have the secret die with me."

He sat back and listened while the two women started to detail the process involved in giving the cheese its unique flavor. The more he watched Ingrid, the more beautiful she seemed to him. Had he really lived for three weeks in her hut without seeing her for the marvel she was? Was it because they had kissed that something had changed and he was seeing her differently? Maybe. But all of a sudden he felt like a prisoner in awe standing in front of the first sunrise he'd seen in years.

"Do you know, Caedmon," his grandmother said when the cheese's secret had been thoroughly exposed, "some time ago, I bumped into your old friend, Frigyth. You'll never believe it but she, too, is married to one of the Norsemen living in the village yonder. I could scarcely believe my ears when she told me. And then her husband came to join her and it was my eyes I couldn't believe. Little old Frigyth married to such a handsome giant! Who would have thought it?" The old woman chuckled. "I bet she's not bored at night with a husband like him next to her!"

He gritted his teeth. His grandmother had always been blunt, and he'd always loved that about her. Right now, though, he wished she would keep her observations to herself. He already knew that Frigyth was getting what she needed in Sigurd's bed. He didn't need to hear it.

"Did she tell you where her sisters were?"

"Dunne is in the village, too, married to another Norseman whose name I don't recall, and Birgit has gone all the way to Mercia." She waved the information away and he didn't insist. He already knew where his old friends were. He'd only asked to avoid having to hear what she thought Frigyth and Sigurd were up to in bed because he knew she was not above telling him. "But what about you? What have you been doing all this time?"

There wasn't much he could tell her. The misadventure with Mildred was out of the question, so were his years of misery looking for fulfilment and his fake marriage to Ingrid. That left only one thing.

"I'm a goldsmith now. I learnt the trade with an old Londoner who took me under his wing when his only son died."

"A goldsmith? Well, I suppose I shouldn't be surprised." She turned to Ingrid and winked. "He's always been very good with his hands, that one. Although I suppose I don't need to tell you as much. As his wife, you probably know."

Caedmon rolled his eyes. Really, she was unstoppable. "Gran, please. You're making Ingrid uncomfortable."

"Tuh! You're not uncomfortable, are you, my girl?"

"Talking about your grandson's skill in bed? No, of course not, why would I be?" Ingrid murmured.

Caedmon could see that his grandmother missed the sarcasm but he felt his lips curl up. This woman was incredible.

No one he knew would have handled the odd situation better. In fact, the way she fit in so easily, gave him pause. It was as if she had always been a part of his small family. As if to prove it, she started to clear the table as naturally as if she had grown up in the house. Gesturing to his grandmother to stay where she was, he stood up to help her. Everything felt easy with this woman.

Kissing her that morning had been a spur of the moment thing and it could, and should, have been awkward. It had only been natural. It was the aftermath that had been difficult. Mercifully, though, they seemed to have recovered from it.

"Time to sleep, methinks," his grandmother announced once everything had been cleared away. Night had started to fall while they ate but it was not dark yet. "You two are going to share my pallet and I—"

"I will not hear of you sleeping anywhere other than your own bed," Caedmon interposed, raising a hand.

"Of course, not!" Ingrid sounded just as outraged at the notion. "You already offered us a splendid meal, we cannot possibly—"

"This is my house, so it will be my rules. As I was saying, you will share my bed and I will go sleep in my neighbor's house. She is away tonight, tending to her daughter, who's just given birth to her second son, so it is the best solution. I will not hear any protest," she added before anyone could say anything else. "Now, I know it's still early but my old bones urge me to get into bed. All the emotions of the day quite tired me out. Good night, you two."

Once they were alone, he and Ingrid looked at each other, slightly stunned. Caedmon cleared his throat, not knowing what to say or what to do. He felt as if he'd been picked up by a whirlwind and deposited somewhere far away from home. Now he had to get his bearings and decide on the best course of action in strange surroundings. It was all the more disconcerting that he was in a familiar place. This house, with its comforting smell, was where he most felt at home.

And yet he was utterly at a loss.

"So, shall we..." Ingrid started, eyeing up the pallet behind him.

"No," he ruled. "You've already done more than I could have expected of you by pretending to be my wife. I cannot ask for anything else. I will sleep on the floor, next to the fire pit, like we did in your hut."

"And if your grandmother comes back before we wake up and sees us sleeping separately? How will you explain that?" She shook her head and sat on the fur-covered pallet without further ado. "I trust you, Saxon. We can sleep next to each other."

She trusted him.

Caedmon swallowed. The question was, did he trust himself? Did he think he could keep his urges to himself whilst lying next to her? Earlier that day he had kissed her, just because they'd happened to be in the place where he had shared his first kiss with Frigyth. Then he had taken her into his arms and pretended to be her husband and felt rather unsettled by their proximity. As if that was not enough, he had spent the whole evening ogling her and marveling at her beauty. There was no telling how he would react when he felt her warm body next to his, or rather, he could predict it only too well.

He would get hard.

He reached out to his boots with the distinct impression that he was making a mistake.

But there was no stopping it now. He had been well and truly swept away by the whirlwind.

CHAPTER TWELVE

Ingrid was cocooned in delicious warmth and finding it difficult to emerge from sleep. She could tell by the light pervading through the window that dawn had already broken but she was not ready to wake up just yet. She tried to stretch, turn to her other side and go back to sleep a moment— and found she could not. Something was holding her.

Some*one*.

A man.

Her eyes snapped open to confirm what she'd already understood. She was nestled against Caedmon's chest, bathing in his woodsy scent and warmth. Why? Even when she'd been supposed to keep an eye on him at night because of his wound they had not lain with each other.

Everything came back to her in a flash. They weren't in her hut but in his grandmother's house in town, pretending to be husband and wife, and sharing a bed as a consequence. It was an odd sensation. She had never slept with a man before, not in that sense at least, but now she found herself thinking that it was the most comforting thing she had ever done.

They weren't simply lying next to each other either, they

were completely entwined. It looked as if she had burrowed into his arms during the night and he had then closed his arms around her to stop her from leaving. They were face to face, her nose was buried in the crook of his neck and her left arm was wrapped around his middle. She whimpered. How was she going to wiggle out from his embrace without waking him up? It seemed impossible but she didn't want him to see them in such in intimate position.

Before she could come up with a solution, Caedmon started stirring. She froze. And then he spoke, his voice hoarse from sleep, deeper than usual. Every single one of her nerve endings caught fire.

"Mm. Good morning."

"Good morning," she croaked back, trying to act as if there were nothing unusual in their position.

As soon as he heard her, he opened his eyes. He blinked like someone trying to make sense of what he was seeing and then scrambled away as if he'd been burned when he saw how close they were to one another.

"I'm sorry, I didn't mean—"

"Forgive me for—"

They spoke at the same time and stopped when they realized they were saying the same thing. Of a common accord, they stood up and put some order to their clothing.

"No need to apologize," Ingrid murmured eventually. Not when she had been the one nestling herself against him after insisting they could sleep next to one another.

Caedmon ran a hand through his hair, looking guilty, and she wondered if he had not been the one to draw her into his arms, after all. Well, it mattered not who had initiated it, the result was the same, the other one had complied only too readily.

Her gaze automatically went to his groin. There was a sizeable bulge tenting the front of his braies, betraying a very masculine state of arousal. Her throat went dry at the sight, even if she knew men tended to wake up hard, no matter where they were. Should she avert her eyes? Should she say anything?

She blinked. No, of course, not! What was she thinking? Caedmon already seemed ill at ease with his body's uncontrollable reaction, she should not add to his discomfort. The only thing to do was to act as if she had not noticed anything, and take a step—or three—back. They were too close to one another, close only as lovers could be. But she didn't seem able to move.

Just then the door opened on his grandmother. She took one look at them and beamed when she saw their reddened faces and unseemly proximity. Evidently, she thought they had just finished making love or had been about to jump on one another. Probably the latter since, fortunately, they were fully dressed. Wonderful. Ingrid had never thought embarrassment could reach such proportions.

"Good morning!" the old woman said with ill-placed cheerfulness. "Instead of asking if the two of you slept well, I will ask if you slept *enough*."

To Ingrid's mortification, she winked. By the gods, it seemed that embarrassment had unsuspected depths after all...

"Yes, thank you, Gran, what about you?" Caedmon answered with commendable effort at breeziness.

She appreciated the way he tried to shield her and take the brunt of the discomfort on to himself. But, of course, it was the least he could do since she was doing him a favor by going along with the pretense that they were husband and wife. She could have exposed the lie by now, she should perhaps have done so. It might have been better received coming from her, as it could more easily have been brushed off as a misunderstanding. Only...It had not seemed an option somehow. The old woman had seemed so happy to be reunited with her only grandson, she had looked at the two of them with such emotion in her eyes. Ingrid could no more have spoiled that joy than she could refuse her little nephew a hug when he ran toward her with extended arms.

"I slept well enough, lad, or at least not worse than usual. Don't worry about me," the old woman said with her usual briskness. Ingrid couldn't help a smile. She would be like that in fifty years time, she decided, telling things the way they were and not worrying about what anyone thought. Pity she didn't have the nerve to do it now. It must very liberating. "Shall we break our fasts?"

"Yes. And then we'll be on our way."

"Of course. I imagine you have much to do at home and I had planned to go visit my neighbor's daughter and see the new babe anyway. I love children. I cannot wait to hold my first great-grandchild in my arms."

As she spoke, she threw a none too subtle glance toward Ingrid's stomach.

Caedmon winced inwardly.

Somehow the whole lie seemed ten times worse this morning. He felt like a child caught doing something naughty and he could not imagine how Ingrid must feel. From the moment he had opened his eyes it had been a succession of awkward moments. When he'd woken up with her in his arms it had taken him far longer than it should have to understand that it was not normal for them to be in such close proximity. Why? It should have been instantaneous. He had never woken up with a woman in his arms, so the newness of the experience should have registered immediately. He had never found himself in that situation, as he usually didn't stay the night when he bedded a lover and Mildred had never wanted to cuddle up at night. Ingrid was apparently different, since she had nestled herself against him. Or...was she?

Had she really been the one initiating the embrace? He could not be sure. It could have been him. Considering what he had done the day before, he could well have been the one to draw her closer, even if he did not remember doing so.

It made little difference anyway, he had not pulled away when she'd come to him, but instead he'd wrapped his arm around her to stop her from moving away. As a result, they had been entwined as only lovers could be when he'd woken up. Thank God he'd realized what was happening before he could start caressing her, moved by instinct. Because he'd been hard, as he always was upon waking up. He was still hard, in fact, even if he'd angled his body away to hide the fact from his grandmother.

As for Ingrid, it was too late to hide anything from her. She knew full well that he was as hard as one of Magnus' pokers. He had not missed the glance she had thrown at his groin earlier—or the color on her cheeks when she'd seen the proof of his arousal.

Ah, well. It was not as if it was the first time it had happened.

They all settled down at the table. His grandmother had bought some hot pies to go along with the gruel she always had in the mornings. Everything was delicious and Caedmon ate with as much relish as if he'd not eaten in days. The only thing missing was a cup of Björn's ale.

Finally the moment to leave came. He and Ingrid glanced at each other, understanding he would have to go back to the Norsemen village with her, at least for a few days. He could not stay in town as he'd intended, not without explaining to his grandmother why they didn't live together. Even if he could muster the courage to do it, he had a suspicion that she would never believe them. Not only did the old woman think they were married and trying for a babe, but she was convinced she had just walked in on them about to make love.

What was happening? Every time he tried to leave, fate seemed to force him back to the Norsemen village. Or rather, to Ingrid. Should he start to heed the signs?

Perhaps. But he wasn't sure he was brave enough.

They left after one last hug to his grandmother, and a promise to visit her again very soon.

"I thank you for what you did," he told Ingrid as soon as they were far enough away from the house. He was uncomfortable about having lied to the old woman but that was his burden to bear, not hers, and she should know how grateful he was to her. "You made my grandmother very happy."

The little shrug she gave was adorable. "From the moment she saw me in your arms and heard you call me your bride, all hope of convincing her that we weren't really husband and wife was lost. And she seemed so happy to see you again, I did not have the heart to tell her the truth. It seemed unnecessarily cruel."

"I know. I felt the same. Still, it cannot have been easy for you to act the part of my bride."

"It was not exactly hard either." She smiled, and went from adorable to stunning. "We once pretended to be lovers and made my brother mad in the process. After that, it was little hardship to pretend to be married and make a kind old woman happy."

"I suppose so."

As they carried on walking Ingrid became wistful. "I never knew my grandparents, you know."

"I had guessed as much, yes."

"They stayed in Denmark when my parents came here, and meeting your Gran made me see what I was missing. I wish I had known at least one of them."

"Yes," Caedmon murmured.

His childhood had not been easy, but at least he'd had a grandmother who doted on him to compensate for the misery at home. And, apparently, time had not diminished her feelings for him. Which was the problem. If she'd cared less about him, he would not have hesitated in telling her the truth. He sighed, overwhelmed by the enormity of the lie he'd told. What was he going to tell her when he came back to town without his "lovely bride"? He was going back to the hut with Ingrid because not doing so would have given the lie away, and he had nowhere else to hide, but the situation could not last indefinitely. What would he do in a few days' time? What could he tell the old woman to explain the fact that he was not married anymore? He would have to find a way, one that did not present Ingrid in a bad light. Saying that his wife had left him or that she had died was out of the question.

Which left only one solution. He would have to take the blame, make it appear as if *he* had left her.

Yes...and then his grandmother would rant at him, remind him where his duty lay, maybe even force him to go grovel and get his wife back.

What a mess he'd gotten himself into. The whole country seemed convinced he and Ingrid were either lovers or husband and wife. No one they had ever met had supposed they were nothing to each other.

Was that what they were? The thought was depressing to say the least.

"Come, we should not dally," he said, feeling more confused than ever.

"Yes."

Ingrid had a sudden urge to be home, settled with Caedmon, and able to savor the fact that he was staying a bit longer with her.

But she seemed unable to move, unable to believe her luck. Only the day before she had bemoaned the fact that he was leaving her. Now, against all odds, she had been given more time with him. Pretending to be his wife had been surprisingly easy, felt so natural. What would it be like to be married to him for real? To be his lover in truth? It would most probably be wonderful, be everything she had never thought she never wanted and everything she secretly craved for. He was so thoughtful, so protective, so handsome...Perhaps with him she could—

"Why are you looking at me like this?"

Ingrid blinked. "Like w-what?"

"Like you are trying to puzzle out something."

"I..." In a way, she was trying to solve a puzzle. Just how many colors had he captured in his amazing irises? "I'm sorry. It's just... I've never seen eyes like yours. They fascinate me." He shrugged, as if he thought them perfectly ordinary. They were anything but. But, of course, he had never seen them, had he? Everyone could enjoy them, except him. It didn't seem fair, somehow. "They appear different depending on the time of day or the weather, or even what you're wearing. Today, for example, they are more green, but of a yellowish green that looks almost amber. Perhaps it's the morning light lending them its glow, I'm not sure, it could be..."

Her voice trailed away when he stared at her as if she'd been speaking in Norse.

"My," he said, drawing out the word. "You *have* been observing them."

She could not deny it. "Yes."

"I'd much rather look at yours. Now, there's an interesting color, if ever I saw one."

"Mine? They are blue." She shrugged much as he had done before. "I can think of nothing less inspiring."

He barked a laugh. "That's because you're a Dane. But believe me, before I went to the Norsemen village I had no idea eyes could exhibit so many hues of the color. They're all beautiful but yours...yours is my favorite."

Her heart skipped a beat because he was staring at her intently as he spoke. "Is it?"

"Yes...It's like a deep lake when the sun tries to pierce all the way to the bottom only to have its light illuminate the whole expanse of water."

Ingrid didn't know how to react. A deep lake...She didn't quite know what he meant, as she had never seen a lake other than the one next to the village but his description was fascinating. Were her eyes really like that? She had no idea, and would never know. The reflection she glimpsed in puddles was not precise enough for her to see. She imagined Björn's face if she asked him if her eyes were really as blue as a bottomless lake. He would think her mad and ask if the Saxon always spoke such nonsense. Her brother had still not accepted the fact that she had a lover. Not that she really had, of course, but as far as he thought she and Caedmon had—

In the corner of her eye she spotted three men coming toward them. Three men she had last seen lying on the ground, unconscious and bleeding.

"The men from the forest," she said to herself, her voice barely audible.

"I'm sorry?" Caedmon frowned.

Her decision was made in a heartbeat. The men could not be allowed to see him. If they recognized him for the traitor who had foiled their plans and caused them to get the beating of their lives, they would pounce. And this time no help would come. He was on his own, for she would not be able to do anything to stop the attack.

Before she could think, she threw Caedmon against the wall and placed herself in front of him.

"What are you—"

"Hush." She was too small to act as an efficient shield but she would do what she could to hide him. Placing both her palms on his face to hide his features, she forced his head down. Damnation, too much of him was still visible. She had to make sure the men could not see his face when they walked past. If they recognized him, it would be a disaster.

There was only one solution.

Hoisting herself up onto her tiptoes, she kissed him.

***

Ingrid was kissing him.

Caedmon's mind registered the shocking fact only briefly before his senses took over and he responded like any hot-blooded man would. *Why* she was kissing him didn't matter, what mattered was that she was kissing him. He didn't want to know her reasons, didn't need to know them, as long as she did kiss him. There would be a reason behind the impulse, and he was sure to hear it in a moment, but for now he just wanted to enjoy the experience.

Ever since they had kissed the day before, he had obsessed about it. The smell of her, the heat of her, the softness of her. He wanted more of everything. And finally, he was getting it.

When she moaned he switched their positions so that she was the one with her back against the wall. With her where he wanted and unable to move, the kiss took on a new dimension. She moaned again, the sound causing arousal to shoot up his spine. Unable to resist, he wedged his leg between hers and started to rub against the sensitive folds hidden under her skirts. This was way more than a kiss, it was a whole body experience.

Delicious. The more intimately he touched her, the more he wanted her.

Another moan brought him back to the reality of the situation. What the hell was he doing? They were in the middle of the road, in full view of everyone, and he was all but making love to her. His shaft was pressing against her hip and she was riding his thigh in search of the friction she needed. If they carried on like this he might well erupt and she might well come against him.

He drew back, panting hard. "We have to—"

"—can stop now."

Just like they had this morning upon waking up in each other's arms, they talked at the same time. She sounded just as out of breath as he was and refused to meet his eye.

"I'm sorry."

He arched a brow. She was sorry? Why? *She* had not been the one transforming the kiss into something far more licentious. "I should be the one to apologize," he forced himself to say. His groin was still throbbing, making it hard to focus.

She shook her head. "I took you by surprise. I know I shouldn't have kissed you thus, but there was no other choice."

No choice? Did she mean she had kissed him for another reason than irrepressible desire? Something within him bristled and he had an inkling of how she would have felt yesterday when he had admitted to kissing her because they'd happened to be in the place where he had shared his first kiss with a woman. Why, he almost felt like crying himself.

"What do you mean?" he asked, not quite knowing what to make of her admission.

She threw a nervous glance behind him. "Three men just walked past us."

Hearing panic in her voice, he looked to the place she was indicating and saw a group of men with their backs to them.

The hairs on his nape stood on end when he saw that the smallest one was limping and had dark, greasy hair.

"The bastards from the forest," he said between his teeth.

"Yes. I didn't want them to see you and start wondering where they knew you from. I panicked, sorry. There was no time to hide you or warn you."

Caedmon didn't know whether to be disappointed or gratified. She had wanted to protect him, which warmed his soul, but she had not, after all, kissed him out of desire, which crushed his feelings. He'd been overwhelmed by the moment, while she had only been trying to hide his face from view. The thought was sobering.

"I thank you. You seem to be spending your time helping me."

"It's no issue. The last thing I wanted was for them to recognize you and—"

And beat you up for saving the women they had meant to rape. This time you might not have survived it.

Ingrid didn't finish her sentence but there was no need. It was obvious Caedmon had understood what she meant and was grateful for her help.

"Thank you," he repeated.

He placed his lips over hers, a swift, chaste caress that was nothing like the kiss he had given her a moment ago. It had been unlike anything she had ever experienced or dreamed could exist, wild, intoxicating, fierce, very different from the kiss they had shared the day before. This kiss had been for *her*, not to erase someone else, she had felt it in every bone of her body. She'd initiated it, but he'd quickly taken over, pinning her against the wall and wedging a strong thigh between her legs to rub her on the sweet spot needing friction. And she had relished every moment, almost begged for more. What would have happened if they had not been in the middle of the town?

Ingrid berated herself for the stupid question, for she already knew the answer.

If they had not been in full view of everyone, she would have let him lift her skirts and take her where she stood. She would have begged him to put an end to the need pulsing between her legs. Once he'd put his hands on her, her body had caught on fire with shocking speed. What had started as a means to protect him had bloomed into something out of her control. Was that because she had gone so long without a man's touch? Perhaps. Did that mean anyone else could have provoked such desire inside her? She doubted it. Confusedly, she sensed this could only have happened with Caedmon.

What must he be thinking? He would have felt the way she had rubbed herself against him, without hesitation or shame, heard her lewd moaning, seen that she was utterly overcome with desire. Would he not think her the most wanton creature, like Mildred had been? Would his opinion of her change as a result? She dearly hoped not.

"Shall we?" he asked after a while.

She nodded. Yes. They had better go, before she said or did something she would regret.

As they approached the town gates Caedmon placed a hand on her lower back to steer her into a smaller road, away from the place where her parents had died. Emotion swelled within her. Not only did he remember what she had told him, but he wanted to spare her grief.

It was then she knew that she wouldn't be able to let this man walk out of her life before she had experienced a night in his arms. She would seize this chance with both hands and not worry about what he would think of her morals or what was the sensible thing to do. Against all odds, they had been allowed more time together. Yet again. Every time he tried to leave, something happened to keep him with her. It had to mean something.

Today he was coming back to the village to appease his grandmother and there was no knowing how long the reprieve would last. One thing was for sure. They had kissed twice now, both times for reasons other than the need to taste each other. She wouldn't let him go until she had placed her lips over every inch of his body for the right reasons.

As they entered the forest, Caedmon finally plucked up the courage to ask Ingrid the question that had been bothering him for days.

Being forced to go back to the village once again was surely a sign that he should not let it go.

"The boy who used you so ill when you were eighteen," he started, guessing she would hate talking about it. But he had to know. "Was his name Ivar by any chance?"

Ingrid came to stop, providing him with the answer to his question. It was.

Now he understood why she had wanted to put the man back in his place the day he had accused him of stealing the horses, why she had wanted to parade a so-called lover to his face, why she had appeared so distraught the day he had talked to her in the vegetable patch.

Because he was the one who had hurt her so badly.

Caedmon could not believe how slow he'd been. He should have guessed her attacker's identity earlier, but in his defense, he had assumed the bastard had left the village after committing his crime for fear of reprisal. But it appeared that for five long years Ingrid had had to endure his presence, and perhaps even his taunts. Well, no more. It was time he paid for it.

"Does your brother know what happened?"

But he already knew the answer to that question. She'd told him Björn had been away at the time and the Norseman was very protective of her. If he'd found out how the man had treated his sister, he would have punished him for sure. And yet Ivar didn't seem to walk with a limp and still had all his teeth and fingers, as far as Caedmon could tell.

"No," Ingrid confirmed in a breath. "He already hates Ivar. He would kill him if he knew."

"So?" What was the problem with that?

"So he has a wife who loves him, and a family to look after," she answered, her voice barely above a whisper. "I will not have him becoming a murderer for me or risk being killed, in turn, when someone wants to avenge Ivar. Too many people need him. I need him."

Yes. She was right. Björn should not be asked to place himself or his family in danger. But *he* didn't have a wife, loving or otherwise, he didn't have any children who would suffer if he died, and he would be leaving the village in a few days anyway. People who wanted to avenge Ivar would not know where to find him. He was the perfect choice to be her champion. Not that he would tell her what he intended to do.

"There wasn't any..." He bit his lip. How could he word the delicate question? Should he even ask it?

Yes. Otherwise he would only torture himself over it in the next few weeks. If he overstepped the mark, Ingrid could always refuse to answer.

"There wasn't any child from the...encounters?"

He didn't think so, as he had not seen any, but he doubted Ivar would have exercised any restraint while he was bedding her, and he was certain the bastard who had come to her while she was blindfolded had no intention of curtailing his pleasure to protect her either. If he'd had time to reach his release, she could well have fallen with child.

"N-no."

The answer should have been reassuring, but he sensed there was something she wasn't telling him. He didn't push her. It was obvious the topic was a painful one, and he should leave it at that, now that he knew what he needed to know. But she surprised him by carrying on with her explanation.

"As you can imagine, I waited anxiously for my courses after that night. I dreaded the prospect of finding myself with child, because not only would it have been imposed on me, but..." She swallowed. "I would not even have been able to ascertain the father's identity. The idea was torture to me. The night I started bleeding, though the pain was just as crippling as usual, I wept with relief."

Caedmon's fingers bunched into fists. If she'd thought she might be with child, it meant that her attacker *had* had time to reach his pleasure inside her. Hatred threatened to boil over. "Of course," he said, not knowing what to do to stop it from erupting.

"It made me...Well, scared, of anything to do with pregnancy. It's one more reason never to get married."

Those three bastards had done more than violate her body that night, they had taken away her trust in men and the ability to choose whether to bear a child or not. They might not have inflicted pain on her body, but they had left indelible scars none the less. The trauma they had caused was why she was alone and not looking to change her situation, why she didn't need a family. But was she really happy about it? Choosing something because the alternative was too frightening was not a solution.

"Are the two other men still here in the village?" If they were, he would have to find them and exert his revenge on them as well. He could not bear the idea that the three accomplices had been allowed to get away with what they had done.

"No. They were two brothers and they left soon after."

Brothers? Dear God, it was getting worse and worse.

"And...Do any of your friends know what happened?"

"No."

No. Just as he'd feared. She had heeded the men's advice and kept quiet about that night's events, in case it reflected badly on *her*. So it would be up to him to give Ivar what he deserved. And he knew just how. Caedmon straightened his spine.

Damn it all. He would have to go see Sigurd and ask for his help.

CHAPTER THIRTEEN

The opportunity Ingrid had been waiting for arrived that very evening.

As she entered the hut, cradling a log for the fire, she collided with Caedmon, who was on his way out. They fell into each other's arms and she dropped the log, which narrowly missed their feet. For a moment, they froze, then instead of releasing her, Caedmon licked his lips. It was not a conscious gesture but everything within her surged.

This was it, the opening she needed. She might not have found the courage to throw herself into his arms but she was here already so she would not let the chance pass. There might not be another.

"Careful," he murmured against her temple.

Careful. Yes. Always, she had to be careful, and do what was expected of her. But she wanted to throw caution to the wind for once.

"What if I didn't want to be careful?" she breathed, grinding herself against him. "What if I just wanted to follow my instinct? What if I didn't want to be wary of men anymore?"

Her hand slipped between their two bodies and snaked to

the bulge at the front of his braies. She had to act before she could lose her nerve, because she certainly wasn't scared of *this* man. Her whole body felt on fire.

"What are you doing?" Caedmon asked in a strangled voice.

She gave a tentative stroke through the fabric, wrenching another groan out of him. He was already hard, as if desire had flooded him as soon as their bodies had touched. The realization that he wanted her, despite his talk of caution, inflamed her. Surely he wouldn't refuse her if she made her wishes clear? Surely he wouldn't deny her what she craved? What they both craved? He was a man, after all.

"Make love to me, Saxon," she purred.

The hold around her tightened and he let out a growl. "I don't think you—"

"I do. I've wanted you for days." If she were honest she would add that she'd wanted him ever since he'd asked her to ride him so crudely. Her senses had been brought back to life that day. Then she'd gotten to know him better and her mind had been seduced by his generosity and his thoughtfulness, his love for his grandmother. And then they had kissed and her heart had started to beat differently. "Please don't make me beg."

Beg.

That one word sent fire to Caedmon's loins. He wouldn't make Ingrid beg for attention, not when he was already hard, and he had been desperate for her for days. He wouldn't refuse her, not after the fiery kiss they'd shared that afternoon. This woman had done what she could to save him from trouble, she had won over his grandmother, she had made him happy. Over the last few weeks she had come to mean so much to him.

"Are you sure?" Even though his conscience forced him to ask, he hoped with all his might she was not about to change her mind.

She did not.

"Yes. I want you. I need you."

It was more than he could bear. When she reached out to her bodice to tug at the laces, he didn't try to stop her. He watched, entranced, as she let the dress fall to the floor in a heap of folds. The shift was next. Because it was a warm day, she wasn't wearing any stockings, and because she did not hesitate, soon, she was standing naked in front of him. All he could do was stare, awed, at the beauty revealed to him. The skin, so pale and creamy, the curls at the apex of her thighs, woven in pure gold, the nipples, of the most delicate pink, everything about her was arousing as hell.

"I've never seen a woman like you," he said, his mouth dry. So beautiful, so desirable, so confident.

"Well, I've never seen a naked Saxon," she retorted, "so you had better start undressing."

"It won't be anything you haven't seen before," he rasped. Even if, admittedly, he doubted any man had been harder, he was not certain his body would please her as much as hers pleased him. In fact, he was sure he would compare unfavorably with Norsemen, who tended to be taller, and more muscular.

Ingrid let out a low chuckle. "I doubt that. You are different from the men I am used to. It both intrigues and arouses me. I can't wait to see a male member nestled in dark curls. I'm thinking it can only be more masculine, more enticing than framed with blond hairs."

Caedmon gave a shiver. No woman had been so bold as to admit to being aroused or talk about his cock whilst looking at him in the eye. She wanted to see it? Well, she would.

He was unashamedly erect but he saw no fear in her eyes when he bared himself, only desire. Thank God she hadn't lied when she'd claimed to be unafraid and aroused.

"Lie down on the pallet." Her voice sounded different. All the air seemed to have left her lungs.

Caedmon was only too happy to comply. In that moment, she could have asked him to crawl on all fours or rub his body all over with coal and he would have done it in a heartbeat.

"Come lie with me," he growled, feeling on the edge of madness. He needed her close, needed to feel her skin.

She knelt next to him and said the most erotic thing anyone had ever told him. "Please let me touch you."

"Yes. Touch me."

Ingrid was beside herself with need. The sight of Caedmon's glorious body naked on her pallet was almost too much to handle. He was magnificent. Even the pink scar on his stomach was beautiful, because it was a reminder of what he had done, risking his life so that she and the other women could be safe. She wanted to kiss it, kiss him everywhere.

Kneeling next to him, she placed her open mouth on his chest, the chest she had fantasized about for days. At the same time she reached for his manhood and wrapped her fingers around it. By the gods, it was so soft, yet so hard and so hot, so compelling. She allowed her fingers to slide up and down the shaft slowly, learning the feel of him. Did the daring caress please him as much as it pleased her? She dearly hoped so.

"Ingrid, stop! You're going to kill me," he growled when she started to stroke him faster.

She released him and made a face. So much for pleasing him. In her inexperience, she was causing him pain. "I'm sorry, I didn't mean to hurt you. I know I'm not—"

Before she could finish her sentence, he rolled her under him. "You are. And you didn't hurt me, quite the opposite. If you carry on like this you'll unman me. I wouldn't exactly mind but I need this to last. I've wanted you for too long, and our kiss this afternoon did not help." He nuzzled at her neck. "So. Now that I've finally got you in my arms, tell me what do you want me to do to you?"

The unexpected question sent her wild with anticipation. *He* wanted to pleasure *her*, just like he'd said the day they had met. She had guessed he would be a generous lover, but to have it confirmed so unequivocally made her shiver.

"Touch me," she rasped, driven to the edge of madness by the feel of his naked body over her and the seductive tones in his voice.

"It will be my pleasure." He closed one hand over her breast and squeezed. The warmth of his palm spread like wildfire into her whole body. She moaned and allowed him to play with her nipple a moment. Then she wanted more.

"Kiss me."

He growled as if that was what he'd been dying to do and took her mouth. At the same time, he started to stroke her body slowly, grazing her skin with the tips of his fingers. Ingrid closed her eyes at the impossibly arousing sensation. She was naked under him, their bodies sharing their heat, hers smooth and soft, his hard and compact. It was perfect.

"And now?" he asked, his voice reduced to a low rumble.

"Kiss me again. Everywhere." She was dizzy with the need for more.

"Everywhere? Here first, then." He took her nipple in his mouth and teased a series of moans out of her with his slow suckling. "Now here." He lifted her foot and started licking her toes. The feeling was so amazing that Ingrid felt herself go liquid inside. She gave a little squeak when Caedmon's lips traveled to the back of her knee, raising her leg high in the air as he did. His fingers grazed along her inner thigh, soon followed by his mouth and then his tongue.

"Everywhere, you said?" he murmured darkly, his lips moving against her flesh.

Her whole body was pulsing by now, begging for release. She gave what sounded like a sob when she realized that she would come as soon as he kissed her intimately. She was too aroused to last very long.

"Yes, everywhere," she managed to answer and just as she'd thought, as soon as he put his mouth on her, everything disappeared. A few flicks of his tongue was all it took to make her lose her mind. A sharp cry reached her ears and it was only when she fell back onto the furs that she understood it had been her, shouting in pleasure.

"Well, you are one responsive woman," he whispered, laughter and desire in his voice. "I'm going to enjoy being deep inside you." The purr in her ear somehow prolonged her ecstasy.

"I thought *I* was supposed to tell you what I wanted," she teased.

"Don't you want me inside you?"

"Oh yes." Definitely. "But not yet." She smiled. She wanted this to last as well. "First I want to kiss *you*. Everywhere." She'd been dying to, she had promised herself to place her lips on every inch of his skin. This time she would not let him stop her. "Lie down," she ordered, pushing him flat onto his back.

"Mm, you like to give orders, don't you?"

"With you, I do."

She lay on top of him and kissed him deep, every inch of her touching him, their naked bodies writhing as their skins explored each other. In one corner of her mind she knew he was stronger and bigger than she was and could have overpowered her at any moment but, far from frightening her, the difference in size only excited her. She was in total control, guiding their lovemaking and dictating the pace. Unlike Ivar, he seemed happy to let her indulge her every whim, and take the time to explore his body before taking her.

It was deeply arousing.

Breaking the kiss, she moved on to his neck. Under her lips she felt the blood pulsing in the vein at his throat. It sent her wild and she nipped at it playfully.

"Calm down, Ingrid, I don't fancy facing your brother tomorrow covered in bites," he scolded with a husky laugh. "Or, at least, he should get to see that I saw to your pleasure as well. Come here." He drew her to him and mimicked the soft bite she'd given him on his neck.

"Oh." She shivered. If she'd provoked half the effect on him as he was doing on her she would die a proud woman. "Wait! This is too much!" she protested when he deepened the bite.

"You'd better get on with what you were doing then," he warned in a dark tone.

Nothing would please her more.

Carrying on with her exploration, she trailed kisses along his silky soft shoulder, moved on to the muscly bicep adorned with a thick vein, then licked the crook of his elbow, humming in delight all the while. He tasted and felt just as good as she'd imagined he would, warm and spicy, the intoxicating scent making her want more.

When she moved lower down to stroke his taut stomach she couldn't help a gasp at the strength of his erection.

"Don't sound so shocked. What did you expect? Surely you know full well what you're doing to me?"

In truth, she hadn't dared to hope she affected him to that extent. She looked again at the smooth length she coveted and smiled. "Now. Kisses everywhere, didn't we say?"

A grunt answered her.

Closing her eyes, she placed her lips on him.

Under her palm, she felt Caedmon's stomach muscles tense up. She opened her eyes just long enough to see him throw his head back in pleasure. Desire flared up between her legs at the sight. She was making him mad with longing, just as he had done to her earlier. The thought was dizzying, arousing beyond belief. Over and over again she welcomed him into her mouth, savouring the silky smoothness gliding over her tongue and the feeling of power she had over him.

"Ingrid, by God, give me a chance." He stilled her head and lifted her up, settling her over his hardness. "Enough, or I won't make it further," he warned, running his thumb over her bottom lip. "That was too good but I need to be inside you. I'll be in charge now, whether you like it or not."

She met his gaze squarely. "I might like it. It depends on what you have in mind."

"I think you know. Would you prefer to be on top?" he asked, stroking her hair in an unexpectedly tender gesture.

Ingrid nodded. How had he guessed she would prefer to be in control, at least at first, while her mind caught up with what her body was telling her, that this was a man she knew and wanted taking her, a man she had chosen, a man who would not hurt her?

"Yes." She was already panting with need, her insides throbbing at the thought of feeling him enter her.

"Fine by me," he growled. "Ride me until you come. Then I'll take over. But don't worry, I won't spill inside you."

With those words, Caedmon lifted her to position her over his waiting hardness. Then he slid inside her in one smooth stroke, making her catch her breath at the perfect fit between them. It was as if their bodies recognized that they were made for each other. After a moment of awe she started moving slowly, her fingers digging into his flesh, holding on to him. He filled her again and again, groaning when she started grinding her hips more urgently, riding them to the very edge of reason.

She came in a hot rush of mind blowing pleasure, while they clung to each other, Ingrid weaving her fingers into his silky chest hair, Caedmon circling her waist in an iron grip, holding her close until her body had stopped spasming.

Then, as promised, he flipped her over and reached his own release. At the last moment he withdrew and lay on top of her, trapping his manhood between their two bodies. He moaned her name as he emptied himself in scalding spurts.

For a long moment they lay side by side, catching their breaths. Then his voice, languid with satisfaction, reached her ear.

"I think you may have lied about your lack of ability at fishing."

Ingrid gasped. The wretched man! "You knew!"

"I suspected, it's not the same. And then your not so subtle comments confirmed it." He laughed, then stroked her cheek. "I hope I didn't frighten you too much, making such crude advances to you?"

"No. But...I think you took me for someone else."

He tensed, as if he didn't remember that part. "How do you know?"

"You wanted us to do things...We have never done before."

Had never done at the time, she amended privately. Now, of course, she could not make the same claim. They had explored each other's body thoroughly.

"I'm sorry," he sighed. "I did think you were Mildred."

"Oh." After he'd told her about his misadventure in London, she had wondered if that was who he'd thought she was that night. Now she had an inkling of how the selfish woman might have ensnared him. The thought of them in bed together, doing everything they had just done, made her insides wither.

"She knew the only hold she had on me was in bed so she made the most of it. I have often wondered what her lover thought of the fact that she bedded me to ensure his subsistence." He shook his head. "But as determined as she was, she never gave me half as much pleasure as you did."

"Oh," Ingrid said again, feeling herself relax. He was right. Without some sort of feelings, sex was just a mechanical act. What she had felt in Ivar's arms, before his betrayal, had never compared. It had been pleasant, nothing more. But then again, she had not felt for him half of what she felt for Caedmon.

He drew her against his flank and she surrendered to the warmth of his embrace.

"You never wear any jewelry, do you?" he asked, a lazy finger tracing a path between her shoulders. The caress made her shiver. And then she smiled. Of course, a goldsmith would notice something like that.

"No. No one has ever given me any."

"Mm." Ingrid wasn't sure what that meant but before she could ask anything, he placed a swift kiss over her lips.

"Sleep now."

CHAPTER FOURTEEN

In the morning, Caedmon woke up alone, and still naked. The light pouring into the hut indicated it was at least mid-morning. He could not remember ever sleeping so well, or for so long. Then again, he had never almost died in a woman's arms before. What had happened last night would force him to redefine what he thought of lovemaking.

It had been more, or rather, nothing like it.

As he got dressed, he listened, wondering if Ingrid was by the door, milking her goat or churning butter but he didn't hear anything. As soon as he was ready, he exited the hut, seized by the need to see her. Why hadn't she woken him up? Why had she left before they could talk? He could not help but worry over it. He knew he had not forced her hand last night but equally, he knew that she prized her independence, and why. Now that her senses had cooled, was she regretting their tryst? Was that why she had left the bed before he woke up?

He found her by the chicken coop, gathering eggs as she did every morning. The sight was a relief. Nothing had changed despite the intimacy they had shared. Life was going on as usual.

"There you are." The words left his lips in an exhale.

She turned to face him and smiled. He received that smile like a punch to the gut. Dear God, this woman might force him to redefine his views on feminine beauty as well. It had little to do with a harmonious arrangement of features, he realized now, it was much more than that. A woman's beauty was in the sparkle in her eyes, in the joy behind her smile, in her sighs when they touched, in her moans when they kissed, in her laugh, in the way she moved against his body and beamed at him when she saw him.

He thought back to Sigurd mocking him for speaking like a poet. For certain the Dane would choke on his tongue if he ever heard his fanciful musings.

"Of course, I'm here," Ingrid said, mercifully oblivious to what was passing through his mind. "Where else would I be?"

He stayed silent, feeling like a prized fool. Indeed where else would she be? This was her home. If one of them had to leave, it was he.

A delicious color crept up her cheeks, causing his groin to stir. "You thought I'd fled, too ashamed about what we'd done last night, is that it?"

"Well, yes." He had thought exactly that but had not expected her to be so honest about it. Would she ever cease to surprise him? He hoped not.

"I told you, Saxon, I wanted you. I'm hardly going to change my mind now, when you gave me so much pleasure."

This woman really was like no other, talking so openly about pleasure and what she wanted. Because she was like no other, he dared ask the question that had been lurking at the back of his mind.

"Why did you ask me to make love to you last night?"

She seemed to ponder this a while, as if she wasn't sure herself. He forced himself not to take personally the fact that she had not immediately responded: "Because I just can't resist you."

"When you kissed me the other day, you told me you wanted to change a memory from the past," she answered eventually. "I suppose I wanted to do the same. It seemed even more important that I did, as, unlike yours, my memory was a bad one. I didn't want to keep thinking of men as selfish creatures looking only for their own pleasure in bed, I didn't want to think of lovemaking as something degrading for the rest of my life. And now thanks to you, I won't."

Relief and pride blossomed through him. He'd made her see that some men considered their lover's pleasure a priority, made her change her mind about lovemaking. It was the best thing he had heard in his life.

"Thank you. I'm humbled. Why me, though?" He could understand her reasoning, understand why she'd wanted to alter her opinion of men and lovemaking, but he was not sure why she had chosen him to do that. He didn't feel he deserved that honor, when he had not promised her anything and up until recently his mind had been occupied by another woman.

What would she think if she knew he'd once been in love with her friend, Frigyth?

He frowned. *Had once* been in love? Where had that thought come from? He was still in love with her, was he not? They hadn't argued or anything, and people didn't fall out of love for no reason, did they? But perhaps they did...What did he know? Perhaps the fact that he wanted to start living a different life proved he had indeed fallen out of love with her.

Ingrid sighed and placed a light hand over his chest, the gesture intimate. "I came to you because you're a good man, I sensed you would treat me well and give me pleasure. I knew you would respect me and ensure I didn't fall with child because you know the idea scares me. And I was right to trust you."

Though she undoubtedly meant all this as a compliment and he should have been flattered, Caedmon bristled.

A good man.

Again.

That was all he had ever been, all his life.

Harmless, dependable, sensible Caedmon. Frigyth had only ever seen him as a friend, preferring a fierce, daunting Norseman to him. With Mildred it had been even worse, she'd only used him for her and her lover's benefit. The women he'd met in London had only been after sex or protection—or even simply pretty jewels—but never commitment. They had come to him because he was a good man. Even that blasted Sigurd, who should hate him, had taken to calling him that. Women who came to his bed only ever saw what they wanted to see, took what they needed from him, not what he wanted to give them. He was always the best friend, the helper, the protector, never the one they wanted to marry, spend their life or even wild nights with. They came to him because they knew he would treat them well and not make them with child, they knew he would forgo his own pleasure and instead ensure their reputation was safe, because he was honorable, trustworthy.

A good man.

Something within him snapped. Perhaps he didn't want to be a good man anymore, perhaps he wanted to spend a wild night for once, worry about nothing but his own pleasure, not think about the future but just enjoy the present.

Before he knew what he was doing he had lifted Ingrid into his arms.

"What are you doing?" she cried out, her hands coming to grab his neck.

"I'll show you just how much of a good man I really am," he growled, marching her back toward the hut.

"Caedmon!" She sounded breathless, though not with fright.

"Yes, that's my name," he confirmed, kicking the door open. He would make sure she screamed it over and over again until she was hoarse. He dropped rather than deposited her onto the pallet where, the night before, he had been so careful, made love to her so gently, where he'd been a good man.

Well, not today.

"On your hands and knees," he ordered, already removing his shirt.

Her eyes widened and for a moment he feared he'd gone too far. She would get back up and usher him out with a curse. It would be nothing more than he deserved, as well. What was he doing, treating her thus when he knew what she had been through and she wanted to believe men could be trusted?

Heart thumping, he waited. Then she bit her lip, her arousal evident, and obeyed. Once she was in position, she slowly gathered her skirts up, revealing her perfect, rounded backside, giving her agreement.

Everything within him roared.

Not a good man. Not today. Today he was going to be a wicked man.

"Why did you do that?"

The question hung in the air between them.

Outside it had started raining. Ingrid was lying by his side, her body covered with a thin sheen of sweat, one arm draped over his chest. Caedmon stared at the wooden beams above. What could he tell her?

The truth, a small voice within him barked. *She's asked a question, she deserves a real answer. She can take it.*

"Because I am tired of only ever being a good man, never more than a good friend, never the passionate lover. I am tired of being overlooked in favor of more assertive men, men who tumble their women in bed whenever they want, not when they're asked, men who just take what they need and don't worry about it."

There. Now she knew. He was not a good man, could not be, if he harbored such shameful feelings. Why had he told her? She was the last woman to whom he should have exposed the dark side of his nature no one knew about.

For a long moment Ingrid didn't say anything.

"You think that's how I see you? You think I—"

"Isn't it?" he cut in before she could lie and claim that was not what she thought. "If it's not, then what did you mean when you said you knew I would treat you well and ensure I didn't get you with child?" She stayed silent, as if that point was inarguable. "So in answer to your question, I did what I did because for once I wanted to think of what *I* wanted to do and nothing else, to behave like no one thinks I will. No one seems to credit me with the same urges and needs as other men, but I do have them. I wanted to reach my release inside a woman for once, not withdraw, and experience the full glory of it."

Glory. Yes. It had been glorious.

He sighed and finally turned to look at Ingrid. Unsurprisingly, she had gone bright red. Perhaps he should not have been so honest and claimed he'd simply lost his mind for a moment. This might be excused. Instead he had just admitted to being a crude individual harboring shameful desires, and he feared there would be no going back from there.

Well, perhaps it was for the best.

"I didn't know it was possible to do what we did," she said eventually. "No man has ever possessed me in that way."

"I should hope not," Caedmon growled. Considering who her other two lovers—if one could call them that—had been, he would have hated to hear she was familiar with what they had just done. "And, in truth, I shouldn't have done it either, but—"

"I liked it." The color on her cheeks had reached alarming proportions. She was embarrassed by the admission but still brave enough to make it. Caedmon could scarcely believe his ears. "You thought last night you had to be gentle with me after what happened with Ivar and his cronies and I thank you for the intention but...I loved to see the real side of you."

Real? Could that have been the real side of him?

No. Caedmon recoiled. It was the dark side, the side he had always fought to keep hidden, the side he'd always thought people would reject. It had started with his mother, whom he hadn't wanted to disappoint, then carried on with Frigyth. Because of her drunkard father, she'd been afraid of violent, impetuous men and he'd done his best to provide her with the reassuring company she craved. Intent on impressing her, he had made sure never to let his emotions out of control, going as far as never swearing in front of her.

And in the end it had been for nothing. She had married a hot-headed, menacing looking giant with a foul mouth. True, now that he knew Sigurd better, he knew that for all his bluster and menacing appearance, the Norseman would never hurt her, but it went to show he'd been wasting his time trying to be the man he thought she wanted. For the first time he considered what his life would have been like if she'd accepted his offer of marriage.

He would have played a role all his life. Never allowing his instinct to take over would have been exhausting.

In London he'd made the same mistake. He'd been a good

friend to everyone, a gentle lover to the women who had allowed him in their bed. Yes. And where had that taken him? He would have ended up as the husband of a schemer who had taken advantage of his good nature, a woman he had never known or even wanted.

But now he had revealed his true nature to Ingrid and, unlike what he had feared, she had not fled in horror. Even better, she had liked what he'd done, if her claim was to be trusted. He wasn't sure what to make of that, or even if he could accept it, because this darkness was a side of himself he was not comfortable with.

"As you know, I grew up on my own with my mother." Though Ingrid seemed puzzled as to why he might mention this now, she waited. *Why* was he talking about this now? He wasn't sure. She had told him she'd liked what he had done, shouldn't he leave it at that? Probably. But the guilt was not so easily forgotten and he wanted to make her understand. "She kept telling me she wanted me to grow into a good man, not someone like my father, the wastrel who had treated her like his property for months and then left before I was born, or her lovers, who only ever wanted one thing from her."

A good man. Again. It always came back to the same thing with him.

A light hand landed on his chest. "Why are you telling me this?"

"Because I can't stand the idea that I'm turning into them. Those bastards who were only interested in bedding her." He took in a deep inhale. "My father, who hurt and abandoned her, instead of providing her with the love and protection she wanted."

There. He'd said it. All his life he had been terrified he would be one of those men who treated women like a commodity and finally today, after years of exerting iron control, he had snapped, allowing his baser urges to take over with a woman who did not deserve it. After what she'd been through already, she should have been spared his crude attentions.

Ingrid lifted herself up onto one elbow. "You're not turning into your father, Saxon, or these selfish men. You need not fear it, it will never happen. You're nothing like them."

"Aren't I?" A glance at her naked body made his meaning clear. He'd just possessed her relentlessly. She blushed but stood her ground.

"That is not the same at all. A good man is entitled to be wicked in bed and give himself and his lover pleasure in any way he sees fit. It doesn't mean a thing about his character."

He rewarded her answer with a kiss to the temple then extended a hand to stroke her cheek. The reassurance meant the world to him. He would have hated to lose her esteem. "You don't think I—"

"No. I think you acted in the way you've wanted for years and gave me immense pleasure in turn. I will never think less of you for being yourself. I could have said no, and we both know you would have accepted my refusal. But I didn't want to say no."

Caedmon's whole body relaxed. He'd been so worried she wouldn't want to have anything to do with him again after what had happened. He'd made her pay for doing nothing more than call him "a good man," something dozens of people had done throughout his life. He had used her to alleviate the frustration others had created within him. She should be incensed but here she was, telling him she didn't resent him for it.

Even more puzzling was the fact that she seemed to like to see this darker side of him. Certainly she hadn't shied away from his caresses, and he'd felt her spasm for him twice, the undeniable proof that she wasn't lying about having had pleasure.

"Thank you."

Ingrid was relieved when Caedmon extended an arm to draw her against his flank once more. Peace was restored.

For a moment she'd feared he would be too ashamed of what they had done to look at her in the eye. Or worse, be disgusted by the fact that she had liked every moment of it. Perhaps she should not have admitted to such a thing but she had. He thought he'd been crude and selfish, when in reality he'd been assertive and generous, pleasuring her extensively beforehand, whispering in her ear, preparing her carefully for his possession, soothing her afterward. He'd been unashamedly male, forcing her to take amazing pleasure she had no idea existed.

She was not lying when she said she had enjoyed what he had done to her. When he'd ordered her to position herself on her hands and knees, her heart had almost stopped. She had heard about that position, but she had never experienced it. It had only taken her a moment to decide that she trusted him and wanted to see for herself how it would feel.

And, oh, how right she'd been to surrender control over to him!

He had not tried to trick her, he had made his intentions clear and even asked for her permission. She could have said no. She had not. As soon as she had felt his fingers on her most secret opening she'd known she would agree to anything he wanted to do, however forbidden, however licentious. He'd been so gentle, so careful, he had created so many sensations within her that she already knew she would ask him to do it again.

It had been perfect, a proof that he trusted her to accept him as he was.

But it had not lasted long. Once his body had recovered from the fit of lust, he had been assaulted by doubt and self loathing, thinking he'd shocked her. His explanation had torn her heart out. Having had such a happy childhood, having been so loved by her family, she found it difficult to understand how he could feel, weighed down by the weight of expectations, never free to give his feelings and desire free rein. To think *she* had felt frustrated just because no one expected her to be whimsical!

What could she do, what could she say to make him understand that she liked him the way he was?

She didn't know.

Soon Caedmon succumbed to a deep sleep. Once Ingrid was assured he'd fallen asleep she tightened her hold around him, relishing the intimacy of the contact.

For weeks they had pretended to be lovers, and now that was what they were in truth.

The only question was, how long would that last?

Not long, in all probability. She suspected Caedmon would not dare bed her again, even if she asked. He would be too afraid of losing control. Besides, he was supposed to leave in a few days, for good. Would he want to prolong his stay? This was far from certain.

Well, for now, he was here, and she was in his arms. She would enjoy what she could.

CHAPTER FIFTEEN

"I need you to do me a favor."

The Dane would no doubt be surprised by the demand but he only crossed his arms over his chest, the very image of composure. "Let's hear it, Coldman."

Caedmon started to explain what he had in mind. After a night in Ingrid's arms, he had gone to find Ivar at dawn, as he'd intended. Now that he knew who was responsible for what had happened to her, he could not just walk away. Before he left the village, he would lead the man into a trap and avenge her, using his injured pride as a pretext. In truth, he cared not about what the Norseman had accused him of the day they had met but he could not let what he had done to Ingrid go unpunished. Someone had to do something. That someone would be him.

"You accused me of stealing your horses the other day," he told the loathsome man, whom he'd cornered in a narrow alleyway. "I cannot let that accusation lie. The whole village knows I didn't commit the crime but now that I am recovered from my injury, you will pay for insulting my honor."

"Pay how?"

"You will meet me later in the forest and we will sort this out together once and for all."

The bastard had had the audacity to smile. "With pleasure."

Caedmon clenched his teeth. Soon that smile would be wiped off his face.

"I don't care about him accusing me of stealing the horses, of course," he told Sigurd. "It's all just a pretext."

He could tell the Dane was intrigued. Perhaps despite the latent animosity between them he would consent to help him. "What do you care about then?"

"I will tell you in good time. But I need another man first, someone you can trust to be discreet. Not Björn," he specified quickly. "This is about his sister, so we cannot have him involved. He may well kill Ivar when he knows why I intend to fight him."

A pause. "Would that be such a bad thing? It seems to me that you're on a punitive expedition. Perhaps the man deserves everything he would get."

"Perhaps." Caedmon conceded. "All the same, I'm sure Ingrid would not like that."

Sigurd nodded slowly. "You're probably right. Women are much more generous than we are. Let me go get Wolf. He can be relied on to keep a cool head. Then you can tell us about your plan."

When he'd finished telling the two Norsemen what Ivar had done to Ingrid, they looked about to run off in the direction of his hut and put an end to his miserable life without further ado.

"I had no idea the man was such a weasel," Wolf said between his teeth. "I should have seen it, I should have done something."

Caedmon knew the Icelander was the acknowledged protector of the village and would see this as a failure on his part. "You cannot know what goes on behind closed doors," he argued. "And Ingrid made sure never to tell anyone. It's not your fault." Still, the man didn't appear convinced.

"Where do we come in?" Sigurd growled, exhibiting the temper he was renowned for.

"I'm going to give him a taste of his own medicine."

"Don't tell me you want us to rape him?" The Dane arched a brow. "That's something I'm not sure I would be—"

"No, of course not. But he agreed to a fight with me. He will actually find himself having to handle three men at once."

"Very clever," Wolf approved, nodding to himself. "A most fitting punishment. Shall we?"

Caedmon afforded a smile. Handling three men at once, and all without warning. Ivar had thought Ingrid wouldn't mind.

Let's see how *he* liked it.

"WHAT IS THAT?"

Ivar stared at Wolf and Sigurd, who had just emerged from their hiding places behind the bushes, a scowl on their faces. No wonder he sounded worried. Never had two men looked more menacing.

"The fight we agreed on." Caedmon spoke with terrible calm. In that moment he felt exactly like the "Coldman" Sigurd always called him. "Or is your memory failing you?"

"No, but this is not what we—"

"You agreed to it so you cannot complain now." He used the words Ivar had had the gall to tell Ingrid that night.

"I agreed to fight *you*, you mongrel Saxon, not to have to face three men on my own!"

Caedmon unveiled his teeth in a feral smile. The man had walked straight into his trap. "Precisely. How rotten of me to take advantage of you thus, and have you deal with three men when you expected only one. Perhaps you'll consider that in the future, when you want to play games. Let it be a lesson for you."

Ivar's body stiffened. He'd finally understood what was going to happen—and why. "What is this really about?"

"Oh, I think you know, or you wouldn't look so panicked," Caedmon hissed. He was having the hardest time controlling his temper. For the first time he understood why Sigurd just snapped when his emotions ran high. It was the only way to stay sane. Though he'd had a lifetime of practice at being sensible, he was on the verge of explosion, and the only person his restraint was hurting was himself. "I care not if you accuse me of theft, I know my conscience is clear and I didn't steal those horses. But I care when I hear you raped an innocent woman."

Even if Ivar had not yet guessed what he was talking about, he would know now. After all, Caedmon was supposed to be Ingrid's lover. It stood to reason that she would have confided her past with him.

"There was no rape," the man started to protest. "She agreed, she said she would let me blindfold her, I only—"

"She agreed to a little game with you, her chosen lover, not to have you offer her up to your bastard friends without her knowledge, to use as they wished!" he barked.

His temper was about to explode but he noticed that the two Norsemen behind him made no move to stop him, as if they agreed Ivar would get nothing more than he deserved if he lost control and ripped him to shreds. Neither did they make any move to take over, for which he was grateful. This was important to him, and he wanted to be the one doling out the punishment.

He needed it.

"Let us see how you like it to have to deal with three men at once."

Ivar recoiled. The smirk had well and truly been wiped off his face. A small satisfaction. "It was years ago, I was only—"

"This is no excuse! Had you been only ten you would have been old enough to know what you were doing was wrong. Now enough talking, you will pay for your crime."

Because Ivar was both determined to defend himself and more experienced than him, Caedmon found the fight hard going. Good man that he was, had never fought a single fight in his life and his inexperience showed. He received a great deal more blows than he would have liked. All the same, he could have kept punching all day. Forget making necklaces, this was what was needed to take the pain and frustration out of him. Each strike helped to rid himself of some of his doubts, each grunt took away some of the disillusioned man he'd been for so long.

The new Caedmon apparently fought bare knuckle fights and bedded his conquests in the most uncompromising manner.

And he enjoyed every moment of it, because his opponent deserved everything he got, and the woman he'd taken to bed had loved it as much as he had.

He fought with renewed intent, knowing he would not be able to last much longer. The two Norsemen let him deal with Ivar, only intervening to hammer the point home that he was facing three men at once and making sure the lesson sank in in his maggot brain. It was for the best, of course, because if they had decided to really get involved into the fight, the man would never get out of it alive.

Finally it was over.

Caedmon stood, panting, over Ivar's prone body, trying to calm the roaring in his blood urging him to deliver the *coup de grâce*. His lip was cut and his jaw was throbbing but he didn't mind because he'd succeeded in his task. The Norseman was still conscious but appeared unwilling to move in case the men finished him off. A wise, if cowardly decision. Right now Caedmon didn't know what he wanted to do. Should he let him go? Did he really deserve to be spared?

Sigurd placed a hand on his shoulder, as if he understood he was battling his conscience and for the first time was considering killing a man. It was a frightening proposition but he could not bear the idea of what that man had done to Ingrid. Now that he'd made love to her and seen her for the trusting, passionate, generous lover she was, he could not bear to imagine her in the arms of a man who had used her body against her consent.

"Let's go. Wolf will take care of the bastard. He knows what to do."

They had agreed together that after the beating Ivar would be sent away from the village. The Icelander would see to it that he could not harm anyone else here. Yes. It was probably for the best, because all in all Caedmon didn't want to have the murder of a man on his conscience. He had to trust Ivar had learned his lesson.

"Come, Caedmon. Our work here is done."

Caedmon arched a brow. "You are not calling me Coldman anymore?"

The Dane shook his head slowly. "I called you Coldman because a part of me hated you. I was jealous of your complicity with Frigyth when we met. Then when you came back, I feared that you would ask her to leave me and follow you."

"I would never have—"

"You would have, given the slightest chance, because she's an amazing woman and you wanted her for yourself, understandably. You'd be a fool not to want to steal her away. I don't even blame you for it. You're only a man after all. No..." He rubbed a hand at the back of his neck, looking more uncomfortable than Caedmon had ever seen him. It was a sight to see the mighty Dane less than confident, one he was not even sure he enjoyed because he knew how doubts could make you feel. "What I was really scared of was that she would agree she'd be better off with someone like you and leave me."

Privately Caedmon knew that it would never happen. Frigyth was head over heels in love with her husband. How could the man not see it? A part of him, a part he was not proud of, a part of what was left of the old Caedmon, leapt in joy. The Norseman thought it possible that his beloved wife could leave him for her erstwhile sweetheart. To know that he was not the only one battling doubt was a revelation.

If Sigurd, who had actually married Frigyth and should have nothing to fear, could allow his feelings for her to disturb him so, then Caedmon had nothing to be ashamed of. It just meant that she was, as the Dane had said, an amazing woman worthy of admiration.

The difference was, now he knew she was not the only one.

"You're not scared I would try to steal her away anymore?" he asked, feeling as if a weight had been dislodged from his chest. About time too.

Sigurd looked at the bloodied Ivar on the floor and gave a slanted smile. "No. I'm not, because I think you've finally stopped loving Frigyth."

Everything stilled and peace descended inside Caedmon.

He had.

"Yes. I think so too. I'm even wondering if I ever really loved her," he said under his breath.

A bark of a laugh answered him, then Sigurd slapped him on the shoulder. "I wouldn't go that far. You were definitely smitten, man. Now, come, let's get back to our women."

On the road leading back to the village, the two men didn't exchange a single word but Caedmon knew from now on things would be easier between them. When Sigurd nodded to him before veering in the direction of his hut, he didn't feel any pang of envy. Let the Dane go to his wife, he had his own woman to go to.

All he had to do now was to make her see what she meant to him.

He would have to find a way to do that sooner rather than later, because the inner jolt he felt when he spotted her graceful form by the gate leading to the vegetable patch told him he was in a lot deeper than he'd thought.

She turned when she heard his approach—and gasped.

"Caedmon! What happened to you?"

Dropping the basket she was holding, Ingrid rushed out to him. He could easily guess that he had a bruise on his jaw, courtesy of Ivar's blows, and unlike the Norsemen, he had no beard to cover it up. She would be able to see it, as well as the cut on his lip. Damn it all! He had not wanted her to know about the fight. He should have left Sigurd and Wolf deal with Ivar but he had been unable to deny himself the satisfaction of bringing the man down himself.

"'Tis nothing. Sigurd and I got into a fight," he grumbled.

After all, that was the truth, even if they had not been fighting each other and Ingrid was bound to see the bruise on the Dane's face as well. It was the best explanation he could come up with at such short notice because he could not admit to the truth. He wasn't sure she would like it.

"Why on earth would you fight the man?"

"Leave it."

She didn't. "And with your injury so fresh, as well!" She sounded mightily aggrieved. "Tell me you didn't do any damage to the—"

"I'm fine!" he snapped.

The satisfaction of having finally punished Ivar for what he'd done, the realization that sometime in the last few weeks he had fallen out of love with Frigyth and in love with Ingrid, the uncertainty about what the future held for them, everything conspired to make his temper shorter than usual. He needed time to absorb it all and decide on the best course of action.

"I will go and see Magnus. He asked me to help with a gate door he's making and I still have something to finish from the other night."

Ingrid hesitated, then said, her voice full of what he didn't dare hope was relief. "So, you won't be leaving the village just yet?"

"No. Not just yet."

Or ever, if he had his way.

CHAPTER SIXTEEN

Caedmon was not leaving just yet.

Ingrid had so dreaded to see him walk away without a backward glance after their two nights together that she repeated the sentence in her head incessantly, like an incantation. He was not leaving just yet. That meant they would have the opportunity to see where they could go from their nights of passion.

And if he decided to stay a bit longer, they might be able to build something together.

Hope fluttered in her chest. Could a future with him be possible?

He'd apparently started to help Magnus at the forge and even had a project to finish, yet another encouraging sign. Was he actually making the necklace for Frigyth, she wondered, to replace the one Sigurd had made? He had joked about it the day she'd told him about it, but it wouldn't surprise her if he had started on it. Was that why the two men had fought? Had the possessive Dane taken exception to it, thinking that another man had no right to give his wife gifts?

Well, she, for one, didn't care. As long as he stayed with her,

Caedmon could make what he wanted, for whomever he wanted. He didn't trust women and she didn't trust men. And yet, somehow, they seemed to trust—and like each other. Perhaps together they could conquer their doubts?

Unable to contain her joy and hopes, desperate to share them with someone, she set off for Frigyth's hut. Caedmon's oldest friend knew him better than anyone else. Perhaps she could help her make sense of the workings of his mind. She could have gone to Dunne, who knew him as well, but she was loath to confide in her in case Björn got wind of their conversation. She hadn't minded facing him when she'd only pretended to be Caedmon's lover but now that, in effect, that was what she was, she found herself oddly intimidated.

As she drew near the hut she heard Merewen's voice coming out from the window.

"Sigurd did ever so well. Considering his...explosive character, shall we say, I expected him to balk at the sight of a man in love with his wife. But he took it in his stride."

Ingrid stilled. Who had come calling to the village, claiming to be in love with Frigyth? In any case, Merewen was right, Sigurd would not take too well to that. He was very possessive, everyone knew that. Hadn't she just now been thinking he would take exception to the gift of a necklace to Frigyth from an old friend?

She waited, not sure she should interrupt such a conversation.

"I know," Frigyth said on a sigh. "I'm so proud of him. He's come a long way since our wedding day. I'll admit that when I saw Caedmon, I feared he would renew his offer of marriage, or even try to convince me that I had made the wrong choice when I married Sigurd and should have chosen him instead."

There was a pause during which Ingrid had to lean against the hut in support. Her legs had suddenly gone liquid. They were talking about Caedmon? *He* was the one in love with Frigyth? *He* was the one Sigurd would take exception to? And... he'd offered Frigyth *marriage*? This was explosive, devastating news.

How on earth was she finding out about this only now?

"I don't think he ever believed me when I told him we would never suit but I am more convinced than ever that I was not the woman for him."

Another woman spoke, her calm voice at odds with the fluttering in Ingrid's heart. "Well, let us hope he has finally accepted it. He's going to be really unhappy if he hasn't."

Dunne. Frigyth's sister. In other words, one of Ingrid's best friends, someone who should have been on her side, and let her know what the situation was.

By the gods. How many people were in there, discussing this as if it was of little importance? Did everyone in the village know about Caedmon's feelings for his old friend? Know that he'd once asked her to marry him? And if that was such common knowledge, why had no one deemed it necessary to tell her? Everyone thought that she and the Saxon were lovers, they should have warned her that she was wasting her time, told her that he would never want more from her than a quick and convenient tumble because he was in love with another woman.

It was awful.

She felt ridiculous and betrayed.

To think that just a moment ago she had congratulated herself on the fact that he was making a necklace for Frigyth, because it meant he was not leaving yet! Well now she knew why he was in no hurry to leave the village, why he was making jewelry for the woman. Because he was in love with her. Because he was trying to prove to Sigurd that he could do something better than him. Because he wanted to show Frigyth that she had chosen the wrong man. Which went to show that he was a deluded fool as well as a deceitful schemer. Frigyth would need more than a necklace to fall into his arms and Sigurd would endure a thousand beatings before he surrendered his wife to anyone.

Ingrid wiped the tears pooling in her eyes. She'd been right all these years. Men were only ever interested in one thing. Bedding her. They were not interested in giving her the kind of life her parents had had. Even if, admittedly, Caedmon had gone about it with a lot more skill and thoughtfulness than Ivar, worrying about her pleasure while bedding her, the fact remained. He had never been interested in her beyond what her body could offer. While she had started to dream about a life she had ruled out years ago, he was only playing with her, waiting for a woman who would never be his.

How pathetic!

Hadn't she decided to be alone for that very reason? Because men could not be trusted to want to make her happy? Because she knew they were unreliable and would only hurt her in the end? Ivar had hurt her but it had not been the same. The pain and humiliation he and his friends had inflicted on her could have been inflicted by anyone else. She had been hurt in her pride, but her heart had not suffered because she'd not had any feelings for him.

With Caedmon, well...it was different.

Her heart had most definitely been struck.

She did have feelings for him and it had taken this betrayal for her to understand just how deep they were. Why hadn't she found out about his infatuation for Frigyth before? If she'd known from the start that he had come to the village to win his old friend around and only had eyes for her, everything would have been different. She would not have...

She stopped, realizing how stupid she was being.

If she'd known about his intentions, what would she have

done differently? Nothing. She wasn't sure it was possible to stop yourself from falling in love with someone. Rant as she might, it seemed that she had been destined to fall in love with the Saxon.

And have her heart broken.

When Caedmon came back from the forge Ingrid was waiting for him. It was late afternoon already and she'd had ample time to mull over what she'd heard outside Frigyth's hut. Which was not a good thing because the more she thought about it, the more incensed she became.

Someone *should* have told her! Whichever way she looked at it, she could not understand their motivation for staying silent.

Just as the sun started to sink below the horizon, Caedmon walked in through the door, looking preoccupied. Earlier that day the look on his face might have worried her, and she might have asked him what the matter was. Now it only made her furious. What did he have to worry about? The best way to waylay another man's wife? How to seduce a woman who was in love with her husband and pregnant with his child? Oh, such deviousness was the mark of a good man indeed! Now she knew why he took exception to the name.

Because deep down he knew he was anything but.

She stood up, and went to plant herself in front of him. The bruise on his jaw and the cut on his lip seemed to taunt her, reminding her of his duplicitous nature. That morning he had fought a man because he'd been caught in the act of seducing his wife and, far from feeling shame at his actions, in the afternoon he'd gone to make a necklace for the woman. No wonder Sigurd had tried to flatten him when he'd realized what his intentions toward Frigyth were. The surprising part was that he had not damaged him more.

In that moment she wished she had the strength of the mighty Dane. Caedmon would not get away with just a bruise and a cut if she could swing her fists to devastating effect.

"The fight you had with Sigurd this morning," she started, knowing she would not be able to pretend nothing was amiss. It was better to address the problem right now.

He hesitated, as if reluctant to talk about it. Understandable, as it pertained to a secret he was trying to keep from her...

"Yes. What about it?"

What about it? she wanted to roar. What sort of a monster was he? Did he really feel no remorse over the fact that he was trying to seduce a married, pregnant woman? Didn't he care that he was using her to slake his lust while he waited for the elusive moment when Frigyth would fall into his arms? Did he really think it acceptable to behave with such cynicism?

Ingrid turned and stormed to the window, overcome by a fury such as she had never experienced before. She had to calm down before she confronted Caedmon, however. In the state she was in she would only ridicule herself. The last thing she wanted was to show him how badly he had hurt her. An outburst would serve no purpose other than to place herself in the position of the victim, a position she refused to be in ever again.

Caedmon walked over to where she was. A moment later she felt two hands on her shoulders. She steeled herself against the pleasure that simple contact brought her. Why, oh why, did he have to touch her? It was the one thing guaranteed to make her defenses fall.

"What's up, Ingrid?" Slowly, he made her turn around. "Are you suffering with your monthly courses again? They're due round about now, are they not? Is that what it is?"

The question, as well as the genuine concern in his eyes, threw her. He knew she was approaching her time, he remembered that it had been more than three weeks since she's had her woman's flux? But, of course, he did. He would be keeping an eye on such things, because when she started to bleed then he would have to put a stop to their intimate encounters. A tumble in bed was all he wanted from her, so he needed to know what the situation was.

But he was wrong. Unfortunately this time the crippling sadness weighing on her chest was not due to her approaching menses. She raised her chin.

"I'll tell you what's wrong, shall I? I went to see Frigyth this afternoon." Let's see what he made of that.

He tensed. It was slight but unmistakable. She might have missed it if she had not been watching for his reaction but she *was* watching, with an eagle eye. And she saw how he stiffened, as if steeling himself for an uncomfortable discussion.

"And?"

"And I overheard a very illuminating conversation between her, Merewen, and Dunne." Her friends, who had not thought it worth telling her about the sort of man she was bedding.

Bile rose in her throat. If she didn't get this over with soon, she might well be sick. It was just too painful, too humiliating. So she launched her attack. "Is it true you're in love with Frigyth?"

The way he closed his eyes, like a man whose most precious secret had been unearthed, was enough to tell her the truth. Oh, what a fool she really was! In spite of everything, she had hoped to hear that she was mistaken, that she had somehow misunderstood the conversation she had overheard, that there was only one woman he was interested in.

Her.

But now all her hopes were dashed. Whatever the two of

them had shared had been based on a false premise. There had never been a possibility for more, only she'd not suspected it.

Caedmon ran a hand through his hair. "Frigyth and I grew up together and I—"

"Please," Ingrid interrupted. Suddenly she didn't need to know what he felt for the other woman. It would make little difference to hear that he'd been in love with her all his life, and why. She wasn't sure she could take the humiliation, the pain of it. "You're in love with her. That's all I wanted to know."

He grabbed her shoulders again. "No, you must listen to me."

"I 'must' nothing!" she shouted, shrugging herself out of his hold. "Let me pass, Saxon!"

Pushing him out of the way, she ran out of the hut.

Now it was clear why he had stayed in the village for so long, even though he intended to live in town. It was not to be with her at all, it was because he was in love with Frigyth and wanted to be close to her, so he could try to win her around. Now she knew why Sigurd and Frigyth had wanted to put an end to the conversation about first kisses the other day. Because the "sweet, warm, delicious girl" Caedmon had kissed as a youth was none other than Frigyth, and they both knew it. Now she understood why he he'd fought with Sigurd and gotten injured this morning. Because he'd tried to steal Frigyth from him.

All along it had been about her.

Ingrid had tried to convince herself that she could mean something to him, that they could build something now that they had slept together. She'd even been ready to give him a chance. Against all odds, and after years of convincing herself she didn't need a man to be fulfilled, she'd considered giving up her independence and give family life a try. And all that time the man she had chosen had been lusting after another woman. All that time he'd been biding his time, lurking in the shadows, hoping to waylay his childhood sweetheart. It was so pathetic she could have laughed if she wasn't hurt. Had he not seen that nothing would ever come between Sigurd and his wife, that he was fighting a lost battle?

He had no chance of luring Frigyth away from her husband. But still he'd remained fixated on her, the girl he had loved all his life, and not even seen the other women who wanted to offer him more.

Women like her. Fools.

She bunched her fists.

A distraction, that was all she had been to him, nothing more. That was why he had allowed his wild side to shine through with her. Because in the end it didn't matter if she thought him crude or depraved. She'd never meant anything to him and she was disposable. How he must have rejoiced when she'd said she'd loved what he had done to her! He would have thought her the perfect woman to indulge his baser needs with while he waited for the woman he loved.

But then, if that was the case, why had he not tried to bed her again last night? Of a common accord, they had slept in the same pallet because after sleeping together twice it had seemed silly not to, but he'd not tried anything, merely held her tight until they'd both fallen asleep.

Oh, it was an insoluble puzzle, and it was useless trying to make sense of it. The more she thought about it, the more pain it would cause her. She placed her forehead against a tree trunk and closed her eyes.

And then she heard footsteps. Too heavy to be a woman's or a child's. Had Caedmon followed her? No! She didn't want to see him, now or ever again. What would be the point?

Determined not to hear his fumbled explanations, she did not turn around. Hopefully he would get the message and leave.

"Ingrid? What are you doing here at this time?"

She had no idea whether to be relieved the man was not the one she had dreaded to see or disappointed Caedmon had not even deigned come after her. To her dismay, disappointment won. But, of course, he hadn't come. Why would he bother? She was only good to indulge his masculine urges. Any woman could do that, and his heart belonged to someone else. He didn't need her. She would only ever be allowed access to his body, and that would never be enough to satisfy her, now that she had fallen in love with him.

She wanted his soul.

All of him.

Slowly, she turned around to face the Icelander. "Wolf. You—"

The rest of the sentence got stuck in her throat when she saw that he too wore traces of a recent fight. This was wholly unexpected. He was not a violent man and always solved his problems with words. In twelve years, she had never seen him lose his temper once so she could think of only one reason for the bruise under his eye.

"Did you try to defend your friend when he fought with Caedmon?" she asked before he could even greet her. If he'd seen Caedmon and Sigurd locked in a fight, he would have run to the Dane's rescue. The two of them were like brothers.

He frowned. "I don't underst—"

"No need to lie. I know what happened. Caedmon told me."

"He did?" No wonder he sounded surprised. It was true that Caedmon had told her about the fight, but not what it had been about. That had been supposed to remain a secret.

"He did, the stupid idiot," she said with feeling. Why had he not lied? It was conclusive proof that he cared not if she found out about the fight or the reason behind her. He had not even made any effort to spare her from the pain of discovery.

"Don't be mad at the Saxon," Wolf said, coming a step

closer. "He did what he had to do. Even the most controlled of men can lose his head over a woman he cares about. I myself almost killed at least three men over Merewen."

Ingrid sighed. If Wolf, who was the fairest, most measured man she had ever met, thought it reasonable for Caedmon to act in such a dishonorable, underhanded manner, all because he was in love, then she had no chance of making him understand that she felt betrayed. Besides, she preferred not to expose the depth of her despair to anyone. Things were bad enough as they were.

"I'm not sure I agree with you," she said with no small amount of asperity. This discussion was quickly becoming too taxing for her.

"I don't expect you to, but it's all right. As I keep saying, women are always more forgiving and reasonable than men. We have a lot to learn from you. Anyway, the good news is, you won't have to see Ivar ever again."

"Ivar?" The name was little more than a croak. What did he have to do with this? And what did Wolf know about him?

"Once he could stand again, he was sent away. I saw to it." Wolf's face became a mask of barely controlled fury. "You won't have to face him ever again, I swear."

"What are you talking about?" she asked in a whisper.

"What are *you* talking about, if not the beating Caedmon inflicted on Ivar?"

Everything went numb inside Ingrid. Caedmon had not fought Sigurd over Frigyth at all, even if he was in love with her. He had fought *Ivar*—over her. What did that mean? She desperately needed to know.

"I have to see Caedmon," she breathed to herself.

And this time, she would listen to what he had to say, because she had a feeling she had done him a grave disservice.

But when she reached the hut Caedmon was nowhere to be

found. Cursing the contretemps, she ran back out, in case he was in the vegetable patch digging for onions or leeks, by the coop chopping wood for the fire or gathering eggs. She found no one. Her heart started to beat a wild rhythm in her chest. Had he left for good, thinking that if she didn't want to speak to him there was no point in him staying any longer? Where would he have gone? Back to town as he intended, and his grandmother's house? Yes, perhaps. Should she try to go and see the old woman? But what would she say to explain their separation?

She went back to the hut, determined to be sensible this time, and think before she acted.

Night had fallen now. Nothing could be accomplished tonight. First she would get some sleep, then in the morning she would make sure Caedmon had really gone, and only then would she devise a plan of action.

She lay on the pallet, and gave a sob when Caedmon's scent hit her. Had they really woken up side by side this morning, entwined like lovers? Had she really thought everything might work out between them?

Tomorrow she would have to find him, as she feared she would go mad without him.

CHAPTER SEVENTEEN

Ingrid woke up with a strange taste in her mouth, no doubt due to the fact that she had spent a long time crying last night. Judging from the noises reaching her ears, it was already quite late. This didn't surprise her either. It had taken her a long time to fall asleep.

Feeling parched, she helped herself to a cup of ale. And then she heard the commotion. People running, doors being slammed, children crying. Now, these noises were definitely not normal. What was going on?

As soon as she walked out of the hut someone took her by the arm. Arne, one of her brother's friends. He was holding a hammer. Before she could ask him why he was walking around with such a tool in hand, he spoke.

"What are you still doing here? Go hide in the room at the back of the forge with the other women and children while we deal with the Saxons."

"The Saxons?" What was he talking about?

"We're under attack. Now *go*, or Björn will kill me for allowing you to get hurt, even if I survive the attack."

Her legs moved even before she took the conscious decision

to run. Weaving her way through the village in upheaval, she took refuge in the room where Magnus kept his old tools. It was already full with mothers cradling infants and children doing their best to be brave. Agnes looked at her, eyes huge with anguish but didn't say anything. No one spoke. What was there to say anyway? They only had to wait it out and hope the door would not be breached. It was currently guarded by a group of men doing their best to repel the assailants. The Saxons' determination to enter the room where they had taken refuge didn't bode well. They had to hope the Norsemen would hold out long enough for the attackers to give up.

Having no child to comfort and cuddle, Ingrid settled herself by the window to keep an eye on things and report on what was happening.

It was chaos.

The village, usually a peaceful haven, was filled with men fighting with real or makeshift weapons. Thankfully, no woman or child was anywhere in sight. It seemed they had managed to round up everyone in time while she slept, oblivious to it all. The Saxons also seemed to be slightly outnumbered. With luck, they would soon realize it and leave before they were all killed. The Norsemen, who were defending their village and their families, fought with skill and determination, making them formidable opponents.

And then she saw it.

One of the attackers was behaving oddly. Instead of confronting the villagers like the others, he was looking around as if in search of something—or someone—only stopping to defend himself against stray blows when necessary. Not only did he act odd, but he also looked odd. The top half of his face was covered by a soft leather mask that only allowed her to see his eyes, as if he didn't want to be recognized. He was also bare-chested and his chest bore the traces of recent injuries. The hairs at the back of Ingrid's neck started to prickle. His gait was too familiar, and he was a lot taller than the other attackers

Understanding tore through her when she saw that his hair was too blond to belong to a Saxon.

Ivar.

That was why he had covered his face. He didn't want the villagers to recognize him and fall on him all at once when they understood he had betrayed them. Wolf had said he'd been sent away after the fight with Caedmon. Now he wanted revenge for what had been done to him, he wanted to find the man responsible for the beating he'd received and his subsequent banishment from the village. In his bitterness he had gone to a group of disgruntled Saxons, probably the same ones who had stolen the horses and abducted the women and asked for their help in making the Norsemen pay for disavowing him. Once a sizable force had been assembled, he had given them all the information he could to make the attack a success. That explained why they seemed to know where the women and children were hidden.

But Ivar was not interested in rampage.

He was after one man only, the one who had attacked him on her behalf.

Caedmon.

How the Devil had the Saxons guessed where the women and children would be hiding? Upon descending on the village they had headed straight for the smithy's workshop, as if they'd known that was where they would find them, even if it wasn't the most obvious choice. The main hall would have made more sense, but the attackers kept trying to reach the room at the back of the forge as if they knew what the room was being used at the moment. The barrage of men defending the door was barely enough to keep them at bay.

Should he go help them? Before he could make the decision, a Saxon ran at him, dagger drawn.

There was no time to think, he had to fight for his life, against his own people.

The assailants had seen he was not a Norseman and seemed intent on making him pay for what they saw as a betrayal on his part. Would he always find himself fighting on the other side? It appeared so. Well, he could not help it if his countrymen insisted on behaving with such violence, could he? He would always be on the side of the victims, whoever they were. The Norsemen had done nothing to provoke this attack, and he would never condone the raping of women or the hurting of children.

Fueled by rage, he sent the man to the ground with a well-placed kick. For good measure, he then knocked him unconscious with the butt of his knife. As much as he despised what they were doing, he was loath to kill another human being.

It was then that he heard a voice from behind him.

"That one's for me! We agreed."

He swiveled around, blade at the ready to face who had spoken. A man whose face was covered with a leather mask was walking toward him. He'd spoken in his language but with a strong Norse accent. Caedmon did not need to see the bruises on his ribs to understand who he might be.

"Ivar," he said with icy certainty. Tall and blond, it had to be him. "Why don't you remove your pitiful disguise and come fight me like a man?"

"It will be my pleasure. I'm on my own, just like yesterday, but I have an axe this time. I won't need another two men to dispose of you."

Yes, he was indeed armed with a fearsome axe, when

Caedmon only had a knife. This could well end in disaster. He tightened his grip on his dagger, determined not to falter. He could not, not today, not when he still had to explain himself to Ingrid. He would not die before he had told her that the woman he was in love with was not Frigyth anymore but her. There was no telling what she would make of this declaration but he had to say it at least.

There would be no peace for him otherwise.

"Ready to meet your maker, whoever he is? Be sure to tell him who sent you to him." Ivar smiled a sinister smile. And then he lifted his axe.

Caedmon instantly understood he was not going to make it. With an axe, Ivar's reach was ten times that of him with a dagger. But that was not even the problem. Instead of engaging in close combat, the coward intended to throw the weapon at his chest. It would be impossible to avoid being hit. They were just too close. He took in a deep breath.

"No!"

From the corner of his eye he caught a blurry shape moving. A woman. More precisely, a blonde woman armed with a fence post. Ingrid. His insides dissolved in horror. What was she doing outside the room, in the midst of all the fighting? She could be killed!

Before he had time to do anything, she charged at Ivar. Alarmed by her cry, the Norseman had turned to face her. The tip of the fence post caught him square on the chest and the strength of the blow sent him reeling backward. The axe went flying out of his hand, landing on the ground behind him. After that, everything happened with slow inexorability. Caedmon could only watch as the man tripped over the weapon and then fell, arms flailing. The back of his head hit the edge of the well with a sickening thud and he crumpled to the ground, where he lay, utterly still.

Caedmon and Ingrid stared at each other, then at Ivar, thinking he would stand up and demand retribution. He did not.

Around them the village had gone quiet. The fighting was over. For a moment, nothing existed but the two of them, breathing hard next to the Norseman's lifeless body.

And then Ingrid dropped the post and fell into Caedmon's arms.

"He'd dead. But I-I never mean to—"

"I know." He kept her face cradled against his chest so she didn't have to see the blood seeping onto the dust. Framed by the leather mask, Ivar's eyes had already gone glassy. He was indeed dead.

"I saw him with the axe, and you with the d-dagger, and I just—"

He placed a kiss over her hair. "I know, sweetheart, and I thank you. You saved my life." That was not in doubt. Without her, he would be the one lying on the ground right now, with an axe buried in his chest.

Ingrid started sobbing. "Oh, Caedmon, where were you last night? I thought you'd gone and left me."

"I would never do that, not without an explanation. But I knew you did not want to see me, so I went to Sigurd and Frigyth." At the name of the woman she thought he still loved, she stilled against his chest. His heart leapt in hope. She would not be jealous if she didn't care about him at least a little. All he needed now was to make her understand what he had understood the day before. "Listen, I—"

"Are you both all right here?" Armed with a bloody sword, Wolf was coming to them, every inch the formidable Norse warrior who had terrorized his country for generations. Caedmon nodded.

"Yes. Thank you. Ivar is dead." He indicated the crumpled

body by the well. "I think he was the one who organized the attack on the village."

The Icelander's nostrils flared. "Yes...I thought something was odd. The Saxons seemed to know the lay out of the village and where to strike first. It was as if they'd had an informant. Well, I doubt they will try their luck any time soon, or ever again. Half of them are dead, and the other half fled like coneys."

"I killed him," Ingrid said, her voice trembling as much as her body. She had left the protection of his arms to come stand in front of Wolf. "But, it was an accident. I swear I-I only wanted—"

Caedmon wrapped an arm around her shoulder in support. He would not have her feeling guilty for killing a man who had allowed his friends to rape her, who had turned against his own people and almost cost the Norsemen community dozens of lives. Besides, she had not actually delivered the blow that had killed Ivar.

"She saved my life," he told Wolf. "He was coming at me with an axe and I only had a knife. She struck him. There was no other choice. If she hadn't intervened I would be dead."

Wolf nodded as if he had already understood as much. He told Ingrid something in Norse. She mumbled something in response and it seemed to Caedmon that some of the tension left her shoulders. His own body relaxed.

"Take her home now," the Icelander instructed before walking away.

As soon as they were alone Caedmon swept Ingrid into his arms and brought her back to the hut. She did not protest or utter a word, instead allowed her head to rest on his shoulder. Hope surged through him again. If she wasn't angry anymore, perhaps he could make her see that she didn't need to worry about Frigyth. Because he was now sure that he was not in love with her anymore. Last night, he had found himself laughing and being genuinely happy for her and Sigurd. Even the sight of her swelling stomach had failed to stir any jealousy. All he had been able to think was that he hoped Ingrid would manage to overcome her fear of pregnancy and one day have a family of her own.

With him.

Careful not to jostle her too much, he deposited her onto the pallet. When he would have straightened back up, she took hold of the front of his tunic. Her eyes were huge in the sunshine, bluer than ever.

"I know everything. Wolf told me yesterday."

What was she talking about? "Yesterday?" What had the Icelander told her?

Ingrid bit her bottom lip. She couldn't wait to tell Caedmon she'd been a fool and ask his forgiveness for her behavior. She should have listened to him when he'd started to explain himself last night. In fact, she should have guessed who the fight had been with and why. He'd been so insistent when discussing what Ivar had done the other day, she should have known he would not let the deed go unpunished. How did she feel about it? Angry? Touched? She didn't know. One thing was certain, she would now listen to everything he had to say.

"After our argument yesterday, I saw Wolf by the river." Her voice started to crack but she carried on. "He explained you had not been fighting Sigurd over Frigyth, as I thought, but Ivar over what he had done to me. You fought him for me, to avenge what he did all those years ago."

"Yes. Sigurd and Wolf helped, in case you were wondering why they sport bruises too."

"Three men," she whispered, understanding what he had tried to do. He nodded and placed a kiss on her temple. She closed her eyes, relishing his touch.

"Three men. It was the only way. Forgive me, I know you didn't ask anything of me, and might even resent my intervention, but I just could not let it go. I only wish I could find those two brothers and give them what they deserve as well." He paused. "I didn't tell Björn and asked Wolf and Sigurd not to mention it to anyone, either. I thought you would prefer it that way."

Emotion flooded Ingrid. He'd thought of everything. It was perfect. "It's all in the past. You should try to forget it, as I did."

Touched as she was by his support, she didn't want him to risk his life for her ever again. She just wanted him safe, even if it wasn't with her.

Caedmon leaned in toward her, stopping just before their mouths touched. Tentatively, she placed a finger over the cut on his lip. Was it too painful for a kiss, or had he stopped for another reason? Could she initiate the kiss and see? Should she? Would her heart bear it if he refused?

"So thanks to Wolf you know most of it but you don't know everything," he murmured before she could make a decision. "You don't know the most important thing. You don't know that I'm in love with you."

"You—Pardon me?"

Had he said he was in love with *her*? She stared at him in incomprehension. "But you cannot be. You're in love with Frigyth." That was the whole problem. The fact that he had wanted to avenge her, wonderful as it was, did not change that.

He sighed and gave her cheek a stroke. "I was in love with her once, yes, but not in the way I am with you. It was a childish infatuation, nothing more, I see that now, one I clung on to, for lack of a better alternative but I'm certainly not in love with her anymore, not in that way at least. I love *you*, Ingrid. I could not help but fall in love with you, with your kindness, your beauty, your eccentric side as you call it. You're like no one I've ever met, that's why I keep coming back to you, that's why I could not help kiss you in town. And after we slept together and I saw how wonderful it was to make love to you, I just had to..."

Instead of finishing his sentence, he took her hands in his. He seemed wary of what her reaction would be.

"You just had to go to Ivar," she said simply. "I understand." Tears stung her eyes. Perhaps he was not lying when he claimed to be in love with her, perhaps that was why he had felt the need to avenge her. Oh, could she be so lucky as to be loved by the man she loved?

"I could not bear the idea of what that bastard did to you, or that he had gotten away with it. I had to do something." He closed his eyes. "I don't regret it, but I should have gone about it a different way, because my actions put everyone here in danger. Without me, he would not have brought destruction to the village."

"It was not your fault, and no one was killed," Ingrid said in a breath, realizing only then that he wouldn't have understood Wolf's words of reassurance earlier. She could understand why he would feel guilty, but she also knew that he had not forced Ivar to betray his people and place dozens of people in danger. "And the Saxons might have come anyway. You know trouble has been brewing for a while. They stole the horses a month ago, then they abducted the women. It was only a question of time before they mounted a full attack on the village. Ivar merely gave them the excuse to do it now. None of it is your fault. You certainly did not force them to arm themselves with axes and swords to come and kill innocent children."

Slowly the tension in his body relaxed. He believed her. Ill-intentioned people always found a reason to wreak havoc.

"I love you," he said, before taking her mouth in a fierce kiss. Oh. Obviously the cut was not painful then...Good.

Reassured, she allowed her desire free rein.

"I love you too by the way," she whispered once she got her breath back. "I think you might have noticed it."

"I did." He gave a slanted smile. "You were the first person to see me as more than 'a good man,' you know. You allowed me to be myself, freed me from that prison and made me see that I could live my life without Frigyth in it. You saved me, in more ways than one. I cannot thank you enough for all you've done for me."

She gave a shaky laugh. My. The man had a way with words. In his mouth they became pure poetry, just like metal became precious jewels.

"No need to thank me. You freed me from a different kind of prison. You were the first one to find me remotely exotic and take me as I really am, instead of what you expected to see. But even if you had not, I would have fallen in love with you. You are one fascinating man, Saxon."

He stared at her as if he could not make sense of the declaration. But she knew it was no wonder she should have fallen for such a handsome, intelligent, caring man.

No one renounced years of conviction in such a short time, unless they have fallen in love, she had once thought. Well, she'd been right about that. It had taken her less than a month posing as Cademon's lover to forget her resolve never to be with a man.

"Everything between us has been a mess." His eyes were glowing in the sunshine, a silvery gray she had never seen before. "I met you because I had come to the village to see a woman I thought I loved, I kissed you for the wrong reasons, I bedded you in the most animalistic way, then allowed you think you meant nothing to me. No more. I love you, and I want to do this right. I want to spend the rest of my life with you, to kiss you for the right reasons, to make love to you the way you deserve, to—"

"Oh, no. Don't tell me that you intend to behave like a 'good man' from now on? I can't stand those, and I rather enjoyed having a wicked man in my bed if you must know."

The silver in his eyes melted to gold. "You will get him, I swear, every time you need him."

Another kiss sealed that promise. Just when Ingrid started to pant, and hope he would show her just how wicked he was, he drew back.

"I know you said you never wanted to marry and I myself once swore that I would never ask anyone else to marry me. But...Do you think we could forget all those silly promises and get married anyway? The sooner the b—"

"Yes. Let's get married. The sooner the better."

He kissed her again, even deeper. Just like before, she melted. And just like before, he drew back when she was readying herself for more.

"I have something to give you," he said, ignoring her moan of protest.

"Mm. I was hoping you did." With a smile she placed a hand over his crotch. What she felt there caused her whole body to jerk in anticipation. He was ready for her.

"Not that," he groaned, sounding strained. Ruthlessly, she gave a slow stroke, then another, hoping to persuade him to give in. He closed his eyes and for a heady moment she thought she had won. Then he grabbed her wrist and stilled her. "Wait, Ingrid, I really need to do something first."

First.

That was all she needed to hear. He did intend to make love to her, only he had something he wanted to do first. Assured she would get what she needed in due time, she released him. He sat back up and retrieved something from the pouch he always carried at his belt. Something he placed in her hand.

"This is for you."

Ingrid gasped. It was a silver chain, the most delicate one

she had ever seen. It flowed like water on her palm, and sparkled in the sunlight when she wiggled her fingers. "Did you make this?" she asked, even though she already knew the answer. No one she knew would be able to make such an object.

"I did."

"For me?"

Caedmon hesitated. Should he tell Ingrid the truth? He had set out to make the necklace for Frigyth, admittedly, but as soon as he had started on the chain, he'd sensed he would never give it to her. In the end he had made it for Ingrid. Why else would he have chosen a Norse design? Never had he created anything like it, or even wanted to. It marked a new chapter in his life, on every level.

He hadn't made a necklace charged with disillusion, pain and lost hopes, as he'd first intended, he had actually created something interwoven with love, gratefulness, and hope for the future. And such a necklace could only be worn by one woman. The woman who had made his life complete and who was waiting for his answer.

He wanted to be honest with her. How else would he convince her he was not in love with Frigyth? He could not start lying to her now.

"I originally meant to give it to Frigyth, to replace the necklace Sigurd had made for her," he admitted. Ingrid was not an idiot, she would already have guessed as much. "But the chain had other ideas. It chose you, just as I did. Only it realized before I did." It was always the same. His instinct knew what he wanted before his reason had accepted it. "If you don't believe me, take a look at it. It is a Norse design. Would I have chosen something like that if I hadn't intended it for a Norsewoman?"

A pause, during which his heart almost stopped beating. "No. I guess not."

And then, to his relief, Ingrid beamed at him. Despite the

pain he had caused her, she believed him without question, she was ready to trust him. Why was he even surprised? From the start everything had been simple with her, as natural as breathing. She just fit in his life, like the part he had always missed. What had he done to deserve such an amazing woman? He could not wait to stop pretending they were lovers, pretending they were married, and make her his for good.

A smile curled his lips. It seemed that his grandmother would be spared the pain of being told he and his lovely wife had parted ways.

"Will you please put it on me?" Ingrid asked, handing the chain back to him. She had gone a delicious pink color.

"I would like nothing more. And I love that I am the first to give you jewelry," he answered, fastening it around her neck.

"You are the first to *make* jewelry for me. It's even better, don't you think?"

"Yes." She inhaled when he placed a kiss on the soft spot by her temple and then licked her earlobe. "And now, I'm going to take everything else off. You're going to sleep in my arms with nothing else on than my chain around your neck."

She arched a brow, mischief written all over her beautiful face. "Sleep?"

That one word sent him hard as wood.

"Eventually. But first, you're going to let me show you just how much I love you. Every part of you. There will be no denying me."

She let out a tinkling laugh. "No need to threaten me so. I'm sure I can accommodate that wish."

CHAPTER EIGHTEEN

How would he look with long hair and a beard, Caedmon wondered as he rinsed his clothes in the stream? Would it feel weird? Would Ingrid like to see it? He would have to ask her when he got back home. Of course he would never look like a Norseman but now that he lived in their village and was married to Ingrid, he almost felt like one. With them he'd found the home he'd been looking for, at least. They had welcomed him with open arms. He had already started to learn the language and working with Magnus at the forge had helped to make him an integral part of the community. It turned out that a good number of the men here wanted to lavish their wealth on their wives and having a goldsmith on hand had proven to be what they needed.

Wolf had been his first customer, commissioning a pair of silver earrings for Merewen, and only the day before Sigurd had come to ask if he could make a bracelet for Frigyth, to be given to her at the birth of their child in a few months' time.

"No," Caedmon had answered, enjoying the scowl on the Dane's face. "I'm going to show you how, but you are going to make the bracelet yourself. We both know that's what she would prefer."

Something had flashed in Sigurd's eyes. Anger? Amusement? Gratitude? Probably a mixture of all three. "Bloody hell, you can't help it, can you, Coldman? You really are a good man, down to the marrow."

"Apparently so." He afforded a smile. It was not such a problem anymore. "Now let us see if we can do something that bears no resemblance to vegetables. One turnip is enough for anyone to have to wear, I think."

"It's a bird," the Norseman grumbled.

"If you say so."

There had been only one uncomfortable moment, when Björn had drawn him to one side on the morning of his wedding to promise to tear him limb from limb if he ever caused his sister any pain. His answer—that he would gladly allow him to geld him if that was the case, as he would deserve nothing less—must have pleased his brother-in-law, because they had since become the best of friends.

Caedmon looked at the sky and took in a deep breath. Yes. His new life promised to be a happy one, filled with all the things he had gone all the way to London to try and find. Who would have thought he should simply have gone to the other side of the forest?

Oh, well, it was done now.

Just as he was wringing out the water from the last of his shirts, Magnus appeared through the bushes, a rod in hand, and called out to him. "Caedmon! I'm going fishing. Would you like to come with me?"

Fishing.

He smiled to himself, remembering his discussion with Ingrid the day after she had stitched his wound and how she had pretended he had asked her to go fishing while out of his mind with the healer's potion. How had she hoped to get away with such an outrageous lie? As if he would not remember being desperate for a woman's touch.

He shook his head. "No, thank you, Magnus. There is only one person I would ever...go fishing with."

And he would go to her now. With luck, she would feel better. The last few days had been hard, for both of them. Despite being newly married and happy, Ingrid had suffered from irrepressible sadness two days before her flux started and then from crippling pain when she'd started bleeding. Although he had not had to endure any of it himself, it had crushed him to see her in such a state.

He found her still lying down but smiling. She also looked more rested than she had in days. A wave of tenderness crashed through him. This woman was his whole world, and right now, he needed to hold her. Unable to resist, he took all his clothes off and fell down next to her on the pallet, engulfing her into his arms. She instantly snuggled up against him, all warm and sweet-smelling.

"My love. How are you feeling?"

"Like myself again. Forgive me, it's been a rough few days," she murmured against his throat.

"Don't worry about me. As long as you feel better now."

Seeing how much she suffered, physically and mentally, was agony. He'd only seen it twice but it was twice too many. Knowing there was nothing he could do to help made him feel useless. He'd asked Helga the day before if she could not think of a solution but the healer had admitted to having exhausted her knowledge.

And then something his grandmother had told him had given him an idea. The old woman, whose only obsession was the conception of her first grandchild, had warned him in her usual blunt manner that he would have to keep his distance from his wife for a few weeks after the birth, if not months, and ignore his masculine urges.

"Giving birth is no mean feat, you know. Her body will need to recover so you will have to be patient." She had waved a finger under his nose. "Or see to your needs yourself, my boy, because you had better not let me hear that you went to another woman while your wife waited for everything to go back to normal."

Normal. But that was precisely what neither he nor Ingrid wanted. Normal for her meant suffering.

"I might know a way of stopping your monthly pains, at least for a while," he murmured in her ear.

"Oh?" She didn't sound too hopeful. "Old Helga has tried everything, as well you know. Some things help marginally, but as to stopping them..." She shook her head. "I'm afraid it can't be done."

"Helga cannot have done what I'm thinking." Talented as she was, the healer did not possess something *he* did. It was worth a try in any case, as he knew he would not be able to spend the next twenty years watching Ingrid suffer agony with each new moon without doing anything.

"What are you thinking?"

He rubbed his nose in the crook of her neck. "I could make you with child. Then at least for a year you would be free from your monthly courses."

A child!

The was the last thing Ingrid had expected him to say. She gave a breathless laugh then stilled when she saw that Caedmon was serious.

Every time they'd made love since their wedding he'd spilled outside her body, as he knew she was dreading the idea of falling with child. She'd been grateful for his thoughtfulness because, yes, she had dreaded it until now. But with this man...

With her husband, the man who wanted to alleviate her suffering, the idea was not as frightening.

He wanted to help, he wanted a child with her, a family, and he would be there all the way. He would not abandon her or the babe, he would love her and raise their children like he would have liked to be raised. Emotion welled in her chest when she imagined him cradling their newborn son or daughter against his naked chest. Yes, perhaps pregnancy was a solution for both of them...

To hide her reaction, she decided to make light of his offer.

"I've never heard a worst seduction ploy in all my life," she said, shaking her head in mock disgust. "But you know, you don't need to resort to such devious methods to get me into bed. I am more than willing. Aren't I here already? Didn't I marry you?"

"You certainly did." He drew her atop him, forcing her to straddle his lean hips. Despite the teasing, his face was serious. "But this is not a ploy. I mean it. If you gave me a child, you would make me the happiest man in the world and, as a reward, it would earn you months free of pains."

Reward...The reward would be the child itself, of course. A little boy with his smile or a little girl with his eyes. The idea was irresistible.

Caedmon's hands stroked her hips longingly, lovingly. "I know you said you were scared of pregnancy, but I think you were more scared of having to deal with it on your own, of not knowing who the father of your babe was or whether you could rely on him to raise it with you. With me, your husband, you won't have to worry about those things. I will be the father of your baby, in all the ways I can be, and love every moment of it." The hands at her waist gave a small squeeze. "So what do you say, love? Is it worth a try?"

"I suppose." Definitely. She placed a hand over his straining hardness, eliciting a groan from him. It was obvious that he, at least, was ready to try. Not that she was overly surprised. He always responded to her proximity, as she did to his. "Let's see what you've got, then, Saxon."

Desire flashed through his eyes. "Let's see you first. Take your shift off. I need to touch you, I need to see you."

Before he'd finished his sentence her shift was thrown to the other end of the hut and she was naked, poised above him, ready for his possession.

"Now, you are going to ride me. You are going to use me for your pleasure and you are going to let me watch." One devilish eyebrow arched. "And then you're going to let me touch. Everywhere."

She moaned. Oh, how she loved it when he took charge.

"Anything you want, but..." she started, pretending to be confused. "I don't understand. Don't you want to reach your pleasure as well? How are you going to make me with child if you don't come?"

"Ah, you minx, don't you worry about me," he growled, tightening his hold around her waist. "I will hold my end of the bargain and fill you up. I can't wait to feel your heat around me while I erupt. It might happen sooner than either of us would want, in fact."

She could well imagine. Up until now he'd had to stay in control when they made love, and make sure he did not spend inside her but today he would be able to let go and enjoy their joining as much as she did. The mere idea brought her close to release.

Slowly, she lowered herself onto the hardness waiting for her. This position had always been a favorite of theirs. She loved the feeling of power it gave her, as well as the sensations it created in her body and Caedmon liked to be able to watch her while she was exposed. Nestled between her breasts, warm and smooth, was the pendant he had given her on their wedding night.

"Here," he'd said, placing it in her hand after they had made love for the first time. "A dog rose to hang on the Norse chain. My favorite flower. Now you and I are linked forever, just like the chain and the pendant."

She had cried and then cried some more when the following day he'd presented her with a ring adorned with a blue stone.

"The color of your eyes, as blue as a deep lake in the sunshine," he'd told her. "It took me a while to find it."

"I'm going to be dripping with jewels, at this rate," she'd whimpered while he'd slipped the ring on her middle finger, next to the chiselled band he had given her during their wedding ceremony.

"That's the idea. I will have my wife unable to move without being reminded of how much I love her."

"I'll forget my own name before I forget that."

How could she forget, when he looked at her as if he could see the sun rise in her eyes, when he touched her as if he wanted their skins to fuse together? Just like he was now, while they were joined as one?

"So beautiful," he murmured, cupping a breast in one hand. With the other he grabbed her hips with possessive eagerness, lifting her slightly. "Move for me, wife. Let me give you what you need."

She did. While he held her, she undulated above him. Despite the slow, languorous movements, or perhaps because of it, it was not long before an unbearable heat invaded her. Caedmon was panting as well, helping her movements, driving her higher and higher into ecstasy.

"Tell me what color my eyes are when I'm inside you, love."

Ingrid almost swallowed her tongue. He really wanted to talk? Now? He had slowed down, and she knew she would not get away with not answering. If she wanted to come, she would have to tell him.

"When you're inside me it's not the color I see, it's the brightness," she rasped. "They are...lit up from within."

"Yes." He gave a lazy thrust, making her body quiver anew. Oh, she was so close! This new rhythm was doing wonders for her. Usually their couplings were rather frantic and she loved it, but this...This was something else. "I'm not surprised. I *feel* lit up from within when I'm inside you."

Yes. And so did she.

"Please, I need more," she whimpered.

Taking pity on her, Caedmon placed his thumb over her sensitive bud and started to rub. It was too much, just what she needed to tumble into the abyss. In a rush, she started to squeeze him, her body spasming with unprecedented force. On and on it went, draining every ounce of energy out of her, replacing it with joy. Just as her orgasm was subsiding, she felt his, powerful, hot, and deep inside her. She cried out, surprised at the pleasure it gave her to have him come while they were still joined. Never again did she want him to leave her when he reached his pleasure. It was too good to know he found completion in her body, to feel his warmth flood her.

Exhausted, she fell onto his chest. "I love you, Saxon."

She felt rather than saw his smile. "I love you too, wife."

EPILOGUE

"Time flies. I can't believe it's been a year since the twins' birth." Dunne sighed, leaning back into her chair.

"Me neither," Ingrid agreed with a smile.

In the end, Caedmon's ploy had worked. Less than a month after the night he'd offered to make her with child, she had missed her courses. For the first time in ten years she'd seen the new moon rise up and not felt any suffocating sadness or pain in her stomach. It had been a revelation, like she had been given a new lease on life.

Grateful beyond words for his help and understanding, she had spent the night making love to him with slow tenderness. Usually, and despite her best intentions, she ended up getting carried away by desire. But that night she had taken them both to unprecedented levels of ecstasy. At dawn, as they lay exhausted on the pallet, she had whispered in his ear that she was going to give him the family he craved. She would never forget the way he'd engulfed her into his arms and cried into the crook of her neck.

Eight months later the twins had been born.

Ingrid had gotten both her wishes that night, giving birth not just to a little boy with her husband's smile but also to a little girl with his amazing eyes. And now, for almost two years, as Caedmon had promised, she'd been free of pain. Her courses had returned in due time, when she had started to wean the babes, but without the pain accompanying them. It was as if pregnancy had altered something inside her womb and now she suffered no more than other women did when her time came.

It had been nothing short of a miracle.

"You changed my life for the better, Saxon, you know that?" she'd whispered in his ear as they lay in bed the night she'd bled for the first time after the babes' birth. "In all the ways that matter."

"And you, mine."

Tonight the children were under the supervision of Bee and her eldest cousin Elwyn, who were looking after them while the whole village gathered to celebrate the winter solstice around a mighty fire.

Suddenly a warm hand settled on her shoulder.

Caedmon.

"If you don't mind, I will take my wife home now," he said in Norse, his accent causing all the hairs at the back of her neck to tingle. How she loved it when he used her language. "I'm afraid she didn't get enough sleep last night."

Sympathetic nods answered him. Ingrid thanked the darkness preventing her friends from seeing the flush on her cheeks. They all assumed the babes had been the ones to keep her up all night, when in fact it had been a demanding Saxon.

"Ah, girl, your husband is such a good man," Helga enthused, patting Caedmon lightly on the forearm.

"That he is," his grandmother concurred with a smile. After

their wedding, the old woman had left her house in town to come to live in the village. She and the healer had created a strong bond in the past year. "He's always been my favorite grandson."

"Thank you, Gran, but you know full well I am your only grandson, so that is hardly an endorsement."

Caedmon gave a benevolent smile, the very image of graciousness. Ingrid's lips quivered. He'd hated it once when people called him good, thinking it was all there was to him. But thanks to her, he'd started to make his peace with it. Because he *was* a good man. The only difference was, it was not all he was.

Making their apologies, they disappeared into the star-studded night. Around them the village had gone silent. Ingrid had never felt so happy, so at peace with her life. Before they could enter, she took Caedmon by the hand to lead him to the back of the hut, and into the shadows.

There she pushed him against the wall and gave him a long, lingering kiss, grinding herself against him. It was all thanks to him that she felt so good.

"I thought you would be tired after last night, love," he growled. "That's why I took you home."

"Ah, husband," she moaned while he nibbled at the tender flesh of her throat. Right now she felt anything but tired. Could she persuade him to give in and make love to her, here in the shadows, as if they didn't have two children already but were two young people courting in secret? A smile stretched her lips. Perhaps. And she knew just how. "Helga is right. You're taking such good care of me, you're *such* a good man."

Heat flared in Caedmon's eyes. That sentence had become a signal between them. Every time she wanted him to revert to the assertive lover she craved, she only had to say those words. To her delight, he complied every time.

"I *am* a good man, who aims to please his wife." White teeth flashed in the moonlight. "So drop to your knees."

Next, Seducing the Warrior
Read about Moon and Eyja

ABOUT THE AUTHOR

As far back as I remember, I have been attracted to the Middle Ages, to knights in shining armour and their ladies in spectacular dresses. Now I get to write about them, I feel like the luckiest woman in the world. Being French and married to a Brit makes each book I write extra special, as our countries share a long and sometimes painful past. But in the end, in life as well as in fiction, love conquers all!

I have published several medieval romances under my own name, including series, and also have a pen name, Judith Falcon, for spicier projects, still in historical romance.

Join my newsletter and check out my other books on virginiemarconato.com.

www.ingramcontent.com/pod-product-compliance
Lightning Source LLC
Chambersburg PA
CBHW050306110726
47899CB00007B/2127